Sir Les

Sir Les

THE AUTOBIOGRAPHY OF

LES FERDINAND

HEADLINE

First published in 1997
by HEADLINE BOOK PUBLISHING

10 9 8 7 6 5 4 3 2 1

British Library Cataloguing in Publication Data

Ferdinand, Les
  Sir Les: the autobiography of Les Ferdinand
  1. Ferdinand, Les 2. Soccer players – England – Biography
  I. Title
  796.3'34'092

ISBN 0 7472 1997 4

Typeset by Avon Dataset Ltd, Bidford-on-Avon, Warks

Printed and bound in Great Britain by
Mackays of Chatham PLC, Chatham, Kent

HEADLINE BOOK PUBLISHING
A division of Hodder Headline PLC
338 Euston Road
London NW1 3BH

This book is dedicated to the memory of my mother
Adrianna. I wish she had been here to see where
my career has taken me.

Contents

Acknowledgements

I'd like to thank my dad Austin, my two lovely kids Aaron and Lauren, my sister Anna-Marie, my half-sisters Nola and Rachel and friends Andrew, Kevin, Earl, Danny, Warren, Clive, Incey, Wrighty, Clive B and Ray Wilkins. Thanks must also go to Phil and Jon at First Artist and in particular Nicki for sorting out my whole life from day to day. Lastly, thanks to Simon Greenberg for putting up with my comings and goings.

Sir Les

THE AUTOBIOGRAPHY OF

LES FERDINAND

CHAPTER ONE

A Revelation

It was the moment that Kevin Keegan told us he was going to quit – except none of the players realised for one moment what he was really saying or that he was serious.

It was almost a throwaway line during the half-time break of our match at Blackburn on Boxing Day last year. In fact, he had just had a go at me and a couple of other players in the changing-room for a poor first-half performance. There was nothing unusual in him being critical of us if we were playing badly – Kevin Keegan always spoke his mind and it hadn't been a good first-half display.

But this time he said something that seemed out of context with the game.

Just as we were going out for the second half, he said to us all that if he felt the team were not playing for him and he couldn't motivate his players anymore, then he knew when it was time to call it a day.

When he said it, I looked around at the other players, most of whom had their heads down because they didn't want to be criticised by the manager. I thought to myself that his comments were a bit strong – the first half had been poor, but it wasn't a question of us not being motivated for the game or not wanting to play for him, so it was a strange thing to say.

However, in that particular game he seemed to be more upset with us than I had ever seen him. It was not that he was shouting – in fact, when he talked about quitting he said it as more of an aside, just thinking out loud almost, and it was not directed at

1

anyone in particular. He had said some harsh words in the past, but normally he was very passionate in the way he expressed himself and this time he was strangely subdued. We had not won a league game in seven matches and that wasn't good, but there wasn't a crisis as far as the players were concerned. I remember thinking at the time, and regardless of how events developed later, that it looked like something had got to him. He was withdrawn, and his enthusiasm for the game had been getting less and less for some time.

None of the players talked about this incident afterwards. Even though it was a very unusual thing for him to say, no-one seemed to pay any attention to it. Maybe we should have done, because it was there for all of us to see. We had heard the news first, even before the board had (he told them after the game), but no-one read the signals.

I came into training on the morning of Wednesday 8 January expecting just an ordinary day. However, something immediately struck me as odd: I walked past Keegan's office door and it was closed. It was the first time I had ever seen it closed at that time of the morning, so I assumed he must be having a serious meeting. Maybe we had signed a player, or something like that.

Then Peter Beardsley said that everyone had to be upstairs for a meeting at 10am. As we were gathering, I noticed that all the coaches were there, the trainees, the first-year pros, all the professionals were up and I thought to myself, 'This looks ominous.' I had seen it a number of times at QPR when someone had either been sacked or resigned. Then the whispers started, the gaffer must be gone. But most of the people there couldn't believe it, his was the safest job in football. Then Terry McDermott and Arthur Cox came in. Arthur hadn't been seen around for some time, because he was now chief scout. It was strange that he should be there. I asked him what was up and he tapped the side of his nose and said, 'Wait a minute and you'll find out.'

Terry Mac came forward and said he had something to tell us. 'The gaffer has resigned today, it's a sad day and he's decided he can't do the job anymore,' he said. Everyone stood there open-mouthed. Terry read out a public statement that Keegan had put out, and that was basically it. In fact, it was very low key for an event of such importance for the club and its supporters. Someone asked whether Keegan would be coming in to see the players and we were told he had decided not to, because the whole place would be like a carnival with all the media attention. Terry Mac and Arthur Cox were going to be in charge for the moment and the players were happy with that, because we respected them both, especially Arthur, who I had a lot of time for.

I was surprised that Keegan hadn't told us himself. There are always press people at our training ground, but that morning there were only a couple. No-one knew anything about it and the press statement wasn't going out until 10.30am, so I thought that if Keegan had wanted to, he could have got himself in, told us face-to-face, jumped in his car and shot off. But he decided against it. That was one thing mentioned among the players. We would have preferred it if he had said, 'Sorry, but I had to do this,' and explained the reasons to us. Everyone was greatly disappointed he was going, but they felt let down that he hadn't come in and faced us. The majority of the lads I spoke to felt like that. He should have come, because we had so much respect for him and we thought he had a lot of respect for us, as a team and as individuals. After all that we had been through together, it would have been nicer had he come to see us himself.

Most people were in shock. I'm not sure if this is the right scale to put it on, but with everything that had already happened, it felt similar to someone in your family dying over a long period. You try to prepare yourself for the moment, but when it happens, it is still a great shock. It was kind of like that. We knew something was wrong, but we never thought it would come to this. I thought back to the Blackburn game and that one line, 'I'll know when it is time to go.' Obviously Keegan felt that now was the time.

I began to think of the reasons why he might have done it. Was it just the pressure, which is what everyone assumed straight away, or was there another reason that would only emerge in time? In his statement, Keegan said he had taken the club as far as he could and that he didn't want to be a football manager at this point in his life. Maybe that was all there was to it, only time would tell. I heard that he had walked out of the press conference after the FA Cup match at Charlton three days earlier when someone asked him about a story in one of the Sunday papers that he had quit. My mind then flashed back to his television interview after the Leeds game the previous season, when many people thought he had cracked under the pressure of us having such a big lead at the top and Manchester United slowly catching and then overtaking us.

At the time, it was impossible to know what the critical factor in his decision had been. Since then, we have heard claims that the board forced him out. They wanted him to sell players. They couldn't go into the stock-market flotation in the knowledge that he was going at the end of the season, which is what he had told them. They wanted him to sign a new contract, which he had refused. Players were never party to any of that. Only when Keegan decides to say what happened will we really know.

The players never knew he had tried to resign before the end of the previous season and had been persuaded to stay. We were shocked by that as well. We had come so close to winning the league, yet he had tried to resign while there were still some games to go and we were still in contention. I remember him saying, after we eventually missed out on the title, that we might not have done it this time but the people at Newcastle deserved something, and he would be here until he had delivered that silverware they longed for.

Apart from the shock, the other feeling was one of great disappointment. We were halfway through the season, in the UEFA Cup quarter-finals, still in the FA Cup and fourth in the league, so we had a lot to play for. It was confusing, you couldn't really understand why someone would do this given the position we were in, unless they had really had enough and had to get away from it before it cracked them up. If that was the case, then Keegan had every reason for wanting to quit.

The players' committee of me, Peter, Rob Lee, John Beresford and Lee Clark – and they asked Alan Shearer as well – had to go to the ground after training and speak to the board. By then, there were a lot of supporters outside and they were totally devastated by the news. For days afterwards, fans would come up to me and say that it was as if someone in their family had died, the reaction was incredible. They would say that this was the man who took us to the top of the Premiership when not so long before, the club were at the bottom of the old Second Division. The fans never forgot that, he meant so much to them. The board were obviously very disappointed – they knew what Keegan meant to the club and the supporters – but did not really tell us anything new. As professionals, we just basically had to get on with it and they said that as soon as they had any more news, they would tell us. We knew, with the stock-market flotation coming up, that they would have to appoint a big-name manager pretty soon, and there was obviously a lot of speculation straight away about Bobby Robson, Kenny Dalglish and John Toshack.

We now know that in the end, Dalglish was appointed. I read some time after Keegan's resignation that Kevin had said Dalglish would have to change things, because you couldn't win championships the Kevin Keegan way. I suppose you have to agree with that, because we never won anything apart from a lot of admirers who loved the way we played. In all the time we played under Keegan, people were saying that if we could just get our defence sorted out, we would be OK. But in order to do that, we would have to have changed the way we played.

Looking at it objectively, you could say that Keegan did get it wrong, because sometimes teams scored against us and we were not able to break them down. Maybe it was a flawed ideal. He believed we had so much talent that we would score more times than the opposition. Keegan wanted us to play that way, and he was the manager. We got very close and we almost won the championship doing that. If we had won it, people would have said this was God Almighty as far as football managers were concerned, because we'd won the title playing the most sensational football. Kevin would have proved all the knockers wrong, and that was a big thing for him. But I think he realised in the end that it just would not work. The sign of a good manager is being able to look back and say, 'I got that wrong,' and Keegan will do that eventually. The players would have been willing to play in a less flamboyant way to win the championship, without a shadow of doubt. Everyone else associated with Newcastle would have settled for that as well. If the attitude had been, 'We are 12 points clear, we'll defend,' I don't think there is one player who would have disagreed with that. But it was not only that Keegan was convinced his way was right; he also maybe felt he did not have the players to do it any other way, who could have adapted like that to a more defensive style.

While a lot of the lads had phoned Keegan after he left, I hadn't spoken to him. But in April, he was away in South Africa doing some coaching with my agent Phil Smith. I was speaking to Phil and he said Keegan was there, have a quick word. Keegan came on the line and we had a quick chat. He said he had been pleased with what I had achieved at Newcastle and that if there was anything I wanted, I had his number and could give him a ring. If I decided not to pick up the phone, that was up to me. There were no hard feelings either way, but I haven't spoken to him since.

CHAPTER TWO

Growing Up

I was born at St Mary's Hospital in Paddington, west London, in December 1966. In the early part of my life, I grew up in a place called Faraday Road in Ladbroke Grove, where I lived with my sister Anna-Marie, my mum Adrianna and my dad Austin, in a two-bedroom flat at the top of a four-storey house.

I remember it vividly, it was like a big old Victorian town-house and there were all sorts of people who lived below us. An old woman lived on the bottom floor, but in the two floors in-between it was constantly changing. There were families from different places all over the world – I remember there was a Portuguese family who, when we moved to our next house in Latimer Road, also moved to the same estate as well.

Both my parents came from St Lucia in the Caribbean but only met when they came over to England in the 1960s. A lot of people from St Lucia seemed to stay in the Paddington area, just like a lot of Jamaicans moved to Brixton and places round there where there was already a Jamaican community.

Obviously the Caribbean influence was always there, but it wasn't particularly important in terms of how I was brought up. All my sister and I knew at the time was that there was this place far away that my parents came from, but we had never been there. We heard many stories about it and how beautiful it was.

I suppose the main influence that was always with us was the traditional Caribbean cooking, and I think the same probably goes for a lot of the communities that come from abroad. It is especially true of the Caribbean community because you can buy so much of the food in London at the various markets, and we used to enjoy that side of the culture. Both my parents went back to St Lucia on occasions, but I never did until I was 18 or so.

We all lived together until I was about eight, when my mum and dad split up. That was a difficult time for me and my sister, although she was younger than me and probably doesn't remember as much about it as I do. Dad didn't move too far away, but I was used to coming back from school every day and waiting for him to come home around five o'clock. When you do that every day and then one day it doesn't happen anymore, that is obviously a difficult thing to come to terms with.

I never talked to my parents about the reasons for the split, or how it made me feel, for a long time, until I was much older. They tried to explain it in the best way they could at the time. There were a lot of tears. I remember especially my mum crying many times over it, and seeing her cry naturally affected me and my sister too. We cried a lot about it as well but, slowly and surely, time was the healer.

It was not long after that we moved to the Lancaster West Estate on Latimer Road, not far from where we used to live. My dad was living in Paddington and he used to come round every other day or so, but he wasn't there all the time. He got married again, to Vanessa. She is a lovely lady and I get on with her very well. She has looked after my dad and has been like a second mum to me, especially since my own mother died. I also now have two half-sisters, Nola and Rachel. Both of them used to play football and Nola still does, for QPR. It must run in the family.

Back then, though, moving away to a new house was like starting afresh with my mum, who was more like my best friend as well as one of my parents. I would say that I was brought up by my parents, especially my mum, in a very strict way. I don't really remember much of my dad being there, because I was so young. My mum basically took over the role of being the father and mother, and she was very determined to bring us up in what she would call 'the right way'. Whether it was right by anyone else's standards I don't know, but I think it was important and I have carried much of it forward to teach my children.

She would always make sure we both had good manners. She always used to say that she wanted to be able to take us anywhere and leave us there in the knowledge that we would always behave ourselves. That's how I feel with my son now, and I think it is an incredibly important thing to have instilled in you when you are young. Sure, all kids get up to a bit of mischief every now and again, but as long as you don't misbehave badly and aren't rude to people, that is the main thing.

Certain memories of my mother stick with me now from all those years ago. I can always remember walking with her and my sister every day to school. Mum would turn off on the Harrow Road about a mile or so from home one way to go to work, and we would turn the other way to go to our school, called St Andrew's. We would always be on our best behaviour with her, but once we were on our own, we would run down the road playing and things like that. Those are good memories.

When I look back, I suppose my mum struggled to bring us up in financial terms. She always worked, as far as I can remember, to try and bring us up in the best way possible. I will always be grateful to her for that. She could have gone the other way, like a lot of mothers, by letting us do what we wanted all the time, but she didn't. It made me very appreciative of what football has given me.

Where we lived in Ladbroke Grove is probably one of the trendiest areas in London now, but back then it had a lot of problems between the black community and the white teddy-boys and later the skinheads. There was also a place nearby in Notting Hill called All Saints Road, which at the time was seen as one of the centres for drugs in London. So it was generally regarded as a bit of a rough place, but I really enjoyed my time growing up round there. It made me really streetwise, which is important in this day and age.

There were places that young black kids couldn't go because it wasn't safe, due to the skinheads, and I suppose there were some places in the area where white kids would not have felt safe. Living in that sort of environment teaches you a lot of things.

In an area like that there were tensions between the black community and the police, as there still are now, and a lot of kids used to get into plenty of trouble with the law. I only ever did once, and it never happened again. I remember that my dad was away in St Lucia at the time, and I was going to play in a football match with the guys from the Harrow Club in a local park called St Mark's. We always used to knock for each other at the flats and walk down there together as a team, where we used to meet the manager.

We were on our way and there was a large cable-drum lying empty at the side of the road. Some of the guys started pushing it down the street, just having a laugh. Me and another guy in the team got fed up after a little bit and decided not to push it anymore, but the others continued and it was going faster and faster down the road. I was watching and the drum was going all over the place, they couldn't control it. We were shouting at them to be careful and they told us to shut up. Just then, the drum went into the side of this big American car; I remember it was summer and the roof was down. We were near some garages and it quickly became obvious that it belonged to one of the mechanics who worked there. There was a massive thump and the car had a huge dent in the side.

The mechanic came rushing out and said, 'Oi, what are you lot doing?' He grabbed three or four of the boys and told them he was taking them down the police station in his car. He then turned to us and said we were going as well. 'Like hell, we weren't pushing it,' we said, and off we ran down the road.

It was then that we started to panic. We didn't go to the game and I didn't dare go home just yet. Eventually I went home and as I walked through the door, my mum was standing there and she was glaring at me and I thought, oh no. She didn't ask any questions and just started hitting me and shouting at me. Obviously the other guys had said I was there as well. I was supposed to be going on a school holiday but now I couldn't, because my mum had to use the money to help pay for the damage. She had to take me to the police station and they said they were going to caution me. She was so embarrassed to have to go down there. But a few days later, one of the other boys who did it came round and told her I didn't push the drum into the car. Years later, I would always remind her about how she gave me hiding without giving me the chance to explain! She used to laugh about it.

But at the time, it made me stop and think how hard she struggled to bring me and my sister up properly. I decided I didn't want to put her through the ordeal of going to the police station or the courts to get me out of trouble.

My dad had said to me once that if I got into trouble with the police for whatever reason, he would bail me out twice but the third time I would stay there and would be on my own. So even though in my own mind I knew I could get into trouble twice and still get bailed out, I had too much respect for my mum and dad to put them through that, so I didn't.

I was one of the lucky ones to have been brought up that way. I lived in an area where it would have been easy to get involved in crime and drugs and bad scenes like that, but fortunately for me I didn't. I know some who are not so fortunate as me.

Even the drugs and stuff like that, which you do when you are young and just having a laugh, didn't interest me. A lot of my friends used to take drugs and probably still do. But it was something that just never interested me. There were some people I knew who got into trouble with that sort of thing, and I could see what their parents were going through when it happened.

I always saw myself as a particularly strong character, which I think had a lot to do with my father leaving at such a young age. The oldest son will always tend to look on himself as the man of the house in that situation and that was probably the way that I saw things.

I used to be pretty good at football, so my friends used to respect me for that. If I said to them I wasn't doing something with them, when I knew they might be getting into potential trouble, they never used to say 'you this-or-that' to try and make me go with them. For some reason they respected my wish. They would go their way and I would go mine, and the next day we would meet up again. Sometimes they would come back with nice things and sometimes nothing. It's only natural at that age that sometimes you think that what they have come by – and I knew how they had got it – was nice, but I never got into that. The fact that I was good at football, and was always busy playing or training, helped me from that point of view.

But as I've said, there was also one other important factor in all of this. My mum and dad splitting up had made me quite a strong character anyway, but if I had got into trouble it would have made their whole situation worse. My mum had gone through enough emotional turmoil already without me adding to that. That was one of the reasons I stayed out of getting myself into bother: I didn't want to give her any more heartache.

I look back now and think I wish I could buy a house in Ladbroke Grove, but it is a very busy area and I probably wouldn't get a quiet life. I still have a lot of friends there and when I go back to London I go out around there sometimes. I think it's important not to lose touch with where you came from.

I never really started playing football out of school until I was quite old, certainly not until after we moved from Faraday Road. I was a pretty good footballer around the playground but we never really had a school team. There was an adventure playground just down the road from where I used to live and I would try to sneak in there whenever I could (my mum never used to like me going in there), but football wasn't really an important part of my life yet. No-one in the family played it, so I never really had anyone to look up to, to push me into it. My dad used to do a lot of weight-training and got to be quite a big size, but that never really interested me either.

I can't say I remember wanting to be a footballer then. I don't even remember watching it on television. But once we moved to Latimer Road, there were a lot more kids about and we started to play these massive 20-a-side matches on the grass areas between the blocks on the estate. That's when I first began to play for my first real side, when I was about nine or ten. I used to play for two teams around that time. One was called the Barandon Eagles, which was made up of some of the guys who lived around our walkway (which was called Barandon Walk).

Then there was a youth club down the road, called the Harrow

Club, which is still there now. We used to play five-a-side in the gym there and we got really serious about it, playing other teams from the area. I remember going there with some of the boys from school. It was in an old converted church and my mum didn't mind me going there, because at least she knew where I was most of the time. It meant we weren't hanging around in the streets and kept us away from the sort of problems you can get involved with if you get bored. One of the guys I used go down there with, Elvis Burke, who used to live on the same walkway as us, I am still friendly with now. Our biggest rivals then were a team called the Rugby Club, which was where Dennis Wise, the Chelsea captain, used to play, along with another guy called Bobby Dixon. About a year later, we all went to the same school and were in the school team together. They came from Shepherd's Bush and they were a good team. They used to beat us most of the time and you could see even then that Dennis was a good player.

That was my first taste of competitive football, where I first began winning things and bringing home medals. I used to play outfield for the Harrow Club but at school I used to play in goal. My mum was pleased I was getting involved with a team. We used to spend most of our free time at the Harrow Club; it was a good youth club, with table football and other games as well. It was at this time that I began to get more interested in football, and I suppose certain people began to influence my thinking about becoming a footballer.

This was the era of people like the late Laurie Cunningham, Cyrille Regis and Brendan Batson, who were at West Brom and were all black players. I can remember seeing them on the television and they gave me my first real impressions of professional football. There was also Glenn Hoddle, who I used to like. I'm making him sound really old now and he's my England manager!

Funnily enough, the other person I remember very clearly is Phil Parkes, who was the QPR goalkeeper at the time. He was in goal at the first game I ever went to, which was QPR v Leicester. My cousin's husband took us, just to get us out from under our mum's feet. We stood in the Loft end and QPR won.

I always remember Phil Parkes because he saved a penalty. But the real thing that sticks in my memory is that professional goalkeepers were going through a stage when they didn't wear any gloves. I remember somebody was really smashing the ball at him and he was catching it, no problem. I turned round to my cousin's husband and said, 'Look at that, he hasn't got any gloves on!' I couldn't believe it. The latest thing at the time were these new keeper's gloves with dimples on, every kid wanted a pair; but here was this really famous goalkeeper not wearing gloves.

I must have been about 10 – certainly I was still at primary school – and it was then I first thought to myself that I would like to be a footballer. Just to be in there in that atmosphere, seeing all the supporters cheering for those guys on the pitch and wanting them to win, made me want that for myself. (I didn't know whether I was good enough or not, and I suppose most boys go through a stage of wanting to be a footballer.) But I also noticed that, for me, there was something a bit uncomfortable about the whole experience as well. I was really nervous going to the game. In the stadium itself, when I was standing in the Loft, I felt like it wasn't the right place for a black person to be, especially at that time when there weren't that many black players and you never saw that many black people in the crowd. I remember feeling really intimidated by it and thinking to myself, 'Should I really be here?' It wasn't a nice feeling at all for a young kid.

Because of that, although I used to like football, I never really had a great desire to go to matches. The reason we went to that game at QPR wasn't because I'd said I wanted to go to the football, it was my cousin's husband saying, 'I'm taking you.' So I'd ended up being there and as it turned out, we didn't get any problems – but generally, it wasn't a place where young black children went. In those days, most of us used to support Brazil because their players looked black and there weren't that many black players in England for us to relate to. That's why when the World Cup used to come around, they were the sort of players we would support. We liked their skills and everything else they had about them. We identified more with them than with the England team, as there were no real role models for us then.

It was when I went to the Christopher Wren School in Shepherd's Bush – it's now called the Phoenix High School – that I really got into sport. I was a really good sprinter, played rugby and of course football, although for the first three years I used to play in goal. Rugby wasn't my game, that's for sure, but it was really a rugby school and we all had to do it. We used to call it 'roughby'. It was always cold whenever we played, and I suppose you are either into it or you're not.

I always remember how whenever we used to play, we would take about 15 jumpers each out with us. We used to play at a place called Warren Farm, in Greenford, which was the biggest open space you've ever seen and the wind used to really howl around there. It was so cold. It would always make me laugh seeing all of us run out with so many layers on, because we could hardly move. Your hands would be freezing and you couldn't catch the ball.

But there was one particular incident where I decided that was it as far as rugby was concerned. I used to play out on the wing, so I used to get really cold. The ball came to me during one game and I started to try and run with it, but I had so many layers on I could hardly get going. The opposing winger grabbed hold of one of my jumpers and held on. As I tried to break free, the jumper was almost strangling me round my neck, really digging into the skin, and I went that's it, no more rugby for me. I haven't played since. At the time, it was compulsory but in the second year, you could do football, so rugby went out of the window. Without me knowing it at the time, it was one of those moments that helped shape my life. I decided that football was going to be my game from then on.

CHAPTER THREE

Wisey and the Boys

I became quite well-known in the area as having one of the hardest shots around. Elvis Burke and I used to have a competition over who could hit the ball hardest in the games at the Harrow Club. We used to roll the ball back from the halfway line from the kick-off and smash it as hard as we could towards goal. Once, I actually broke one of the goalkeeper's wrists by doing it and no-one else would go in goal! Paul Mortimer, who now plays for Charlton, was playing that day and they said he should go in goal, but he wouldn't. The next week, Elvis hurt someone doing the same thing, so after that we stopped doing it.

Our school, Christopher Wren, was just round the corner from QPR but not many of us supported them, which was strange. A lot of the black folk around Shepherd's Bush felt that QPR never supported anyone in the area – there were always a lot of Irish and Scottish boys on their books, but none of the talent from around the Shepherd's Bush area. If you were to go back to my school and ask the teachers, they could give you a long list of talented players that went to the school. A lot of the boys at our school were associated with Southampton, like Dennis, and we used to think, 'How can Southampton come here and take our players when QPR is right on our doorstep?' So a lot of us didn't see why we should support QPR if they didn't support the area.

I used to like Tottenham, they were my favourite team. I used to like the way they played, with players like Hoddle and Ardiles, although my cousin Tony – who I used to spend a lot of time with, we were basically like brothers – used to support Liverpool, so I probably supported Spurs to be different to him as well. Because he was the only boy in a family of five sisters, he got spoilt a bit and he used to have all the different Liverpool kits. I never had a football kit – my mum couldn't afford one – but even from that young age, I was never jealous of anybody. Sure, I wanted one, but I never resented Tony or anyone else if they had something nice.

For as long as I can remember, both my mum and dad were always working. Dad used to work as an engineer for London Transport and my mum worked as a secretary for a firm on the Harrow Road. When they made her redundant, she found another job almost straight away. They were both very proud of their desire to work and that is something they instilled in me. I suppose that's why when I left school, my thoughts were about getting a job so that I could support myself, rather than being really ambitious and trying to become a professional footballer. The work ethic was very important to them and that taught me that if you want things in life, you have to work to get them, which is an important attribute to have.

Some of the guys I went to primary school with ended up at Christopher Wren, but I made a lot of new friends there. Of course, there was also Dennis and Bobby Dixon who used to play for the Rugby Club against us in the five-a-sides, and we were all in the same class.

At that time, as I've already said, I was a goalkeeper. I suppose it was a phase I was going through: I just felt like going between the sticks, throwing myself about and having a good laugh. I seemed to be pretty good at it, so they picked me for the team and there I was, in goal for the school. I would play for them in goal and then on a Friday night I would be at the Harrow, playing centre-forward and smashing goals in from all over the place. We lost only one game during one season when I played in goal, and at that time I had no reason to think that my future lay elsewhere. I was happy playing in goal, not at centre-forward. Then finally, in the fourth year – I must have been 14 – my life changed.

We had a school game and our centre-forward got injured.

Because a few of the guys also played on Friday nights, they said: 'Les can play centre-forward.' Luckily for my future, we had a reserve goalkeeper, a boy called Troy Tubrick, standing on the sidelines. (I'll never forget Troy. He used to have a very successful mobile-disco business when he left, and used to sponsor my kit every year when I was with QPR.) So Troy went in goal, and I went outfield and whacked in a few goals. At the end of the game, the year master came up to me and said: 'Les, you'll never play in goal for the school again.' And that was the humble beginning of Les Ferdinand, the centre-forward.

I used to play football for a number of teams, on Saturdays, Sundays and midweek . . . in fact wherever I could get a game, I used to enjoy it that much. One team was called the Jaguars. It was made up of lads much older than me that I used to see around the estate. They were the sort of guys you used to look up to, and I played for them for probably a season. It was good football because it got me playing against men for the first time – most of them were in their twenties and thirties – which helped me develop my game a lot. It was also around this time, when I was 14, that five or six of us started to train in midweek with a team called Viking Sports, whose pitch was down on the A40 near Greenford. They used to have astroturf, which was a really big thing in those days. But the thing that really impressed me was that they had dug-outs by the first-team pitch!

At our first training session, we were there but all we were doing was looking over at the dug-outs, because it all looked so professional. When the training finished, we went straight over there to sit in them! We all decided straight away that this was where we wanted to play, so that we could sit in the dug-outs regularly. I suppose that was the start of me taking football more seriously than just playing at school. Most of the good players from school went to train at Viking, apart from Dennis. Because I used to play against him before we were in the same class, I always knew what a good player he was and he joined Southampton as a schoolboy when we were 14. We had a really good school team. There was Bobby Dixon, the captain – I thought he was definitely going to make it as a pro – and another guy called Gary Hall, who I still think is one of the most skilful players I have ever seen or played with. If he could have taken what he had at kids' level to the professional ranks, he would have been a world beater but unfortunately, other things began to come into play, like girls. It is inevitable that when you start getting to that age, people will go their different ways and get interested in different things. They get into girls or music, things like that. Sometimes you think, 'I don't fancy going to training on Tuesday night, I will miss this one and go out for a laugh,' but before you know it, you are missing too many and are out of the side. Then you bang it on the head completely, decide there are other things in life, and that's what happened to a lot of my friends.

All the players respected Dennis because he was such a good footballer. He was also an excellent long-distance runner at school and always used to win the cross-country races, which I hated. His dad used to really help and encourage him all the time. He used to be out training more than us and his dad was really behind him 100 per cent. My parents were different when I was at school, and maybe that is one of the reasons why I came into the professional game so late. Don't get me wrong, they thought it was good that I was taking something seriously, which I was committed to and which you needed to be disciplined at to do well, but they never really took an interest like Dennis's parents or other people's.

My dad would come and watch the odd game every now and again, when I got to a final or something like that. They started seeing me come home with medals when I was playing for Viking. My mum was obviously pleased for me, but she didn't come and watch me until I started playing non-league.

When you look at our school, it produced some good sportsmen – Linford Christie also went there – but we weren't really getting the backing locally to push them on. Most of us came from the same sort of background where our parents never really had money to help push us onto the next level, which you do need in most sports. So everything most of us did, we had to really work hard for.

I was really enjoying it at Viking because it was my first real taste of proper football. We had a good year where we won the local league cup, but the manager left and the side broke up. I was about 16 at the time and still a youth player. Some of the guys were going to play for another team called Southall, so I went as well. There, I spent a year in the youth team, one in the reserves and one in the first team.

It was around this time that I also left school. I remember enjoying my time at school immensely and I got on well with my teachers, but I never really applied myself as I should have done. I used to hear people say to me that I would regret it when I was older, and of course, like all kids, I never believed them. I did my work, but generally, school was one big playground to me, where I would see my friends.

There was one incident at school that I will never forget and it involved knocking out one of my teachers in a staff versus pupils football match. It was an art teacher called Mr Lynch. Every year, we used to have a fifth form against the staff game, and through-out the year, we used to joke with the teachers that they couldn't play football and how we would sort them out in the game at the end of the season.

The funny part about it was that we were in an art lesson, drawing some still-life stuff, and lying on the table amongst other things was this really old pair of football boots. I said to Mr Lynch, 'Cor, those football boots look old and crusty. Did they come out with the ark?' And he said to me, 'What are you talking about? They are my football boots.' I thought he was joking, but he had them on in the game. They couldn't have been washed or polished for years, as long as he had them.

Anyway, the ball broke loose during the game, we both ran for it to challenge and bang – he went over and that was the end of his game, they carried him off. It wasn't a foul or anything but at that stage, when I was 16, I was quite big and physical, although it *was* just an accident! He always swore that he would get me back but he never did, because I left the school and never played in one of those games again.

I was mostly well-behaved at school. Recently I saw an article that Dennis did, where he said that the only person who used to bunk off more than him was Les Ferdinand! He must have been having a joke with the journalist, because that is totally untrue.

Anyway, if he was hardly at school, how would he know whether I was there or not? I used to really enjoy it. I was generally good at the artistic things like woodwork and I did Maths, English and Science, which I enjoyed because you could blow things up. I think I could have done a lot better at school than I did. When I got to the fourth year, I started working part-time at a steam-cleaning company called West Ten Steam Cleaners, where we cleaned taxis. The guy that ran it was called Conrad and he used to say to me that when I finished, there was a job there for me if I wanted. So I always had that in the back of my mind – I would think to myself that I didn't need to take my exams seriously and do well. I was just thinking about getting money and being able to look after myself. As a result, I probably slacked in my lessons a bit. There were occasions when I did bunk off, but I wasn't really bad – only once in a while, like a lot of kids. I used to get plenty of detentions for turning up late and talking in class, but nothing too bad.

I suppose the worst thing was that I actually got suspended once for swearing at a teacher. I thought she hadn't heard me and it was one of those things where it was in front of my mates. She asked me what I had said and I couldn't back down, so I said: 'You heard what I said.' I never forgot it, because we had a cup final at school that night – that was when I was still the goalkeeper – and I got banned from playing. I had all my kit with me and the headmaster said, 'I don't think you'll be playing tonight, Ferdinand. Go home and don't come back until your mum comes with you.' I suppose at that age I was now a bit big for my mum to give me a good hiding, so I got in and explained to my mum what had happened. She wasn't too happy about it. She had to come to my school and said, 'Don't ever make me do that again.' I must have been about 14, and I heeded the warning. When you are that age, you do things because you want to impress your mates, just like every normal teenage boy.

As I said before, going to Viking was the start of me taking football more seriously and I suppose from then on, it was my ambition to be a footballer. But things didn't go all that well, and pretty quickly I thought that the chance to become a professional had passed me by.

I thought my big chance had come when I had a two-week trial with Southampton. They used to train schoolboys from our area down in Slough. Numerous boys from school got sent down there – Dennis was already training there, and there was also Bobby Dixon and Ken St Louis. We all used to travel down on a Monday night, straight after school, and we never got back home until 10 or 11 at night.

I did it for a couple of weeks, but my mum and dad weren't too happy about me travelling all that way on my own, late at night on the train. They said they would like it for me but it can't happen, so I had to stop. I remember being disappointed, which was a natural reaction. It was a chance to become a pro, and I saw how well Dennis was doing and wanted my parents to support me like his supported him. His dad used to take him to the training all the time, and I thought my dad could have done it for me. (At that age, you never think that maybe your dad might have other things to do!) So I just carried on playing non-league football. If I look back at that time now, I think I was probably overawed anyway and I never did myself justice. If you go into a situation like that, there are all these guys who have been training with a professional club for some time. I tried my best, but when you are tensed up, things don't flow out of you properly. Some people can get through that without any problem, but I wasn't ready for it at the time.

I stayed on at school to take my exams and I got CSEs in English, Art, Maths and Woodwork. Having got to that stage, I left. All I wanted to do was earn a living for myself, so I worked full-time at the steam cleaners. Conrad was great. I had been working there for so long I had a really good relationship with him, and if I ever needed to leave early to play football, he was fine about it.

Looking back now, if I had got more qualifications, I think I would have gone on to do something else. I already felt that pro football had passed me by and I was only 16 or 17. I thought I wasn't going to make it, because the only experience I had of it was people like Dennis, who were already in a club doing an apprenticeship, and if you weren't doing that, you didn't stand a chance. I didn't want to be out of work, even though I was doing something I wouldn't have chosen to do. It was giving me an income and independence, and that was what I wanted more than anything else then. Nevertheless, education is very important. Some people say it isn't these days – because no matter what qualifications you get, you can't get a job – but I don't agree. I often wish my parents had taken a bigger interest in my education and pushed me to achieve more at school.

Of course, things haven't worked out too badly for me – but at the time, I could never have envisaged what was to happen in the future.

CHAPTER FOUR

Wembley

I spent three years at Southall and in my last season, in 1986, when I was 19, we got to the FA Vase final. When I first started there were a number of us from school, but by the time we got into the first team there were only a couple of us left.

Other things came into play like parties and girls, but contrary to what I have read in places, this didn't affect my game. Of course, I enjoyed going out and I had girlfriends, but I also enjoyed my football. There were times when, for whatever reason, I didn't go training, but it was only a few times and it never happened when I was a professional. At non-league level you could get away with it every now and again, because it was still basically fun. But you still had team-mates, and responsibilities to those team-mates if you were playing in that side, and that's the way I looked at it.

I think we were in the Vauxhall-Opel Second Division, as it was known then, when I got my first pay in football. It was about £20 and I remember thinking to myself, 'This is the life!' One of the guys who was still playing in the team at the time was Bruce Rowe. He had been at my school and had also been on Southampton's books as a young player. I'd always thought that if anyone was going to make it, it was him; and if he didn't, what chance did I have? Here was a guy who cared more than I did, probably had a better attitude towards it than me, but he never made it. Because he was involved with Southampton at a young age, he knew what being a professional was all about, how you train and everything else. I suppose I was a little bit slapdash in the way I approached it.

We all used to go in and see the manager on a Thursday to get our wage packets. The first time, I never opened mine until I got home. I probably shouldn't be saying this because of the tax man, but it was so long ago I think they'll probably forget about it . . . we used to get little bonuses for winning as well. At the time, there was a chairman there who we used to call 'Jack the Wad' because he used to have bundles of money in his pocket. He was really flash. He used to say, 'Want a drink, lads?' and he would take out this great wad of cash, and if we hadn't been paid he would lay it out there and then.

I was becoming one of the better-known players down there, so they used to look after me a bit better and pay me more every now and again. As well as people like Bruce – who I don't think is playing football anymore, he has a job high up in the Post Office – there were guys like Roger Joseph, who went to Brentford and then on to Wimbledon, and Tony Lynch, who played for Brentford and then Barnet. But as I've said, out of all of us, Bruce was the one everyone thought would make it. Some people thought he was a bit small, but that never made any difference in any of the matches we played. He never did make it, though.

He always encouraged me and I hope he is happy that I made it, even though he didn't. He phoned me recently to tell me that a journalist was trying to find out some stuff about my early career and a piece appeared in the *News of the World*. It read like Bruce was running me down because I turned pro. But he phoned to say that he didn't say it like that, and I believe him. I remember at one point there was talk of a team from the Vauxhall-Opel Premier Division, I think it was Harrow Borough, being interested in me. Bruce said to me: 'Les, you have done well here. You've come here, you kicked ass. But if you sign for them and do the same, you'll have every chance of turning pro.' Those were his words to me, but nothing ever came of it. In the end, I got into the Premier through a different route, with Hayes, and it had happened for me, so Bruce turned out to be right.

Things went well at Southall almost from the start, and there was always a lot of talk about scouts from league clubs coming down to watch me and some of the other players. You didn't know there were scouts there at some of the games, we were always told afterwards. At one time, I was told that West Ham were watching me and Arsenal had watched me three times. But one of the times that Arsenal came to watch me, I didn't turn up on the Saturday. I can't remember exactly what I was doing, but I didn't show.

Mick Byrne, our coach, was very dramatic and always exaggerated everything, that was just the way he was. He was just so dedicated to football and wanted the best for all his players. (I suppose every one of his players that turned pro would have done his CV the world of good.) Anyway, after I didn't show, I went training on the Tuesday and he went bananas with me. I think I was ill, but I hadn't phoned or anything to let them know.

So he said, 'Arsenal were down here to watch you. I guarantee they would have signed you. They were asking where you were and we had to say we didn't know. How does that make us look?' He was going potty, probably quite rightly. That's why when people said to me that QPR had been down to watch, I was so blasé about it, because I had heard it so many times before. West Brom apparently came down as well, but nothing ever came of these things so I never really took much notice.

I'm a great believer that you have got to be in the right place at the right time. When the scout comes down, he has got to be in the right frame of mind, so a lot of it just depends on luck. Some of the times they came down I didn't play very well, and other times I did. It's just that on a particular day, my 'good enough' wasn't what they were looking for. As I said before, generally I didn't know if scouts were there or not, and to be honest, I don't think I would have wanted to know before the game. I would probably have tried too hard to impress. At that age, the thought of an Arsenal scout watching would have been enough to put me off my game. Not that I lacked confidence, far from it, but it might have made me want to beat seven players and lash the ball into the net, which is not what they are necessarily looking for. I was told so many times that scouts were interested that in the end, I didn't believe they were there at all.

I thought it might just be the manager's way of trying to get a good performance out of me.

It's been said that the reason I didn't get spotted was because I was too laid-back, and that is something I still get labelled with today. There's one story which has been written about in the papers before, which came from Mick when a scout from Spurs was at one of our games. Apparently, the ball went over the fence and I jogged around to get it, rather than jump over. According to the article, the scout said to Mick, 'He's not very enthusiastic, is he?' To which Mick replied: 'What do you want? A bloody hurdler or a footballer?'

When I first went to QPR, that was one major thing that people used to say. My laid-back appearance and attitude gave the impression that I didn't care, which was not true. I just took things in my stride, that's my nature. I didn't lack motivation, or anything like that. When I was playing for Southall, I was getting a train to Shepherd's Bush and then the 207 bus from there down to Southall. I wasn't doing that just for the hell of it – I did it because I was really enjoying my football. I'm not saying there weren't cold nights when I thought, 'I don't fancy training or playing tonight,' because everyone thinks that once in a while. But I did it, and if I was so laid-back that I wasn't interested, I wouldn't have done these things. It would have been quite easy for me to say no, I'm not going this week, especially after some of my friends started to drop out. But I didn't.

In my last year at Southall, when we got to the FA Vase final at Wembley against Halesowen Town, I thought I'd really done it now. I couldn't believe I would be playing there as I was still really young, only 19. Just like anyone else, I used to see Wembley on the television but you can never really envisage yourself there. Now there I was, sitting in the dressing-room ready to go out into the most famous stadium in the world. A guy called Gordon Bartlett was leading us out. (Mick was the manager and did all the team-talks and tactics, but he didn't get on with the committee at Southall.)

I remember vividly, we were in the dressing-room before the game and Mick sat us all down. 'One of you will be fortunate and come back here to play later on in your career,' he said.

'But for the rest of you, you will never play at Wembley again. Don't miss this opportunity to go out and perform in one of the best stadiums in the world.' I remember that really made an impression on me. I looked around at all the other players, guys that I really respected, and all I could think about was which one of them was Mick talking about, who would be the one to come back here? I never for one moment thought it would be me. Of course I wanted it to be me, but I couldn't see how it would be. I was convinced by now, because lots of scouts had already been to see me play, that the professional game had definitely passed me by. It was bound to be one of the others, maybe Bruce Rowe or another guy called Roland Pierre.

Anyway, the talk didn't do much good because we lost 3–0. I remember playing OK but I don't think I was really nervous. In my own little way I probably was, but nothing I can really put my finger on. This was a chance of a lifetime for all of us. We could still say we played at Wembley even if we didn't make pro, and not a lot of people could say that. We were told how good Halesowen were and that there was a chance we were going to get a hiding. But in the end, although it finished 3–0, it was a lot closer than that. They scored two late goals that made the scoreline look a lot worse. I was disappointed because I didn't score and I felt I could have played a lot better, but it was just one of those days.

I played up front with a guy called Paul Swales for that game. Bruce had been my partner for much of the season but he played in midfield for the final. He took the place of a guy called Randy Richmond who was dropped, and I always remember feeling really sorry for Randy because of what happened. Years later, there was a story in one of the papers that Paul was playing number nine and that I pleaded with him to let me wear the number nine at Wembley because it had always been my dream and he eventually gave in. But that's a load of rubbish, because I'd been playing in the number-nine shirt all season and he was in and out of the team; he got in the side for the final after scoring a few goals in the run-up.

Sometimes I get disappointed when I see things in the papers that are supposed to have come from people I used to be involved with in football. As long as they tell the truth, I don't mind. I read somewhere once that back then, I couldn't trap a bag of cement. Well, if that was someone's opinion, then that's fine – but things should not be said that are not true. I suppose some people just want to get their name in the paper.

I'm still friendly with a couple of the guys from those good days. There's one guy called Earl Whisky who I still see, and he would kill me if I didn't mention him. I also used to play in the Greek League on a Sunday for a team called Akna, and last season at the Charlton FA Cup match I saw this guy who I hadn't seen since then.

I used to play on both Saturday and Sunday regularly – the Greek League on a Sunday was just for fun and I was still playing for them when I was at Hayes and under contract, which meant I wasn't supposed to play for any other team. One game, I got sent off for Akna and I was getting really worried, because obviously the paperwork was going to get sent through and Hayes would find out – but I don't think they did.

I really enjoyed it and it meant I could play with some of my mates. I think you were allowed to have three or four non-Greek players in the team. After every game, we used to go back to their clubhouse in Wood Green and have a few drinks and kebabs and other food. It was a real laugh. So I really made my way around London football. I was still of the view that professional football had missed me, so I didn't ever get disappointed that no scout had been in for me, despite what people were saying. My view, as I've said, was that you had to be like Dennis and get into a team when you were 14 or so. If you didn't, that was that. It wasn't a lack of confidence or motivation that worked against me, because I was scoring loads of goals no matter who I played for. It was all about being in the right place at the right time.

It was around this time that I left West Ten and started working for a wallpaper shop on the Harrow Road called Lipmans, where my mum also worked. The steam-cleaning business had slowed down a little bit and I didn't want to be out of work. Conrad was struggling and he was going to have to let me go. I started working at the shop selling stuff and I thought it was OK, another string to my bow, and then I started driving the van and delivering. I think this is actually where I got some of my later injury problems with my back, from having to lift the heavy boxes. But the job enabled me to keep playing football.

After that year at Southall, when we obviously did well to get to the FA Vase final, the first team got dismantled. The club had made a promise to pay us more money, but they turned round and said they couldn't afford it. I was taking home about £100 a week in my job and then there was my money from Southall on top of that, which was a bit of pocket money. I was still living at home with my mum. I didn't want to move out – she used to say I was treating the place like a hotel – but I started to stay more at my girlfriend Angelea's house. At one stage, I was getting everything done there, my meals, clothes washed and things like that, and that used to annoy my mum, who still wanted to cook for me and everything else. I used to give her rent and housekeeping money and I told her to spend the money on herself instead of food for me, because I was away most of the week. She said she didn't want it for herself. I suppose she got a bit protective as I became more independent.

Those were interesting times. It was a really funny part of my life when I started to grow up. Don't get me wrong, I had plenty of girlfriends before that, but those were the first times I really stayed away from home. Sometimes girls used to stay at my house, my mum was totally cool about that. She was very liberated. We only had three bedrooms anyway, but she didn't mind if they stayed. That is why I could talk to her about anything and have always described her as my best friend. Even when I was out at football and my mates used to come round, I would come back and there they would be, sitting in the front room with my mum and sister, having a real laugh. It didn't matter if I was there or not.

Unfortunately, my mum didn't come to watch me a lot: I still feel it wasn't seen as the thing to do for black people to come to football. To a certain extent, it was a racist environment on the terraces at a football match, and I didn't want her to be subjected to anything nasty. At that time, you were still getting bananas thrown on the pitch at players like John Barnes, Luther Blissett and John Fashanu. It was fine for me to hear the chants and everything else, but I didn't want her to feel intimidated by it. I would rather have her stay at home and if I had a medal to show her, I could do that by bringing it back. If my dad went, that was slightly different. He was in a position to look after himself. But I would have hated my mum to have felt intimidated.

My dad used to come to the finals and he used to speak to the managers about me to see how good I was, and it was that summer after the FA Vase final that became a real turning-point in my career. Every manager said the same thing to him, that I could make it if I applied myself. One day that summer, he sat me down and told me that every manager I had was of the same opinion. They said that if Les was to take the game seriously, he would be one hell of a player. I remember it clearly. My dad and I were sitting down watching the television at the place where he lived in Bravington Road. I used to go there most weekends and we were watching the football. He was saying to me what a good living footballers seemed to be having. He didn't know any, but he could see like everyone else what players were earning and the sort of cars they were driving.

He had listened to my managers and now he said: 'Les, why don't you take it seriously? Go out and give it two years, give it your best shot and if at the end of the two years it doesn't happen, you can say at least you gave it your best shot and you can go back to just enjoying it like you do now. If you never do anything else for me in your life, just give me these two years.'

He was serious and sincere, and I could see how much it meant to him. He said he'd seen me play and although he wasn't a football expert, he thought I was good enough to be successful in professional football. I said to him, 'OK, I'll do it for you.' Most of the time when your parents sit you down, you just say yes to keep them happy. But I took on board what he said. That summer after the season with Southall, 1986, I sat at home a lot and thought about what my dad had said. I decided I could give it a go but also still enjoy it. We talked again when I went to St Lucia with him for the first time on holiday that summer.

We went out there with his brothers, two of whom lived out

there already, and with my grandad, who was planning to go back the next year. That was one of the greatest times of my life. I saw my uncles in a different light, they became my friends. There was a kind of bonding between myself, my dad and his brothers, and it was really out there in St Lucia that I decided to have a real go to make it in football.

I had always wanted to go and see all my family in St Lucia, and the way I looked at it was that I was really going into the unknown – I had never been abroad in my life. Ours was a poor background out there. One of my grandfathers, on my mum's side, had money but he was a miser, to say the least. People were asking me whether I could see myself living there and at that age, I couldn't. It is getting better now, but then it was pretty remote. I was totally unused to the pace of life there, it was so much slower than in Ladbroke Grove. No-one was going to die of a heart-attack out there, that was the biggest difference in life. The other thing I noticed was that I would be back in London complaining about this or that, but I looked at the people out there and I would see that they hadn't got much but they seemed so happy. They seemed to be ten times happier with their lives than people at home. It's difficult to put my finger on it, but being out in St Lucia with my family in a really relaxed environment was conducive to sitting down and thinking properly about things. There were no distractions, nobody rushing you.

It was also my first experience of getting on a plane and I remember thinking to myself, 'Just sit there, say your prayers and see how it goes.' It was a long flight over, but I knew that waiting for me at the end of it was a great experience. I was travelling in a suede jacket and a polo neck because it had been quite cold back in England. But when I got off the plane, the heat hit me. Even though we arrived at night, I remember sweating like there was no tomorrow.

I talked again with my dad while we were over there. I told him the Southall side was breaking up and that I didn't know who I was going to play for. He assured me that something would come up but if I was to find another team, I would have to go looking for it. I didn't really know where to start, because I had been at Southall for three years.

When I got back from St Lucia, everything was a bit unclear, even though I had decided to have a real push to see if I could make it. Two weeks before pre-season, I still didn't have a team to play for. Then out of the blue, I got a call from the manager of Hayes, a man called George Gooding. They were in the Vauxhall-Opel Premier Division at the time. He had got hold of my number from somebody – I still don't know who – having heard I was struggling to find a team, and he was hoping I would come down and play for them. I jumped at the chance because I didn't have any other offers and the season was soon going to start. It was a bit difficult to 'give football my best shot' if I wasn't playing! Luckily, it turned out to be one of the best decisions I have ever taken.

CHAPTER FIVE

Into the Big Time

The splitting-up of my parents obviously had a profound effect on my life, my emotions and the way I thought about things. But I didn't talk at length about it with my mum and dad until I was much older.

For a long time, I was told that I had an attitude towards women. I wasn't aggressive or anything like that, but people said I had difficulty relating to them. For example, if I was at school and I had a problem, I could guarantee it was with a female teacher. The headmaster once said to me, 'Les, you have got a problem with women.' To be honest, I never thought I did. But that was one thing that got thrown at me when I was growing up. The school clearly felt that there was something there, because my mum asked me about it as well. The thing was, I always looked on myself as a bit of a mummy's boy and so I didn't really see that I was the person being portrayed.

Obviously there was something about me that formed people's opinion in that way. Thinking about it now, I can't remember anything in particular which would have made me appear to have a dislike of women or anything like that. But it was something that was levelled against me and it was put down to my mum and dad splitting up. I tended not to open up too easily as a result of the split and, my mum and sister apart, I was not very affectionate towards women, and that could have given people this impression of me.

I suppose it was at about the time when I sat down with my dad to discuss my future in football that we really began to talk

35

for the first time about them splitting up. We started to talk about the situation and the reasons for it. I think he had decided that I was old enough to understand what was going on and to see things a bit from his point of view. If I then had any questions, I could go back to my mum and ask her view on things.

Nothing can prepare a child of seven or eight for that sort of shock. Although I saw my dad nearly every day, at that age I felt I'd lost him and that he didn't love me anymore, otherwise he wouldn't have left. Despite that, I was still so close to him that I didn't blame him for the situation; and of anyone, he has had the biggest influence on my career. So it helped to talk things through with him. The way it was explained to me was that the reason they split was a culmination of a number of things, all of which produced a situation where they couldn't live together. They had basically grown apart.

This was a period of major upheaval and discovery in my life. I had just taken a major decision regarding my career and was unprepared for the bombshell that was soon to follow.

It was just after the summer that my girlfriend Angelea became pregnant. I was only 19 and although I had decided to try and make it in football, there were no guarantees that it would be a success. My dad had always told me, as far as women were concerned, that I should be careful, take precautions and everything like that. But he'd had me when he was 19 and he said that if you love your kids, you will devote your life to them whether you live with them or not. They have got to be the main priority. He said that was how he was with us, and with his two girls when they came along. His life probably would have been better than it was – but for the sake of his kids, he had to forfeit certain things and make the sacrifice. I'm sure there were things he wanted to do, but he still had a responsibility to my mum and to help maintain us. He didn't mean it was like a 'trap', but it did take over his life and even though he wasn't with us all the time, the way he was meant that he couldn't just get up and do what he wanted.

I think he wanted me to get my life in order before I found myself in that situation, but things don't always work out that way. When it happened to him, his kids became his main priority and I have picked that up from him, because I feel the same way about my kids: they are the main thing in my life.

I remember Angelea told me one day that she thought she was pregnant, so we went to the doctors and that was it, really. It was all confirmed pretty quickly and there was no going back. My first reaction was that I had done what my dad had told me not to do. Finally, when it sank in after a while, I thought to myself, 'I am still a child and I am having a child.' I was in a panic for a long time.

People say that if you are old enough to do the deed, you are old enough to take the responsibility, but that's a load of rubbish. Age doesn't mean you are able to take on that sort of huge responsibility when it comes down to it. It does depend on what kind of person you are, but how many would have been able to cope with it in those sort of circumstances? It's not an easy thing to come to terms with. Thoughts rushed through my mind, like 'What am I going to do? What have I got to offer the baby?'

To be honest, at that time I really *didn't* have a lot to offer a child. I knew I was working and could support it adequately and everything else, but I felt it perhaps had come for me at the wrong time. Both my parents were concerned when I told them, probably for the same reasons as my dad when he had me. He could see his life all over again, like a mirror image. My mum was a little bit, how can I say, pleased but not pleased. They both felt I was at an age where it wasn't right for me to be having children, but they never said anything openly against it. That was the impression they gave at the time.

My life really changed during that whole period. It wasn't an ideal situation, but I decided to make the best of it. It wasn't easy at all because before and during the pregnancy, a lot of things went on between Angelea and myself that created quite a bit of ill-feeling between us. But we got over that and Aaron was born. I wouldn't swap him for the world and I would give my life for either of my kids now. I have to admit there were mixed feelings at the time and it was a frightening situation to have been thrown into, but you have to cope with it. I was 20, and when Aaron was born I was still going about doing the same things that most guys that age were doing. I was a father by name, rather than by my attitudes. My life was in turmoil. You are about to have a baby and you think to yourself, 'Is this the girl I want to be with for the rest of my life?' We argued a lot, we were at that sort of age where you row and then forget about it quickly. This was obviously something different though, and to be treated more seriously, so in the end we decided to get on with it.

We didn't really live together, because it was only about a year after Aaron was born that I went out to Turkey to play. It was difficult to be away from Aaron but they came out to see me a few times, which made things a lot easier.

This was an incredible period of my life; everything was happening to me, both privately and professionally. When I got back from St Lucia, I went to play for Hayes after the manager phoned me up. Aaron was born in March 1987 and I signed for QPR that same month.

I scored about 20 goals for Hayes that season and things were going really well. Even before things happened with QPR, I had already spoken with Steve Perryman, who was the Brentford manager at the time. He took me down to the club, told me what he wanted me to do and what his ambitions were for Brentford. Then I heard that QPR had come in and had watched me over a series of games.

I spoke to Steve Perryman quite a few times and he was fantastic about things. It was then that QPR made their interest known, because word was getting about that I was talking to Brentford. Frank Sibley came down, so did Chris Gieler, Peter Shreeves and even Jim Smith, the manager, to watch me.

I was obviously very interested in Brentford, and Perryman made me even more keen because of who he was. I was sitting in his car talking to him one day and I was staring at him, thinking this was the guy who lifted the FA Cup twice for Spurs and here I am talking to him and he seems totally normal. It's amazing how many people do come up to you and express their surprise when you are just like them! I suppose it's all part of the business, that we place people in football on pedestals. It gives the impression that they are different from the average guy on the street, but that is rarely the case.

I've spoken to Frank a few times since about what it was that persuaded him to go for me. He had good contacts in Middlesex football and had been hearing about me for some time. Funnily enough, one of the reasons he liked me was that I got sent off in a game he had come to see! The guy who was marking me did something to me – to tell you the truth, I can't even remember what it was now – so I gave him a whack. Unfortunately, it was in front of the referee and he sent me off. But Frank thought that was good, because I'd showed a bit of aggression.

In another game, there was one chance I had – it was an easy chance, really – where I only had the goalkeeper to beat but didn't score. Then in the same game, I picked the ball up near the halfway line, ran past four or five defenders and just smashed one in the top corner. Frank later told me that was the moment he said, 'Yep, we'll have him.' They then came down to watch me a few more times. Jim Smith saw me one night when it was really pouring with rain and I didn't have a good game, but I set off on a run like the last time only this shot hit the bar. Jim said to me some time afterwards that he was pleased I didn't score, because it would have cost them more money.

It was about March time when I got the call saying they wanted to sign me, and it was up to me to decide whether it would be QPR or Brentford. It was a very difficult decision. I was weighing everything up in my mind and I had always been told that QPR was a racist club; they never took many of the black kids from the area who were very good footballers.

So I thought to myself, there was one black player at QPR as far as I could remember and that was Leroy Rosenior, and he was a striker. I didn't know whether that was good or bad for me. All I wanted to do was play football, but I was told by someone at the time that I shouldn't go to QPR because of their reputation. This was from a person who was a coach there. So I thought about what he had said and I spoke to my dad about it. Dad said only I would really know what to do, but he made one very good point. He said, 'If you go to QPR and don't make it for whatever reason, the chances are a team from the Second or Third Division will give you a chance. If you go to Brentford and it doesn't work out, who is going to take you from there?'

I thought that sounded like good advice so I opted for QPR. The money came into it as well, as they had made me a very good offer. I was earning about £150 a week with my job and playing for Hayes, but what with the signing-on fees, that at least trebled. It was a totally different world. Here I was, a 20-year-old earning this sort of money. I thought to myself, 'Yes, I've made it.'

I signed after that game which Jim Smith came to watch at Hayes, for £30,000 in the end. The original fee was £15,000, with another three payments of £5,000 that were staggered after I played a certain amount of games. We went up to the board-room after the game and I signed two forms. The official signing of the contract was at QPR the next day. All the people from Hayes were there and the chairman Derek Goodall, in particular, was really good to me. He knew it was a good deal for me and I remember him saying to the QPR people that Hayes didn't need to sell me, because they could hold their own in the Vauxhall-Opel League, financially. So really, he could have made things awkward – but he didn't, because he knew this was my big chance.

Derek was only interested in how they were going to treat me and he helped me get a good deal from QPR. I didn't know what the ins-and-outs of their dealings with QPR were, but when I signed for Newcastle it came out that Hayes would get £600,000, 10 per cent of the transfer. I was pleased for them, because they had treated me really well. Derek was a shrewd businessman to get that sell-on clause.

I was really excited: here I was, becoming a professional footballer, after I thought it had all passed me by. I remember going down to QPR and telling them that I had to work two weeks' notice at the wallpaper shop! Jim Smith looked at me and said, 'Are you sure?' But that was part of the deal with my job.

I had to leave work early soon after, because I was playing my first game for QPR at Southampton in the reserves. One of my mates came with me to Loftus Road because I was a bit nervous, and the first person I bumped into at the ground was Sammy Lee. He had been a famous player with Liverpool but was at

QPR now and he said to me: 'Hello, Les. Good luck today, and I hope everything goes well in the future.' I thought it was weird that he knew my name, as I had only been there five minutes. I travelled down on the coach with the rest of the players. They made me feel at home and everything, but they were all playing games and cracking jokes. I didn't really know what was going on and still felt like the outsider. It was just really strange and totally different to what I had been used to.

We played the match and got beaten. Jim Smith was at the game and he came in afterwards, steaming. There was a group of players, Clive Walker, Jimmy Carter, Gary Chivers and David Kerslake, who all wanted to get away and they hadn't played well that night. Jim was going potty, saying they all wanted to get to other clubs but on that evidence, no-one would take them. He was going red in the face and swearing, and I thought, 'My God, what have I come to?' I've seen managers do worse since, but at the time it was a real eye-opener.

I thought I had done OK. Then he turned to me and to be honest, I was fearing the worst. But he said, 'I'm leaving you out of this, because you were playing with a bunch of fellas tonight who were not interested.' I just sat in the corner with my head bowed and never once looked up at him – and that was my first match. A fairly inauspicious start to my career in professional football.

There were still a few games left that season and as I had been doing pretty well in the reserves, I thought I might get a chance with the first team. Then one day, I was told to travel down to Wimbledon for a match. I wasn't going to be a sub or play, I was just going down to see what happened on match day.

There was a lot of hype surrounding the game. John Fashanu was at his height then, with his tough, physical style of play. He clashed with Robbie James, although it was a fairly even tussle, to be fair. The game ended 1–1 as far as I can remember, and that was the first professional game I'd been involved with. I saw what went on in the changing-room and things like that.

There were about two or three games to go and we were playing Coventry, who were on a real high at the time as they had just got through to the FA Cup final. Derek Goodall phoned me just before the game to say that if I got on, it would be the first time there had been two former Hayes strikers in a First Division match, because Cyrille Regis was playing for Coventry at the time. We got beaten 4–1, but I came on for the last 15 minutes for my debut in the first team. Cyrille played really well that day and got two of the goals against us.

You could hardly call my first taste of the First Division memorable. We were under pressure during the game and I was warming-up on the sidelines when Jim called me over. (You always see on the television the manager doing that to the substitute, and wonder what they are saying to them.) So I got stripped and was obviously very excited when he said I was going on to take the place of Mike Fillery. 'All I want you to do,' he said, 'is run your bollocks off.' I said to him, 'Is that it?' and he said, 'Yes, just run your bollocks off.'

I'll never forget it. We were coming back home on the coach and I was so disillusioned with what he had said to me. I thought to myself, 'Surely there is more to being a First Division professional footballer than what he has just told me?' I was used to things being a bit more sophisticated than that at Hayes! I thought about that for a few days, because the next game was at Sheffield Wednesday and we lost 7–1. I came on when we were 5–1 down and Jim said exactly the same thing to me that day as well. It really affected me badly.

I remember talking to David Kerslake about it, and I was feeling so disenchanted by my first experiences of first-team football that I told David I was going to pack it all in and go back to non-league. He said I didn't know what I was talking about. I remember we'd been training at the main ground on the astroturf and we were sitting in the bath afterwards. I said I was going to quit and he started to say what a load of rubbish that was, and what the benefits were of being a professional footballer. I sat there and thought to myself that David was the one who didn't know what he was talking about. Maybe I just said it for something to say because I was new, I'm not sure. I had only played in two matches so far, but that's what I felt at the time. Every time I see David now, he reminds me about that day and asks me whether I have quit the game yet. It was a funny way to start my professional career.

QPR had a miserable finish to that season, I think they won just one of their last 12 games. Although I thought I had done quite well in the reserves, I didn't seem to be making any sort of impact at all with the management. It was all a bit of an anti-climax.

CHAPTER SIX

A Turkish Adventure

I got on with Jim Smith pretty well but even though he'd signed me from Hayes, I wasn't convinced he really fancied me as a player. He was a very fiery, passionate person as most people in football know, one of the game's real characters. But at that time I had never really met anyone like him before – although now I have come to appreciate that you meet all sorts of managers in football, all with their own style. Some come in and rant and rave and throw things about, which was very much Jim's style, and then there are others like Peter Shreeves, who was my reserve-team manager at QPR. He was cool, calm and collected at all times, and Ray Wilkins was the same. In those early days I was a bit quiet, shy and laid-back, and Jim's temperament and mine were not exactly compatible.

My first pre-season as a pro was a really strange experience. There I was with an eight-week holiday in front of me, longer than we ever got at school, and I didn't know what to do with myself half the time because most of my friends were working during the day. It was a time for me to reflect on what had just happened to me and I couldn't wait for the new season to start. I had just got a taste of it and wanted it to continue. I was a footballer now, and I didn't need to work to keep the money coming in.

Aaron had been born by that stage and it felt weird being a father. From what I had seen, you were supposed to feel a real bonding with your kid but that never happened for me until he was a lot older. It was strange; I was still very young – and probably very young in my thoughts – and I didn't seem to be thinking the same way, from what I could tell, as other people who had kids. I saw a lot of Aaron, as much as I possibly could. He used to spend weekends with me at my mum's and Angelea lived nearby, so that wasn't a problem. I didn't let my hair down and go on wild binges or anything like that, but I still had a good time like anyone.

At that age I was fairly fit but I did nothing special to prepare myself for the new season. Unlike the boys that had been there for a few years, I didn't realise what was in store for us when we came back for pre-season training and it was a bit of a shock to the system. In the morning, you would do some short runs and some ball-work. But in the afternoon, after having some lunch, you would go on a long run by the river. I suffered, but not as badly as I thought I was going to. There are plenty of stories in football about these nightmare sessions you do during pre-season, but I was OK. I was never a good long-distance runner anyway, so I started at the back and finished at the back! Even though I was a new pro there, they treated me pretty well and didn't really try to play any tricks on me. There were a few players that were sick during training, but I think I was naturally fit so it didn't happen to me – which was lucky because as a new guy there, I would have got a lot of stick off the lads for that. There weren't many other new pros. The only one I can remember was Danny Maddix, who came to Rangers on loan from Tottenham and they ended up signing him.

We went on a pre-season tour to Holland and Norway, which was another new experience for me. I got on in a couple of games and actually got sent-off in one of them. Jim Smith warned me before the game that they would try and wind me up, spit at me and things like that, but that I should keep my cool no matter what the provocation. Anyway, I went into a challenge with the goalkeeper and he lashed out at me, so I smacked him in the face. I ended up getting sent-off and the goalkeeper stayed on. There was a cameraman behind the goal who actually said to Jim afterwards that I was only protecting myself. Jim was obviously annoyed that I had got myself sent-off, especially after he had warned me beforehand. He had also dragged off Gavin

Maguire, who got involved in the incident as well. Gavin liked a good scrap, but Jim said it was bad enough that I had got sent-off, so he substituted Gavin.

At the time, I did have a reputation for being a bit fiery. QPR had seen me get sent-off at non-league level, and now this. I used to get involved with other players a lot then, because where I was brought up you are taught not to let people take liberties with you. You have to stand up for yourself. But I learned from that mistake in pre-season and never got sent-off for a long time after that.

At the beginning of the season I was still in the reserves and I suffered a lot with my back, which kept me out for much of that year, 1987–88. I kept coming back and having problems, so the club sent me to see a few specialists and they said I had a problem with one of my discs. I think it was because I was now training full-time and my body was not used to it. Then I got to a stage where I was playing well again in the reserves but the forwards in the first team were also doing well. The team had a really good season and finished fifth. There wasn't much chance of me getting in ahead of Gary Bannister and John Byrne, especially when Jim also signed Dean Coney and Mark Falco as well.

Then, out of the blue, in February I made my first full appearance for the club. I had not expected to be anything more than a substitute for the rest of the season. We travelled away to Everton and at the time Gary Bannister and John Byrne were in the side and a couple of other strikers were injured. We were in the hotel on the morning of the game and Gary had fallen ill with a bad stomach or something like that. Anyway, Jim came up to me very casually and said I was playing. I didn't really take it in at first, but then he said it again and I realised I was about to play my first full game for QPR. It had been completely unexpected.

It was also the first time I had ever been to Goodison Park, and I went out before the game and looked around. I remember Justin Channing saying what a fantastic main stand they had there, and by the time we kicked off the whole of the stand was packed and so was most of the ground. It was the biggest crowd I had ever played in front of. I suppose I was nervous but once the game got going I felt OK. I played pretty well and Peter

Shreeves came up to me after the game and said I had done well for my first match.

Despite that it was generally a very frustrating time for me; I thought I was good enough, but everything that was happening to me made me start to think that I wasn't. In my mind I knew I just needed to be given a chance, but the people that mattered didn't seem to want to give me that chance. Of course, I had suffered a lot with the injury, but I played only that one first-team game all season and I was beginning to doubt in my own mind how good I was.

It was looking like I wasn't going to get in the side again, and one day Jim came to me and said Brentford wanted me on loan. Steve Perryman had obviously been watching my progress and had come back to get me for a month. I really thought that was the end of my career at QPR – I had come from non-league football and I didn't really understand how the professional game worked. QPR saw it as farming me out to gain some experience and get me used to playing in front of crowds, but I didn't see it that way. I felt rejected, that I didn't stand a chance at QPR. It was never really explained to me what the situation was; I was just told I was going out on a month's loan and that was that.

I played three games for Brentford and didn't manage to score. But I had to go back early because my back began playing me up again.

It was around this time of uncertainty that Jim Smith first talked to me about going out to Turkey. It started off with him saying that he had this pal, Gordon Milne, who was managing a side called Besiktas out in Istanbul. Jim said that Gordon was looking for a forward and how would I feel about it?

I thought it was an opportunity for me. I reckoned that if Jim was saying things like this to me, the chances of me playing for the first team at QPR must be pretty slim. Obviously I had to do something, sort myself out and get some football under my belt. I felt that perhaps he was telling me he didn't want me anymore, and here was a chance to make it somewhere else. I was just thinking about the football side of it, really. If it had been a year before, I probably wouldn't have been mature enough to think of it in that way. But this was my career now, and it was important to make the right career decision.

When Jim initially came to me, I said I would think about it and that was that. There was nothing more said, it was just a relaxed conversation. Then a couple of months later at the training ground, he mentioned it to me again. He said that Gordon was coming over in a few weeks and would I speak to him? I said I would.

I must admit, in my mind I thought I would have a chat with Gordon and pretend I was interested, but there was no way I was going to play in Turkey. It was strange to think of a 21-year-old black guy from Ladbroke Grove going to play in Istanbul. I was going to humour him, show that I was keen to advance my career; but I thought nothing would ever come of it.

Then we drew close to the end of the season and Gordon came over. I remember going out to training and there was this new fellow out there with us. Jim pulled me over and said that was Gordon and would I have a word with him after training? So afterwards, Gordon and I had a quick chat in the canteen and then we arranged to meet at a hotel in Holland Park. We had some lunch and had a good talk. He explained that he had asked Jim whether Rangers had any players they might not need for a year, and Jim had suggested me. Gordon said that Jim had told him I had a lot of potential but that he wasn't sure whether my attitude was right, whether I wanted it bad enough. I was surprised by what I was hearing, because Jim had never come to me and said anything like that! It was strange coming from someone else.

Gordon told me that here was a chance to make some good money for a year, play in front of 30,000 crowds every week and get some real experience, the supporters were fanatical. All the time I was just saying I was interested and would go home and think about it. I talked it over with my mum that night and she said, 'How do you feel?' My first answer was that I didn't really fancy going to Turkey. She said she couldn't tell me what to do, but that it might be an opportunity I would look back on in years to come and wish I had gone for it. She said she didn't want me to go, but if it was for the best then I should go ahead and do it. My dad thought the same, really. None of us knew too much about Turkey, and he thought it was a long way to go just to play football.

I didn't know anything about the country, in fact. My only real impression of Turkey came from watching the film *Midnight Express*, and I didn't really fancy what I saw in that! But I thought about it and in the end I decided yes, I would do it. I had obviously told Angelea this was coming up and she was really good about it, saying I had to do what was best for my career. Gordon told me there would be no problem with my family coming out from time to time; or, if I wanted them out there for the whole time, then that was totally my decision. At the time, I was 21 and I was thinking to myself, 'Just go and do it, don't give it too much thought.'

So I told Gordon I would go and he made all the arrangements. It had all happened right at the end of the season, and all the way through the summer I was thinking to myself, 'Bloody hell, I'm going out to Turkey, what have I done?' Obviously there were a lot of tears shed with all my family. I remember standing on the doorstep with my cases and bags and thinking to myself, 'Am I doing the right thing?' But I had made up my mind and I had to get on with it.

Gordon and I went over together and as we landed in Istanbul, I thought to myself, 'Here we go, into the unknown.' When we walked out into the terminal, it was unreal. There were photographers and hundreds of supporters, I couldn't believe it. Here I was, Les Ferdinand, who had played only three games for QPR's first team, and I was being treated like a god. They hadn't even seen me play yet and my first impression, when I saw all this, was that I had a lot to live up to. They were all there because they expected a lot from me, and I had to deliver that to them. It was only later on that I realised they had such a high regard for English football that they felt any player coming over from England was going to improve their side and the Turkish league.

Gordon had already told me I would be in the team straight away. He felt an English centre-forward would do well in Turkey. He had also explained to me that I was going to play for a big club, but I didn't realise just how big until I got there. On the way to the hotel we drove past the ground and there were loads of people outside. I thought that was strange, but Gordon told me it was the opening ceremony that night for the new season, when the team is presented to the fans. I got changed at the hotel and went straight down to the stadium.

The place was packed; no-one had told me anything about this. There was a big carnival and a parade of all the close-season signings, followed by a training session out on the pitch. There were about three or four new signings from Turkish sides, but I was the biggest from abroad.

The changing-rooms were underground, like many on the continent, and all the players run up into the stadium. I had never been in one of those before and you could hear the crowd, there was absolute bedlam going on. I was really nervous. I was introduced to all the players for the first time, then they called the players out to be introduced to the crowd, one by one. I was last – and this is where the story of the animal sacrifices comes from.

It is a traditional Muslim ritual in Turkey that they sacrifice a lamb for the team, which is meant to bring good luck. But to those players they see as being special, they also give a pigeon to take out into the stadium. They announced my name and gave me the pigeon, and as I went to run out, they dragged me back to dab the lamb's blood on my boots and forehead. Clearly, I had never experienced anything quite like this before. I had half a thought about rubbing it off, but I realised that would be an insult to the fans. They were going mad with excitement as it was. We didn't actually see the lamb being sacrificed in front of us – it was already dead and its throat had been cut – but it was just lying there on the floor in the tunnel. People could see I was a bit uncomfortable with it, but I realised that it was their ritual and I had to respect it. I can safely say, though, that it was very different to what I had been used to at Loftus Road.

However, worse was to follow. When a new player gets to the centre of the pitch, he is meant to throw the pigeon in the air as a sign of good luck. So out I ran and I threw this pigeon up in the air and there was a big roar from the crowd. Everything was going alright, or so I thought. But because the pigeon had been cooped-up somewhere for so long, its wings were closed and it couldn't fly away. It just dropped out of the air and landed with a thud at my feet.

I picked up the bird straight away – thinking, 'Oh no, what have I done now?' – and launched it into the air. There was silence and down it plunged again onto the floor. Now I thought I'd really done something serious and that all the fans were going to run on the pitch and lynch me at any moment. But this young boy came over and manipulated the bird's wings open, then gave it back to me. This time, I shut my eyes and threw it as high as I could. I heard this big roar and the pigeon began to struggle a bit but finally flew away. I just thought to myself, 'What a relief!' My heart started beating normally again and we got straight into the training session.

When it was all over and done with, they took us into a restaurant. As we walked in, there was a lamb on a skewer being roasted, and I remember wondering whether that was the lamb that had been in the stadium. It was really bugging me, I kept looking over at it. A little later, they sliced it up and put it on a plate in front of me. All the players were tucking in and I just couldn't bring myself to eat it. I looked round and everyone was laughing and joking and really enjoying the food, and my stomach was just turning over. They were asking me what the matter was, and I just had to say I was not too hungry because of the excitement of the day and that it had tightened all my stomach up. To this day, I still don't know whether it was the lamb from the stadium or not.

All the new players were living in the same hotel but most of them came from other parts of Turkey and none of them could speak good English, so the contact with them was not great for the first few weeks. After the first day, we went over to Germany for pre-season training. We didn't even stay the night at the hotel in town. We were whisked virtually straight from the meal to a hotel near the airport and then went to Germany early the next morning.

Lying in bed that night, I thought to myself, 'What have I come to?' There was no CD player in those days to take your mind off things. I turned on the television and it was all Turkish TV; it was a long way from Ladbroke Grove. I spoke to my mum

In my early days at QPR.

My mum Adrianna,
who died in 1990. She
was my best friend.

Me (five) with my sister Anna-Marie (seven). Growing up in west London made me streetwise.

On my return from Turkey, again with Anna-Marie.

Playing for Besiktas was one of the turning points of my career.

With a few of my Besiktas team mates. I had a great time in Turkey and tried hard to learn the language.

The QPR line-up in 1989-90, my first complete season with the club.

It was during the 1990-91 season that the QPR fans started calling me 'Sir Les'.

Empics

I had a run of five full first-team games, starting with this one against Aston Villa
in September 1990, before injuries disrupted my season.

Here I am with my dad Austin, my stepmother Vanessa, my half-sisters Rachel and Nola, and my son Aaron.

My son Aaron – I wouldn't swap him for the world.

At the christening of my beautiful daughter Lauren, who was born in November 1996.

Early on in my career I had a reputation for being a bit fiery.

Doing battle with my future England boss Glenn Hoddle in a 1993 FA Cup match against Swindon Town. QPR won 3–0 and I scored two goals.

Scoring on my England debut against San Marino in February 1993.

In my last season at QPR I scored 24 league goals – two of them against my future club Newcastle United.

and my dad for a while and then decided, 'Let's get on with it and see where we go.'

I would never have thought, lying there, that my season in Turkey would be one of the turning points in my career, the year Les Ferdinand really came of age as a professional footballer. This was my football apprenticeship, the apprenticeship I never had as a young player like Dennis had. And to be honest, it was probably a more difficult apprenticeship than people in England had, considering I was a long way from home, without anybody I knew, in a strange country.

Pre-season in Germany went really well because I scored in my first game and went on to score a few more. I got to know the players and Gordon, and it obviously helped a lot to have an English manager. But there was one extraordinary incident that took place in Germany, which had to do with my signing-on fee. Gordon had told me that the people at the club were fantastic and would pay as they said, but the only thing was, they always seemed to pay late.

My first signing-on fee was due and I hadn't seen it, so I went to Gordon and he said he would have a word. He spoke to one of the committee members, who then came to me and said not to worry, they knew it was due but were trying to get the money together for me. I thought that was a bit strange, because over in England you always got your signing-on fee in a cheque to put straight into the bank. But I left them to it.

A few days later, one of the directors came up and started chatting to see how I was settling in. We were in a really nice hotel in the mountains in Germany, and he told me that the club had left a little present in my room to say welcome. I was sharing with our goalkeeper, Rade Zalac. He was a Yugoslav but he could speak English very well and we became the best of friends.

We came in from training and Rade, who had gone in before me, turned round and said there was a parcel on the table for me. It was like a cardboard box, so I opened it up and there was all my money in there – in pounds, cash. I will always remember the look on Rade's face. He said, 'Nice, huh?' with this huge smile, and I said, 'Yeah, it's not too bad.' I counted it all up and there was about £15,000 in cash, although it looked like a lot more.

I thought, 'What am I going to do with all this?' I had nowhere to put it so I locked it away in my suitcase. I couldn't get it transferred to England and I didn't want to put it in the hotel safe. Every time I came in from training I would go straight to my suitcase to make sure it was still there. I was like a little boy with a new bike, but I still couldn't work out how I was going to get it into a bank.

So I went to see Gordon, and I can remember the ex-England goalkeeper Alan Hodgkinson had come over to Germany to take a few training sessions with us. Alan suggested to me that as he was going back to England, he could deliver it to my family so they could put it in a bank. I was thinking to myself, 'I've never met this guy before; he might be a mate of Gordon's, but no chance!' So I said to him that I would sort it out, although I think he realised I was a bit wary of him and that I thought he might do a runner with the money! In the end, I decided to take it back to Istanbul.

As the cost of living was so low in Turkey, and because all the money I was earning was tax-free, I was able to put most of it away, not touch it and live off the bonuses – and because I was playing for a good side, I was guaranteed bonuses every month. The bonus system over there was very different to what we have in England. If we got 12 points in a month, the players would get the full bonus; ten points or nine points, certain amounts; but if we got eight points or less, we wouldn't get any at all; so there was a real incentive to do well. I kept most of the money I got from my signing-on fee with me until I went back to England and put it in a bank. It meant I was able to spoil my mum and my sister a bit. My mum had just been taken ill with cancer and was having a rough time. She was desperate to go back to St Lucia on holiday with her sister, so I was able to send her there. As it turned out, it was to be the last time she went back there.

One thing that was great about my time in Turkey was that whenever I wanted to go back to see my family, it was never a problem. The club always paid for my flights, and today my passport is still littered with entry and exit stamps from Turkey.

CHAPTER SEVEN

Goals and Maggie Thatcher

I got very lonely at times in Turkey as you would expect, especially when I first arrived. The supporters were quite fanatical over there – probably even more so than in Newcastle – and they made me feel very welcome straight away. But obviously, not speaking the language and not knowing the places to go like I would have done in London made it very difficult, particularly since I was out there on my own. I made two very good friends in the goalkeeper Rade and a guy involved with the club called Can Oner, who was the manager of the Hilton Hotel in Istanbul. He became a great friend of mine and used to say that I was like his brother. He took really good care of me. If ever I felt lonely in the flat, he would say, 'Come to the hotel,' and I would go there, have dinner with him and he would give me a room there for the night. On occasions, I used to go out to eat with Gordon and his sons, Ian and Graham, who used to come over from time to time.

I had moved out of my hotel into a two-bedroom flat pretty soon after we came back from pre-season in Germany. The club provided everything. Gave me a car, furnished the flat and made life as comfortable as they possibly could for me. I tried to learn Turkish to help the transition, and of course I learned all the bad words first. But mostly the lads wanted to learn English more than they wanted to teach me Turkish, and I think that was good for me. What got them to accept me into their group was that I was willing to try and learn their language, which is a very important thing to do when you go abroad. They would obviously give me things to say that sounded funny in an English accent. They would all be sitting there in hysterics and I would probably have just insulted somebody. That happened a few times, and even whoever it was I had insulted normally saw the funny side of it and took it as a joke.

After I returned to England, I actually went back out to see Rade and Can a couple of times. But soon afterwards, Rade left for another club, and although I spoke to him a few more times, one day I called from England and he wasn't living in his flat anymore. I lost all contact with him and was never able to trace him again. He had played for Partizan Belgrade before coming to Turkey.

About a year ago, though, I was in the Emporium nightclub in London and this guy came up to me and said he was a really good friend of Rade Zalac. I was really keen to get a number off this guy; unfortunately he didn't have it on him, but he said Rade was really well and I gave him my number to give to Rade. I think he said that Rade had not gone back to Yugoslavia because of all the problems there. Rade was Croatian (he came from Zagreb) so because of the war, he was still abroad.

Although I was occasionally lonely, generally I had an amazing time in Turkey. At no stage did I think, 'I fancy packing my bags and going back to England.' Even at the end of my loan spell, I actually came back to find out whether I could stay there another year. That's how much I enjoyed it.

Even when I got there, my initial thoughts were: 'I'm here for a year, if at any time I don't like it I can go back, and the worst thing that can happen to me is they hold onto my registration for that year and I don't play football for the season.' One thing I had in my favour was that I knew QPR still held my permanent registration and that Besiktas was only a loan period for a year. But the situation never occurred.

When I came back and things started to happen for me in England, people obviously asked me about Turkey, but I felt the things that were written were pretty negative about the country, ridiculing Turkey in some ways (a lot of the articles focused on the sacrifice at the opening ceremony, making fun of it). I never wanted that to happen. It was an excellent time in my life and I often think that if it hadn't been for that year at Besiktas, I wouldn't be the player I am today.

One thing that obviously helped me over there was that I scored a lot of goals, and that started straight away. I scored 21 in 33 games, and any striker will tell you that when you are in that sort of form, you cannot wait for the next game to come along. We finished second in the league, won the Turkish equivalent of the FA Cup and qualified for Europe.

We played in the UEFA Cup the season I arrived as well, against Dinamo Zagreb. I played in the first leg and missed the second, but I went over to Zagreb to watch the game. It was Rade's home town so it was a really big game for him. Because we were only there for two days, we weren't able to see too much of the city. We got knocked out over the two legs, so my first experience of European football was a very brief one. It was certainly very different, but I had gone from playing English football to playing out in Turkey, so I was already playing in a very different style to what I was used to.

The two big games of the season in Turkey were against Galatasaray and Fenerbahce, the other teams in Istanbul. When we came to play them, there was talk of people sleeping outside the ground just to get in the next day. The noise in the stadium for these games was just unbelievable.

I managed to score in my first game against Galatasaray, which obviously made me very popular with the Besiktas fans. I had been out for a couple of games with a damaged cartilage in my knee, and Gordon was coming in for some stick from the supporters because results were not going so well. Then we had the big derby match, with both teams contesting the top of the table at the time. Gordon came to me and said he needed me to play in the match because it was such a big game. It was my first game back and we won 2–1 at home. I scored the first goal, I'll never forget it. Someone took a corner, it flicked off someone's head and I was going to head it but it sort of hit me and went in the net.

Before the match, there had been graffiti and banners around and inside the ground saying 'Go home Milne'. The fans were ready to get rid of him because of a couple of bad results, but as soon as I scored, the banners came down straight away and everyone was cheering. We went on to win the game and everything was forgiven because we had beaten our biggest rivals. The crowd was so noisy and loud it is difficult to describe. The celebrations went straight through you; fireworks, horns, drums, they bring everything into the stadium. I was talking to Warren Barton about it not that long ago and I remembered a game we played against a team called Malatya. One of the players went down injured and the crowd started singing and it was the noisiest sound I have ever heard come out of a stadium. I stood in the middle of the pitch and looked around and I just couldn't believe what I was hearing. Rade's wife was an English teacher and when we got home, she asked him what had happened in the stadium that day. We had won 5–2, so Rade said it was just another game. But I mentioned how loud the fans had been, and she said a friend of hers who lived near the stadium had phoned up frightened, because the windows in her flat were shaking from the noise. Whenever I look back on my time in Turkey – and you obviously remember specific things – that is one of the things that has stuck in my mind. The fanaticism of the supporters was incredible.

They used to come up to you on the street and would give you their last penny just to say hello to you. It became embarrassing in the end, because when I had friends from England over to see me for a while, I would want to take them out for a meal. There were some really good restaurants there and the food was pretty good. It was always a three- or four-course meal with drinks and everything else, and at the end I would ask for the bill and they would bring another special fruit dish with sparklers on it, compliments of the chef. So we would have to eat that and then ask for the bill again, but then the waiter would tell us that the manager was a Besiktas supporter and the whole meal was on him. I would beg to differ and offer to pay, but they wouldn't have it. I got embarrassed because they would always invite you back, but I didn't want to because it would feel like we were taking liberties, seeing as we would not have to pay for anything. But that's what the people were like there. I ended up never going to the same restaurant more than once because of it.

I saw things in Turkey that you would never see anywhere else. A lot of people are surprised that I enjoyed myself so much there, but I'll never forget that year. There were certain things, though, that I would not want to experience again. While the fans were some of the best anyone could wish for, if they decided to turn on you it really could be quite dangerous and I sometimes feared for my safety.

One incident happened just after Christmas. Up until then we were unbeaten and Galatasaray had fallen away, so it was between Besiktas and Fenerbahce for the title.

Now the situation in Turkish football is really weird, because sometimes clubs will offer bonuses to the team their rivals are playing, to encourage them to get a result. It's like Man Utd saying to QPR, 'You're playing Newcastle this week, if you beat them we will give you an extra £X thousand.' That was how it was for Besiktas. The smaller sides we were coming up against, who normally never got bonuses, were really up for it against us. They were playing their hearts out.

In one game, we played this team and it was a draw, but nine times out of ten we would have wiped the floor with them and because we were doing so well at the time, we were expected to win easily. As we were leaving the ground, the Besiktas supporters started stoning the coach. They were throwing what seemed to be these huge rocks at us. I had never experienced anything like that before, it was frightening. I thought to myself, 'What's going on?' It may have been only the first game we had drawn that season! Thankfully, that was the only time it happened.

Later on in the season, we lost to Fenerbahce on a Sunday and came in for training on the Monday. When we arrived, there were large groups of supporters waiting. They used to come and watch the training, but this time they were burning the club's flag and a few of them were saying that some of the players hadn't played their best for the club against Fenerbahce. Rade came in for a lot of stick, fights broke out and everything. It was a really crazy few minutes, but after a while they settled down.

We got our own back in the end, though, when we beat our big rivals to win the Turkish Cup. It was a major achievement for Besiktas, who had lived in the shadow of the other two clubs in Istanbul for some time and had only won the Cup once before. It was also the first senior title that I had won and I scored in the final as well, which made it a really special occasion for me.

It was one of those goals that sticks in your mind. It was in the second leg of the final and turned out to be the deciding goal which won the Cup for us on aggregate. I beat three or four players and then took the ball round the keeper. (The goalie was Harald Schumacher, who had played in two World Cup finals for West Germany, in 1986 against Argentina in Mexico and four years earlier against Italy in Spain.) It was a great way to end the season, which on a personal level had been my most successful ever. You could say that I was very popular with the fans as a result of that, and Gordon said to me afterwards that if I ever walked into the stadium again, I would get a hero's welcome because I was the guy who won the Cup against Fenerbahce.

It was soon time to return to England but the club didn't want to let me go. Gordon was keen to keep me and I actually wanted to stay out in Turkey for another year. Trevor Francis had taken over at QPR by now and we travelled back to see what we could sort out about extending the loan period. We had a meeting with Trevor and Clive Berlin, who was general manager of the club at the time. Trevor asked whether Besiktas could pay a transfer fee for me of about £500,000, but Gordon pointed out that they never really paid fees for a loan player; most of the money goes to the player, who can then leave for free at the end of the contract. That was the way it worked. Francis said that they had heard how well I had done over there and that was the price they wanted, but Gordon made it clear that was impossible. When he realised Besiktas couldn't pay the money, Francis then changed his story and started saying how he really wanted me to come back, having had such good reports about me. He explained how the club didn't have many strikers and he didn't really want to play himself, so they wanted me back.

I thought to myself, 'A minute ago he was willing to sell me but now they know they can't get any money for me, I'm the greatest thing around.'

I was totally fed up with the situation, got pretty angry and walked out of the meeting. Gordon came out and calmed me down. He said that I basically had to come back, so what I had to do now was negotiate the best deal I could for myself. There was no point in being bitter or silly about it. I went back in there and sat down to sort out what I was going to get back home.

It was only afterwards that I discovered the lengths Besiktas had gone to to try and keep me. Gordon told me that people from the club actually tried to get in touch with Margaret Thatcher, who was then Prime Minister, to get her to intervene on their behalf and secure my services for another year. They weren't joking either, it is actually a true story. They sent a letter to her, via the Turkish Embassy in London, asking her to organise it. The club was very well connected into the Turkish Government, and things like that were done all the time over there – the president of a football club could get things sorted because of his connections, and I think they automatically assumed that the same type of thing went on in England. I don't know if they ever got a reply or if the PM ever received the letter. Either she thought they were a bunch of nutcases or Mrs Thatcher was a secret QPR fan. Needless to say, I had to come back despite the best efforts of Besiktas.

CHAPTER EIGHT

Back on the Roller Coaster

Following my Turkish adventures, I started back with the lads at QPR in the pre-season of 1989. It was good to see them all again and renew friendships, although I hadn't been away that long and had been back on occasions during my year out. This was our first pre-season with Trevor Francis as manager, and despite our disagreement over my going to Besiktas for another year, I seemed to get on pretty well with him from the start. While I was in Turkey, I had heard the story about what had happened between him and Martin Allen (he had allegedly refused to let Martin miss a match to be present at the birth of his first child) but you can only judge someone on how they are with you, and he seemed fine.

I came back and felt really good, especially after such a good season in Turkey. But I had to prove myself all over again at QPR to a new manager, so there were no guarantees. Things started off pretty well, although I was in the reserves again at the start. I was playing well and looking sharp, and the year in Turkey had obviously helped me. It wasn't long before I got the chance to prove myself in the first team.

The one thing that still seemed to count against me was that the management thought I was too hot-headed, that I got involved with referees and opponents too much. It had been something that Jim Smith had levelled against me and now I found that Don Howe, who had come in as coach alongside Trevor Francis, was saying the same thing to me again. They felt I was a bit fiery and needed to calm down. I didn't think I had a problem but I was prepared to listen to experienced people to see if they were right.

I was not really disappointed that I didn't get straight in the team back at QPR. I realised that Turkish football was one thing and the First Division another. But I had got a taste of what it was like playing in front of big crowds and enjoyed it, and I have to admit that every now and again I did think about Turkey, playing in Europe and all the big derby matches in front of those fanatical supporters. I also knew, though, that I had to try and be patient, because I did want to make it at QPR.

I was sub for a match at Wimbledon in early November but it wasn't long before I got my chance. A couple of weeks later, I was in the starting line-up against Millwall and then again the following week against Crystal Palace. I hadn't played too badly and the team had beaten Palace 3–0. We then had the local derby against Chelsea in December and this was a huge day in my career for QPR.

I scored twice that afternoon, my first senior goals for QPR. I remember them vividly. The first one was a flick from Mark Falco and I ran onto it, hit a shot and it went through the goalkeeper's legs. They then equalised, but I got a second with a header from a Ray Wilkins free-kick. We ended up winning 4–2 after Falco had hit this fantastic volley for the third.

At the time, I didn't realise how much beating Chelsea meant to QPR supporters. I got taken off with about 10 minutes to go and I always remember on the Monday, Don Howe saying to me how well I had played – so much so, he said, that the manager had a go at him for taking me off (Francis had been up in the stands for that game and Howe on the bench). He told me that he had been telling the manager that I was worth a chance, and that's when he warned me about my temperament and that I needed to control it better.

It was typical of my luck that just when I thought I had got the break under a manager at last, Trevor Francis got the sack the following week. I thought to myself, 'Here we go again.'

I had got those two goals against Chelsea at a time when Rangers were struggling to score. That same weekend, Roy Wegerle signed for £1 million and then Francis left. Don Howe took over and our next game was away at Sheffield Wednesday. Mark Falco and I started that game and Wegerle was on the bench. At half-time, Howe came in and told me that I was playing like someone who knows there is a guy on the bench to come on in his place, and he took me off. (I always remember Ray Wilkins coming up to me and saying whenever you are doing well in this game, there is always someone who'll turn round and kick you in the bollocks. He said I never deserved to come off, and to keep my chin up.) Roy was brought on and that was it for me in the first team for a long time. Don had let me know that Wegerle and Falco were going to be his first choice and that was that. He went on about me not sorting myself out, not being hungry enough for it. I thought if that was his opinion, there was little I could do to change it. I wasn't going to knock on his door and demand to be in the team.

That was a time when I felt I wasn't wanted at QPR and that it was probably time for me to go. Whenever I came into the side – I played only four more matches that season – I used to get a bit of stick from the supporters. I was the boo-boys' favourite for a while. They used to say I was lazy, that I didn't run around enough and the club should get rid of me. I came in for some quite harsh treatment from them but I just kept going and tried not to let it affect me, although obviously it is something you cannot ignore.

I really felt like I was never given a fair crack of the whip under Don Howe. He had made judgements about me that were not correct. All I had ever asked for from any manager was a run in the team and I knew I would prove myself to them if I was given a chance. But Don Howe wasn't willing to give that to me.

So I was quite disenchanted when the new season, 1990–91, started. I began it on the bench, coming on as substitute three times, and then had a little run of five full games in the first team. I scored just one league goal, away at Coventry, and generally the team weren't doing too well so I was dropped. It was around this time that I began to suffer with injuries again, which didn't help, and I was also still having a few problems with Don. He continued to question why I didn't come charging into his office when I had been dropped. I'm just not like that, though. I don't go around thinking I've got a divine right to be in the side – and because of that, I then get labelled with the attitude that I'm too laid-back, and that's wrong.

Looking back, I always thought I could play in the First Division but maybe I did not always believe in my own ability, and what people read into my general demeanour on the field was that I didn't care enough. Nothing could have been further from the truth. I just felt that others had a right to be in the side ahead of me and it took a while to shake that out of my mind, although I did get angry when I came into the side, scored goals and still got left out, or if I was playing well in the reserves and wasn't getting picked.

When I eventually left QPR for Newcastle, I remember speaking to Richard Thompson, who was the QPR chairman then and who I got on with really well. He told me that during the 1990–91 season, when Don was still at the club – and don't forget he was a well-renowned coach who should have been able to spot a player – he had come to the board and said that they should sell me to Millwall for £750,000. Richard and Clive Berlin said they weren't prepared to do that. That conversation, a few years later, seemed to make a lot of sense to me. It was obvious what Don had wanted and it showed in his attitude towards me. It wasn't that we didn't get on, I just don't think he felt I co-operated with him as well as he would have liked. I had a few words with him, disagreements rather than arguments, and maybe he felt it was in his best interests to get rid of me. He said to the club that they had had a few bids for me and maybe it would be good business to sell.

Everything seemed to be going against me and that included injuries. One innocuous incident, especially, looked like it could threaten my career. It was around October that it happened, just after I had been dropped. I still wonder now how it kept me out for so long, about three months in total. One morning, I got a whack in a collision with the reserve-team goalkeeper in training. He caught me on the side of my thigh and I had what I thought was a dead leg. I rested it for a bit, iced it and went out for a run the next day, but it felt like I was being kicked every time I put my foot down. I tried to do a training session but after only a few strides, I could hardly walk. I remember telling the physio that it was so painful, any slight touch on it, even the rubbing of my trousers against it, was causing pain.

They couldn't understand it. After about a week of icing it, I came back to training and they told me just to do the warm-up, not to join in. I was jogging and I could still feel it was sore, but I thought maybe the exercise would run it out. I then went to sprint to the halfway line and as I took off, it felt like someone had smashed me in the leg again. I went in and told the physio, Brian Morris, and he couldn't really understand it, so they sent me for a scan and found out that there was a lot of internal bleeding causing a problem. They thought about drawing the blood out and then talked about an operation – except if I had the op, I would have been out for the rest of the season because of the muscle damage. I decided against that, so I had to go to the hospital every day to have something called Mega Pulse, to make sure the bleeding was stopping and everything was clearing up. All I could do was just rest. I didn't play for 12 or 13 weeks because of it. All over a dead leg.

I was told by the doctors that if I carried on trying to play on it, without proper treatment, it could threaten my career. I wasn't sure myself, because it seemed such a 'nothing' injury – foot-ballers get dead legs all the time. But they said that the more I played, the more it would bleed and the more the bone would grow. I didn't really believe it could be career-threatening but because of the pain I was in, I was willing to go along with anything they said. I thought they must be right, because I'd had dead legs before but nothing like this. I later found out that the reason it was so serious was because where it had been bleeding internally, in the muscle, it had formed in a similar way to how a scab does. The technical term for it is 'calcified' and it had started growing into another bone. It was a worrying time because it had seemed such a normal injury.

It did seem for a while that I was jinxed with injuries and I began to think that maybe QPR wasn't the club for me, because of the amount of injuries I'd had. I was thinking that perhaps if I had a fresh start, my luck would change. I got very down about the whole situation and didn't want to speak to anyone about it. Then, almost as quickly, things began to turn my way again. I got fit after the long lay-off and then had some luck.

In February of that season, because of injuries I got back in the side with Bradley Allen. QPR were going through a dodgy period where they were in the bottom three and looking like they might go down. I came back into the side against Manchester United and then in my second game back, we were playing at Luton and I scored both goals in a 2–1 victory.

One of the goals was a really good header. Bobby Gould was coach with Don and he told me after the game that it was one of the best headers he had ever seen. I really climbed well for the cross and powered it in from just near the 18-yard line. The other goal was a run from the halfway line after the ball was slipped through to me by Bradley. I ran with it, beat a couple of players and smacked it into the bottom corner. Bobby Gould was a funny guy. Most managers seemed to need a buffer who can bridge the gap with the players, and Bobby was ideal in that role. We only had him for a short period of time while he was trying to find another job in management. He is an extraordinary character, very unpredictable, but he was brilliant at scouting players. He brought Darren Peacock and Rufus Brevett to QPR.

That game against Luton was also the start of my nickname, 'Sir Les'. I don't really remember who started it or why – someone later said to me that the supporters started it because I was a gentleman – but it has stuck ever since. They started chanting it at the end of that game and then the players picked it up from there. People still say to me, 'What's this "Sir Les" thing about?' and the players often used to take the mick out of me, saying, 'Arise, here comes Sir Les!' whenever I walked into the dressing-room. People still call me it now.

This proved to be the most successful time I had had in the team thus far in my career. I scored seven goals in eight games, including the first when we won 3–1 at Liverpool, which helped pull us up the table and we avoided relegation. I thought this was going to be a real start for me and maybe would convince some other clubs to take an interest in me. Instead of getting boos, I was now starting to get a few cheers from the supporters.

My contract was up around this time and the club wanted me to sign a new one. I said no, I still thought it was time to move on. Don Howe actually sat down with me, after he had said all that stuff to Richard Thompson. He told me he'd had managers come in for me but they all said the same thing to him: they couldn't understand what was wrong with Les Ferdinand. One week they would see me and think I was a world-beater, the next it was like I couldn't be bothered. Don said he'd told all of them that it wasn't that I wasn't bothered, it was more that I tried too hard and when things didn't go right, I hung my head and got disappointed. I turned round and said to him that these guys had come in there to sign me saying I was a good player, yet the next thing they didn't rate me and I'd got a problem. I asked him why the hell did they want to sign me, then? Don didn't have an answer to that. It was these little things that summed up our relationship. He would put something across to me and I would question it. As far as he was concerned, I was probably trying to be a bit too clever.

Although every now and again I did get really disappointed when I wasn't in the side, and maybe looked like I wanted to get away and make a career somewhere else, at the same time, deep down inside, I wanted to prove everyone wrong: the supporters, Don Howe, and the previous managers who hadn't given me a chance. At the end of that season, Don sat us all down and told us what we would be doing for the next season. A week or so later, it was in the papers that he had been relieved of his duties as manager – and soon after, in the summer of 1991, Gerry Francis arrived.

I didn't know Gerry at all, but during that summer he called in the players that weren't away, one at a time. I went into my meeting with him and he said he had tried to sign me when he was at Bristol Rovers but the club didn't want to do business at the time. He said he rated me as a player and wanted me to know that I was going to be his main striker for the season. That did my confidence the world of good. It was the first time anyone had said that to me at QPR and it helped me a tremendous amount. But when the season started, it didn't go very well for me at all and after a match against West Ham, when I came on as sub, I got dropped. I must admit I knew I wasn't playing as well as I could, so when he dropped me I wasn't really surprised. I missed the next five games but whatever the manager tried didn't seem to work, so I got recalled for the home match with Nottingham Forest at the start of October. It was also the start of more injury problems.

I broke my jaw against Forest without really knowing it. I went up for a challenge with one of the defenders and as I came down, I landed and caught someone's shoulder. I can remember doing it and it being painful at the time, but the physio came on and said it looked OK, there would just be some bruising on the side of my cheek. So I carried on with the game. Afterwards, I couldn't open my mouth too well so they sent me for an X-ray and even when I went to the hospital, the doctor there said he didn't think I had broken it because everything still seemed to be in place.

I had to wait two hours in the hospital to get the X-ray and gradually, as the adrenaline from the game left my body, it got sorer and sorer. I couldn't turn my head to one side, I had to turn my whole body. I was in excruciating pain. After the X-ray, the doctor said he couldn't believe the crack I had along my jaw. I had cracked it all the way from the top right down to underneath my chin. He told me I was very lucky that it had stayed in line, which is why it didn't look broken, as normally a crack like that would have the jaw shifting all over the place. I saw a specialist, who said that really he should wire the jaw and I would be out for six weeks. But if I promised not to play at all or do any running, he wouldn't need to wire it and I could be back in three. So I did nothing for three weeks and was fully fit again for the match against Oldham in November. Although the team lost 3–1 at home, I scored and kept my place for the next match, which was away at Notts County. I played really well in that game and scored the only goal of the match. It was our first win for about five games. It was typical of my luck again that I got hit by some niggling injuries after that, which kept me out for some time. I had a hernia operation and then just as I was recovering, I twisted my ankle in training, which kept me out again for a couple of weeks. It was a very frustrating time.

I was out the side for a while but got back against Notts County in the return fixture. I scored and played well and that game became a real turning-point in my career at QPR. I was never really out of the side again. I played the last 13 games of the season and scored eight goals, which was my best ever run for the team so far. Things were now looking good when not so long before, everything had seemed to be falling apart.

CHAPTER NINE

Lows and Highs

One thing had affected me more than any of the injuries, loss of form or being dropped, and that was when my mum died. It was 12 February 1990, a date that is forever etched on my memory. Her death affected me much worse than I could ever have imagined and had an impact on my whole life, professionally and personally. She was my best friend and because I had been away for a lot of the previous year in Turkey, I felt I had lost a lot of valuable time with her. It was really hard for me, especially because of that and the way that she died: she had cancer and it had hit her over a long period. She became gradually more ill and although she could take care of herself – she was a very independent woman – it eventually got to the stage where she was in a hospice. You know in your heart that once that happens, that is usually it. I tried to prepare myself for it, because I knew she would probably not be coming out of there, but you can never prepare for that sort of thing and it hit me harder than anything else that has happened to me in my life.

My mum had been ill for about 10 years, on and off. She had to have one of her breasts removed because the doctors had found a lump there, and then for the next four or five years she had treatments for it. I remember seeing her coming home from the treatment and going straight to bed because she was so ill. She was such a strong woman that she got over that, but when I went to Turkey she had a fall down the stairs, unfortunately, and hurt her back. I came back to see her and took her to see an osteopath. She was worried that it might be the cancer coming back but he said it wasn't, because he could see where she had put her back out of place in the fall. She said she felt a lot better, but a few months down the line she started to get the pains again and went to the doctor, who told her that the cancer had begun to attack her spine.

For a long spell while I was out in Turkey, she was OK. But from the time when the cancer was diagnosed again, it was a real struggle. I didn't feel guilty about being out there while a lot of this was going on, because I was sure it was what she would have wanted me to do anyway. Now I look back on it and think that was a year I missed with her. At the time, no-one can realise that. I'm a believer that once you develop cancer, that is what you will eventually die from. Even if you beat it once, more often than not it comes back, and that was my experience with my mum.

She was still getting about well, but when I came back from Turkey a few weeks later, she went into the hospice and that was a very difficult thing to come to terms with, because she had been such an active woman. I was more involved with the first team now, going away with them and coming back as soon as I could to go and visit her. If I travelled but didn't make the side, she would always ask why they hadn't played me that day if they had taken me to the game. I was having to explain that to her and it was funny in a way, because she just didn't realise the ins-and-outs of the game but despite her predicament, all she wanted to know was what was happening with my career.

It wasn't a surprise when she finally died. We knew it was coming eventually, but that doesn't make it any easier to deal with. After that, I really lost myself for a while. I went on a wild spending-spree with all the money I had saved up in the bank, just spending money and doing things that I wouldn't have done before. Things like cars, clothes and going out all the time, stuff like that. Thinking about it now, I can't really say exactly what I spent it on. I've got nothing to show for that period of my life. I took the attitude that a lot of people live for tomorrow and go out and save their money for later on in life, but at that point I thought, 'What's the point in that?' My mum was 45, she had struggled to bring me and my sister up for most of her life, and just as we were getting to be in a position where she wouldn't have to struggle anymore, because I could make things good for her, she was taken away from me and my family. I did wonder what was the point to it all. To work hard all your life and for that to happen, to have the closest person in your life taken away from you.

I didn't give up but just thought, 'I'm going to live life and not worry about anything.' I couldn't say exactly how much I went through, but it ran into tens of thousands of pounds. This probably lasted for about eight or nine months, possibly a year even. I felt numb at the time and thought this was doing me some good. I didn't really care if it was good for me or not, I wasn't thinking about the consequences.

In the end, I decided that this was not the way to go about things. I had a lot of chats with my dad; he knew how close I was to my mum. He and my sister tried to get hold of me and tell me that my mum would not have wanted me to be like that. She wanted to be proud of me, for me to do the best for myself, and that wasn't what I was doing then. They told me I needed to calm myself down a little bit. I heard that a few times from them and I suppose it eventually clicked.

Aaron was also a big influence and so was Angelea. She got to grips with me as well and told me that there wasn't just me to think about, there was my little boy. I look back and see a totally different Les Ferdinand to what I know now. Some people would have called it going off the rails. I don't know if it was, but it was obviously something I had to go through to deal with that situation. I think everyone appreciated how close I was to my mum, so they gave me room for a while. They saw that this was something I needed to go through and that no matter what they said, it wouldn't change anything. But at some stage they knew that I would eventually come back into line, because I was not like that before, and it was then that they began to try and calm me down. And to be honest, I couldn't have gone on that wild spree for too much longer. That was the time that I was in and out of the team under Don Howe, so I don't know if the situation with my mum affected my football or not. I suspect that it did. I had nothing to focus on. If I had been in the side more, it probably would have taken my mind off the situation. That was the time when Don used to say to me he didn't know if I wanted it enough; with my mum on my mind, I suppose it could have come across that way.

Getting over that period in my life also coincided with things beginning to click for me at QPR. I began to really flourish under Gerry Francis. He gave me a huge amount of confidence coming into the 1992–93 season, making it clear again that he thought I had the potential to go all the way. My run of goals at the end of the previous season meant I couldn't wait to get started again.

Gerry was very tactically aware and he felt that if the team got the ball to me in a certain way, over the top, or with me coming short and spinning off the defender, then it would reap rewards for me and the team as a whole. Ray Wilkins was in the side and the two of us were almost telepathic. We had been playing together for a couple of seasons and I knew where he would play the ball without even looking at him. I used to run just as he was getting the ball, knowing exactly where it would arrive. It just clicked between us. He just made my life a lot easier as a forward.

I was so looking forward to the new season that I wanted to see if I could improve myself in any way, to get that extra edge, and that is when I began going into the gym and doing weights with my dad. I thought I would do some work on my legs, and for that season it was the fittest I ever felt. I improved my strength in my quads, hamstrings and calves, and I think it did me a lot of good. Gerry had brought in a new style of training where on a Tuesday we used to do box-to-box running, which all the lads used to detest. It was one of those things that we always dreaded, but once I'd done it I would always feel fantastic, like I had really put myself through it.

My dad has been doing weights ever since I can remember and he was always trying to get me to go down to the gym with him. Every now and again, I would go for a week, though I did it more to please him than anything else. But that summer, I fancied going in there and doing a bit of work to keep myself ticking over, because I knew inside that the coming season was going to be a big one for me and I needed to help myself as much as I possibly could. After I got back from holiday in St Lucia, which was now becoming a regular thing every year, I went into the gym every other day and just worked on my legs.

I wasn't convinced it was necessarily going to improve things massively, but my dad had been doing it for years and he always believed that a lot of your body-power comes from your legs. He springs absolutely brilliantly – people always ask me where I get my spring from, and I am sure I inherited it from him. In his heyday, he could jump much higher than me and lift over 500lbs with his legs, so he was really powerful. He wasn't a sportsman at all, he just used to weight-train for enjoyment and as a form of exercise.

The other reason for going in there was because of all the injury problems I had been having. When I was out in Turkey, I'd had a cartilage operation and the doctor that looked after me said the reason why I would get problems like that was because my legs were too developed for my ligaments, which were small and hadn't grown with my body. The only way I could cure that was by strengthening the muscle around them, so that was one of the other reasons I went into the gym. I hadn't taken any professional advice, it was just something that I thought would not do me any harm.

There was no way I could compete with my dad in the gym, he was just too strong. But I remember, going into that pre-season, I felt so strong and powerful. Other people were also noticing it. I looked a lot faster than in previous years, and all I could put it down to was the work I had done with my dad. Things started to go so well that I was more confident and willing to take more gambles on the pitch, which all seemed to work out for me.

Gerry had said to me on many occasions that I could play for England and it was entirely up to me whether I wanted to or not. But although I carried on at the start of the new season in goalscoring form, England was something that still seemed a long way away for me. I thought it might just have been something he said to give me another boost, to keep my confidence up and to try and get a bit more out of me. Sometimes managers do that, rather than tell you the whole truth. After all, I hadn't really held down a first-team place at QPR for that long.

In pre-season, we went to Sweden and I was scoring in all the games out there. Ray Wilkins and I were playing really well together and a lot of my goals came from him. Everyone looked up to him because he had so much experience and had been at some of the biggest clubs in the world, and I began to get friendly with him off the field as well. He used to give me a lot of advice. Another person who arrived, who I became good friends with, was Clive Wilson. I am now godfather to his daughter, Siobhan.

I scored six goals in 11 league and cup matches and then had a little lay-off through injury, but came back and scored the winner against Leeds, who were champions at the time. There was beginning to be talk then about England. The press were starting to mention my name more and more, and I suppose that was really the first time it entered my thoughts that I might play for my country. I was the latest flavour of the month: week in, week out, things like that were being said.

It was in early November 1992 that I got called into the squad by Graham Taylor. England had a World Cup qualifying match against Turkey coming up and there was talk that because I knew Turkish football well from my time out there, I was in with a chance, although I'm not sure in the end that made any difference.

We were at training and Gerry pulled me over towards the end and asked whether I remembered the times he had told me I would play for England. He had just taken a call from Graham Taylor and Gerry wanted to tell me before I got back to the changing-room, because the media would be waiting to talk to me about it. I didn't know what to think. I was happy but nervous straight away. It took a while for it to sink in. We used to train at the Barclays Bank ground on Hangar Lane in Ealing and had to walk through a part that had a swimming pool to get back to the changing-rooms. I remember sitting on the bench for a while by the pool, and Gerry had obviously told some of the boys because as they came past, they were congratulating me. Before I knew it, the media were there wanting photographs of me and Andy

Sinton, who had already been in the squad. I went home to phone my family to tell them, and it was then that it struck me that this was fantastic!

By then, my mum had passed away and I had moved out of Ladbroke Grove to Wimbledon because once she had gone, I didn't feel I could live there anymore. One of the people I thought of first when I heard the news was my mum. I wish she could have been there to see it happen, see my success at QPR and the rest of my career. She would have been very proud. My dad told me that it was nothing more than I deserved. He thought I had been playing well that season and that it was only a matter of time before it happened. He was obviously very proud and pleased.

We did all the normal things you do with England, but clearly it was the first time I had been down to Bisham to train with the squad and stay with them at the Burnham Beeches Hotel. I remember thinking to myself, 'I used to watch all these guys on television,' although I knew many of the team from around the Premier League. David Platt and Stuart Pearce were the senior players, then there were guys like Ian Wright and Paul Ince who I was friendly with from around the London football scene. That helped settle me in and I felt accepted straight away. You are a bit in awe and I was not sure what to expect, but they were fine and made me feel at home from day one.

Graham Taylor was also great to me. He told me he didn't want me to do anything different to what I did for QPR, and not to worry about the other players and what they had achieved. He obviously realised that a new player coming into that situation can feel overawed by the whole experience. He told me I was there because I deserved to be there. I became very friendly with Des Walker when I first got into the squad, and he was a big help as well. I had played against him before, though we had never really spoken. But when it came to England, we just seemed to hit it off.

I didn't room with anybody and I still don't. Some of the guys, especially if they are from the same club, room together. At the time, Tony Adams and Paul Merson used to do that. I have always felt that when you are away for a week, it is completely different to being in a hotel for one or two days with your club. After a week, you start learning about someone's bad habits and that can get a bit annoying. I used to room with Clive Wilson at QPR and he could snore, that boy! I'm the lightest sleeper as it is, and he really used to annoy me. I used to wake him up at all hours of the morning and tell him not to go back to sleep until I was asleep. With England you had the option of rooming with someone, but even though Andy Sinton was there, I still felt I wanted to be on my own, get my thoughts together. There was no initiation or anything like that, no-one played any jokes on me. It was just all friendly chat with the guys in the bar when we met up, and then it was down to business.

I didn't make the final line-up or the subs' bench, but given that this was my first time with the squad, that wasn't surprising. I sat on the bench at Wembley with the rest of the players and the back-up team and just savoured the atmosphere. Being back at Wembley was really strange. As I said before, Mick Byrne at Southall had said to us that one of the team would be back there, and there I was. Although I wasn't playing, I was there and what Mick said came back to me as I was sitting there. Every time I walk out at Wembley, I think of that. Paul Swales has also been back with Yeading in the FA Vase, but I think we are the only two. I heard that Mick went out to coach in Australia, but I have never seen him since I left Southall, to say I was the one who went back to Wembley – and it was with England.

Having played there before, I found it a totally different situation. There were a lot more people and a very different pressure and atmosphere. I remember looking around Wembley, looking at the pitch and the players I was with, and thinking to myself, 'Now I've achieved something.' But it was not until I pulled on the shirt for the first time, which was against San Marino three months later, that I really felt I had finally made it. I could have gone back to QPR after the Turkey game, things might not have gone so well and I might never have got called up again. A few players had been called up for England before and it had gone to their heads and they hadn't played so well after that. I was determined that wasn't going to happen to me. Being called up gave me a massive boost. I went back to QPR, continued scoring a lot of goals and got called into the next squad where I made my England debut, a day that I never really dreamed would come.

CHAPTER TEN

Hat-tricks and England

Things continued to go well for me after I returned from my first England squad. The longest period I went without scoring was eight games, and towards the end of the 1992–93 season I hit a real purple patch, getting two hat-tricks in two days over the Easter weekend.

The first was against Nottingham Forest at home. During the away game earlier in the season, the Forest defender marking me had had a particularly good game and in the run-up to this one, he said a few things in the papers about how he was going to stop me again, especially now I was an England international and was in-form.

That sort of thing always gives you an extra lift, a bit more desire to do well in that particular game. It was my first hat-trick for QPR. None of the goals were very spectacular, but after the game I remember being really excited about it. I got the ball and all the players signed it. There wasn't much time to celebrate, though, because we were off to Everton the next morning for the match on Easter Monday.

The last thing I expected was to score another hat-trick, and I have never repeated the feat of two in a row since. But when you are in that vein of form, you are so confident that you try all sorts of different things. You shoot from places you normally wouldn't, and when your luck is with you, it's with you. Still, I'm not sure I can remember another striker in the Premier League who has scored them in consecutive games so close together. To do it two days later . . . I was getting comments from all sorts of people and if the Lottery had been around then, I would probably have won on that as well that weekend. Everything was just going for me.

The hat-trick at Everton was particularly pleasing because I had always had racial abuse at Everton from their supporters. Doing that to them gave me extra pleasure. There are certain things that stick in your mind during your career as a footballer and the racism at Goodison Park is one of them. When Paul Parker was still at QPR, there was a lot of transfer speculation surrounding him. In one paper it was reported that Everton were in for him, and he would have been the first black player in many years to have played for them. He then got racist hate-mail from Everton supporters, without him even saying he wanted to go there. I thought it was outrageous, the fact that there was a so-called bid for him ending with him receiving hate-mail. There is no accounting for the ignorance of some people.

I ended that season with 20 goals in the league, the most I had ever scored, and nine of those had come in the last six games. It was obviously the best season I'd had as a professional footballer and I put a lot of that down to Gerry. He had given me tremendous belief in myself and my ability, and I had been given a good run in the side. I always knew that once I was given that opportunity, I would be able to show what I could do. In training, Gerry would help me a lot. He had been captain of England and often said that during his career, he had played in virtually every position on the field and with some great players. So he was able to help me make the right runs, and pinpoint the areas on the field where I should be at a given time. He spent a lot of time talking things through with me and when a manager does that, it gives you great confidence. He used to say to me that I needed to improve my first touch, so we worked on that a lot and I improved as a player as a result. He also felt that I was quick enough to be able to hold my runs and still beat the defender. As a young player, I was so eager to get the ball that I would often run offside, but Gerry helped me learn that side of the game. He used to work on the back eight players a lot in training and then he would take the forwards aside and work with us, as a unit or individually. We used to do a lot of exercises where we got into positions to have shots at goal, and the more you do that type of thing, the more your confidence grows so that when you are in a match environment and that situation occurs, it is almost automatic that you know what to do. If you are scoring goals as a striker, you tend to do things that maybe normally you wouldn't. You might hit a shot that nine times out of ten would miss if you weren't on form, but for some reason things just go differently when you are playing with confidence. Confidence is such an important part of the game but is something you cannot always put your finger on, as to why it happens.

That season, Teddy Sheringham was the top scorer in the Premier League and I only finished two goals behind him. But he had also taken penalties as well, which is something I didn't do for QPR; all my goals came from open play. The team was obviously playing well and we finished fifth that season, just missing out on Europe. It was one of the highest places that QPR had finished for years.

It was not long after the Turkey game that I got called into the squad for the match against San Marino at Wembley, in February 1993, when I made my England debut. Graham Taylor told me very early on that I was in the team, about two or three days before the game. He told me straight away that the reason I was in the squad was because I deserved to be there on merit, no other reason. The second thing he said was that I would be playing on Wednesday. He was not one of those managers who kept his team secret right up until the game. I think he told me early in order to keep the press quiet, to give them something positive. They could then go away and write about that for a couple of days and that would leave him free to concentrate on what he wanted to do with the rest of the team.

I went off and did the press conference, but it was only when I got back to the hotel that it really began to sink in that I was making my debut for England. Unusually for me, I began getting a bit nervous, and this was still two or three days before the game. But I then forgot about it, phoned my family to tell them and just did the things I normally do. On the day of the game, I began thinking to myself that I *should* be getting more nervous, but there were still no real nerves at all. The only time it really affected me was as I walked up the tunnel for the first time as part of the team. As we came out onto the pitch, the roar from the fans hit me and that was the only time I thought, 'Shit, I'm playing for England.' All sorts of things race through your mind at that stage. You hope you don't miss a sitter and that you have one of your better games, so that there is another opportunity to come back and do it again. I can remember thinking as well that there was a lot of pressure on us, because Norway had beaten San Marino something like 10–0 and so we were expected to win 13–0. When I was standing in line for the national anthem, my thoughts were totally with my mum, thinking she should be up in the stand there because she was my queen, but unfortunately it wasn't to be. She had always said to me, 'Believe in yourself,' and it was a shame that she couldn't have been there to see how far I had got.

As it turned out, things didn't go so well for the team. In the first half, we struggled to get crosses into the box – and one of the reasons Taylor had played me was because he felt they were vulnerable on crosses into the area. Still, I did manage to score in the second half. The ball came in from a corner and Tony Adams went for it. Some people said it was over the line, but I felt it wasn't so I followed it up and nodded it in. Tony said to me that it was my goal and everyone came over and jumped on my back. It was a great moment, even though it was just a tap-in.

I didn't really celebrate that night because I was still caught up in the whole euphoria of the situation. Strangely, what used to happen to me a lot was that when I had been involved with England, I would come back and be absolutely dreadful at the weekend for some reason. Gerry told me that it used to happen to him too. The build-up to an England game is so intense, the adrenaline starts pumping from the minute you meet up with the squad, and then it is such a come-down to go back to domestic football and a stadium where there are maybe only 10,000 people. Gerry said it was the anti-climax of it all and he understood that, which made me feel better. He also said it was something I would get over, and luckily I have.

That spring and summer of 1993 was a particularly busy one

for England. To be honest, I didn't think I would be selected to start the next game at Wembley, which was a crucial one against Holland. I obviously hoped I would play – I was doing well for QPR and the Holland game came quite soon after I scored my two hat-tricks, so I was the real flavour-of-the-month in the papers again.

I was delighted when Taylor told me I would start against the Dutch. The one thing, though, that I recall particularly from that game is that although I had often seen Ruud Gullit and Frank Rijkaard on the Italian football on TV, I had never seen them in the flesh before, and what struck me about them in real life was how big they were. It was great news for us that Gullit was playing out on the right wing. I thought he did OK, but the Dutch coach took him off and Ruud wasn't too happy about it. We did pretty well in the first half and took a 2–0 lead. I had a good game, without scoring, and Terry Venables, who was one of the pundits on the BBC, said that on that performance, Les Ferdinand has got a big future in international football. (Unfortunately, that came back to haunt me a bit during Euro 96 where he seemed to have changed his view.) My pace seemed to trouble the Dutch defenders during that game and we looked like we would win comfortably. But they got a goal back and then, right in the last few minutes, Des Walker brought down Marc Overmars for a penalty and it was 2–2.

Everyone was very disappointed, because it was such a key game. Had we won that match, we would have been well in the driving-seat in the group. The Dutch were delighted with the draw, I could see by their players' reaction after the game that they were very happy with the result. Our dressing-room was pretty glum: we had performed well and done enough to win the game. Even though I was fairly new to the team, I felt as disappointed as anyone. It doesn't matter how many games you have played for England, once you are in that team environment, everyone is equal. We saw that game more as a loss than a draw, even though Holland were a good side and a lot of teams would have been happy with a point against them. Taylor was very disappointed – that was particularly noticeable. He was very into tactics and the next time we got together, he was pointing out all the things we should have done against Holland but didn't.

I never had a problem with Taylor. People used to say he wasn't a good manager and that he picked the wrong teams. Well, my answer to that is that no manager picks a team that he thinks is going to lose the game, or not perform. He puts a side out that he believes, in himself, will win him that match. Whether it does or not is a different matter, but Taylor believed he was making the right decisions and you cannot call him stupid for that. I have a lot to thank him for: he brought me into international football and picked me for England, for which I will always be grateful to him.

The end of that season was a strange one for England because we had some critical World Cup matches during the summer and then we went off to the USA. It proved to be the turning point of the World Cup campaign and ended very badly for us. The first game was in Poland and I was in line to keep my place after playing so well against Holland. But I had picked up an ankle injury and had to have an injection to see if I could make the game. In the end, the injection needed more time to clear, so Teddy Sheringham took my place in the team. We got out of jail a bit in that game, Ian Wright came on as a substitute and scored a late equaliser. We had been under pressure for most of the match and were fortunate to get a point. We then travelled on to Norway for a game on the Wednesday night, and by this stage things were getting extremely fraught with the press, who had been very critical of the team and Taylor's selection.

I thought that if I was fit, I would probably get back in the team – but as it turned out, it was not in my normal position. Taylor really changed the team around for the Norway game to deal with the opposition. He played Gary Pallister in a wide position to play against their centre-forward Jostein Flo, who Taylor thought would play out wide. But that didn't happen. Taylor set his stall out around what he thought the Norwegians would do and so gave them the advantage, because we didn't play our strongest side. I played the first 45 minutes on the wing, for one reason or another. Norway got a couple of goals either side of half-time and that was it – the game was lost 2–0. We had only managed to pick up one point from two games and would obviously now struggle to qualify for the World Cup.

I thought the decision to play me on the wing was a bit strange – I hadn't played there in all my professional career – but when you are playing for England, you do anything to be in the side. Taylor wanted me to do a particular job and he tried to explain it to me before the game. I adapted to the new role just by staying out wide and trying to be a winger. I didn't really know what to do apart from that. We had given them the psychological advantage by picking our team to suit them, and that affected us badly. We gave them all the confidence they needed and the result went against us.

The aftermath of that game was particularly difficult for the players, because we went straight off to a tournament in the USA which was billed as a pre-World Cup '94 competition – even though it now looked like we wouldn't be there. This was by far the longest season of football I had ever played; we were now well into June. Towards the end of that season I had quite a few problems with my back as well, but I was just happy to be in the squad.

It was during this period that the press criticism of Taylor, and the team, was at its most intense. It's never nice to see or read, but the England players have come to expect it now. There is no point in kidding yourself that it won't come eventually, no matter how well you are doing. It does filter through to the players and it was not pleasant to read some of the things that were being written about Taylor, especially. But increasingly, that is a part of football now.

The players adopted then – and still do now – a kind of siege mentality against it. There is nothing we can do to stop it, so it becomes an us-against-them situation. You also try to use that situation to your advantage. Some managers use it to build up a better spirit within the team, to focus the team's mind on a common enemy! But it is difficult to cut yourself off from it completely. Some of the guys get on well with particular journalists who they are friendly with, and generally, the press need us and sometimes we need the press.

The criticism got so bad that summer that we did actually sit down at one point to discuss it. The view was, 'Why should we talk to them when they are hammering the team so badly?' In my view, it is better to get on with it and hope to prove them wrong through results.

Results had gone badly, though – and were about to get worse. I am sure a lot of the players didn't want to go to the States after such a hard season. There was no real benefit in the tour and because of the results, the morale in the team wasn't great – though it wasn't as bad as it could have been. The lads in the England team are generally in good spirits and don't let too much get them down. There are enough characters around like Wrighty and Paul Ince for that not to happen. We knew what we needed to do and would try to pull things round.

Unfortunately, things only went from bad to worse. We lost the first game against America, in which I was substituted, and then all hell broke loose. The Americans weren't a renowned football nation and when we lost, that was the final nail in the coffin. It is fair to say that the players felt embarrassed by the defeat. I didn't play in any of the other games on that tour – my back was playing up and I was sent home. In some ways it was a relief, because things were beginning to hot up out there with all the criticism and I couldn't do myself or the team justice because of the injury. I was told by the guy who looks after my back that I needed just to relax and not do anything for a few weeks. So I went off to St Lucia just to get away from things.

It had been an interesting first season in international football.

CHAPTER ELEVEN

Racism

My hat-trick at Everton and my experiences with England are linked by one common theme – racism. It is an issue I feel very strongly about.

I first noticed it, in a football context, as a young boy when I was playing in non-league football at Viking and Southall. If you look at my record at those places, I used to get sent-off quite often. Most of those dismissals were due to me smacking someone because they had called me a 'black this' or 'black that.' I used to give them a real good whack and they would struggle to get up. I was young and inexperienced then, and that was how I dealt with it coming from opponents. They were trying to wind me up, I know that, but I am sure they meant it as well. Trying to wind someone up and unsettle them is no excuse for being racist. Most weeks we played against teams that didn't have any black players at all, so we could only assume that the team came from an area that was predominantly white and that was their attitude.

It wasn't confined only to our opponents. There was an incident where one of my own team-mates at Southall racially abused one of my best friends, Earl Whisky, who was playing against us for Hanwell Town. Earl was having a particularly good game and this guy called him something, and I remember Earl smacking this player in the face. He got sent-off and I knew straight away that the only reason Earl would have hit him was if he had been called something. We had it out with this player in the changing-room afterwards. He apologised until really he couldn't apologise anymore, and just said that it had come out and he didn't mean anything by it. From that day, we all kept our distance from him because we knew what he was about. He was just a team-mate, I didn't have to socialise with him and nor would I have wanted to after that.

The older and more experienced I became, the less I got into trouble in that way. But it would also be true to say that as I progressed through the ranks, I used to experience racism less from the players on the field and it has never happened to me in professional football, as far as I can remember. When I made it into the first team at Southall, I began noticing it coming from the crowd, towards me and the other black players we had in the team. There was one game where we were away to Yeovil Town, in Somerset, which was my first real experience of racism coming from rival supporters on the terraces. It was all the usual kind of noises, the monkey chants, the verbal abuse. That year we had four or five black guys in the team, including Bruce Rowe, and I think they had experienced it before at Yeovil so they said to me that I should go out first. When I ran out, I realised why they were so keen to see me go out first – because they knew what I was going to get. I turned round and I could see them having a giggle to themselves. You have to take that attitude to it sometimes, to rise above it, although clearly it is not a laughing matter. We were laughing among ourselves at the joke they had played on me, the fact that they had conned me into going out first, rather than at the abuse we were getting from the fans.

The next experience I can remember came when we beat a side called Wisbech Town, from Norfolk, in the year we got to the FA Vase final. It's quite a remote place and I don't imagine the town is particularly multi-racial. We were playing them in the semi-final. We had drawn the home leg and now we were going to their place, where they hadn't lost for many months. They were well-known for having good support, and I remember getting off the coach and a policeman saying to us, 'Nice of you to turn up today, but you will be going home with nothing.' We went out to warm-up and we got the normal stuff, the monkey chants, etc. By this time, we were well used to it and all you think to yourself is, 'Here we go again.'

We ended up beating Wisbech 3–1. I scored two that day and Bruce Rowe got the other one, and with both of us being black, it did not make the victory too popular. Right from the start of the game, every time one of us got the ball, the crowd started shouting, 'Shoot the nigger, shoot the nigger.' It wasn't just a section, it sounded like it was the whole stadium singing it, and there were about 2,500–3,000 people in there. I'd never heard anything so disgusting in all my life but when you are out there, you are powerless to stop it. There is nothing you can do. So when I scored the first goal, my celebrations were a bit more showy than they are now. That silenced them for a while. Then we scored again, and two or three minutes into the second half I scored the third. Obviously the crowd weren't too happy and they attempted a pitch invasion to get the game called off.

I don't think there was ever any danger of the game being abandoned. Even if the ref had taken us off the pitch, he would have brought us back on to finish the game. The crowd came running onto the pitch saying things, but never came close enough to us because I'm sure we would have been up for it – most of us could look after ourselves pretty well.

The amazing thing about it all was that they had a black guy playing for them at centre-forward. If I remember correctly, I think someone said he was a schoolteacher. You often see this strange kind of racism and ignorance from some football supporters, where they abuse a black player from the opposition team while the one on their side is 'our' player, so that's different. He's not seen as being black, which of course is ridiculous.

After the game, as I was coming off the pitch, one of their supporters carried on the chanting and was saying to me that I was flash and stuff like that. So I said to him, 'Don't speak to me in front of your mates, come and see me after the game by yourself and we'll sort it out between ourselves.' I was in the mood to give him a real good hiding. But of course, when I went out there after the game, he was nowhere to be seen. Those types of people never follow through what they say.

It was quite an experience playing at Wisbech that day but there is a funny story that goes with it, which occurred many years later. Last year, I did an article about racism in one of the papers. It was before Newcastle went out to play Ferencvaros in Hungary, in one of the early rounds of the UEFA Cup. They had a reputation for having a Nazi element among their support, and people were telling me what to expect and asking whether I had experienced such things before. So I talked about Everton and that day at Wisbech in the article. The committee members at Wisbech must have read this in the papers because they sent me a letter, explaining that the club had been taken over by a new committee and that they thought their supporters' behaviour was now impeccable. My experience of a few years ago was a thing of the past. They invited me down to visit the club and see for myself how things had changed for the good. I thought about the letter and decided that I would reply to it, thank them for the offer and put in writing my good wishes and congratulations on the work they had done to turn round the situation.

Then, sifting through the rest of my mail that day, I came across a letter from another non-league club. I couldn't remember having played against this team during my non-league days, so the fact that they were writing to me was very unusual. When I opened it, it was from a committee member of that club saying that when they had gone to play against Wisbech Town that very season, their black players had also experienced what they felt was racist abuse. It was amazing that I should get one letter saying things had changed dramatically, and then another in the same batch saying it was as bad as ever.

Enclosed with the other club's letter was a copy of one they had received from Wisbech. The visiting club had obviously complained, and a committee member at Wisbech had written back saying they didn't think there was a problem with what was being said to the black players, that it was all part of the game and stuff like that.

I actually sent a letter back to Wisbech saying thank you very much for the offer but there doesn't seem to have been too much change since I was there, and I enclosed a copy of the letter sent by this other non-league club. I have never heard anything since.

As I've said, when I got into the professional game with QPR, I think people thought I was hot-headed because I used to react to racist abuse and get sent-off when I was in non-league. I think most people who actually knew me at the time would have said that I was so laid-back, I was almost horizontal. But I never let people take liberties with me, and if that meant I reacted quickly and temperamentally towards someone I thought was trying to take a liberty, then I suppose I did give people that impression. It was a different situation in the professional game. From the time I started with QPR, I don't think I ever experienced racist abuse from an opposition player on the field. I noticed that immediately. It was probably down to the growing number of black players coming into the game. Wherever you are in a minority, be it black, fat, ginger or whatever, people will pick on that. But when there is a good proportion from that minority, attitudes change, and I think that was an important factor in professional football.

Saying that, though, my first full game for QPR in my first season was at Everton and there I experienced the normal racist chants from the crowd, so it didn't take me long to realise that in some places, bigoted attitudes were still very strong. I've always said that football creates an environment where racist people can vent their frustrations towards people like me in a way that they probably couldn't out on the street, face to face. They can get in a crowd, shout something out and no-one will know who has done it, and I certainly couldn't jump in the crowd and confront someone who had called me a 'black bastard.' But if someone called me it on the street, maybe not now but when I was younger, I would have probably got myself into a fight about it. Racism is not a football problem, we have all got to understand that. What football does is give racists a place where they can do what they want without much risk of getting caught or punished. But it is a social problem, not a football problem.

Probably the worst thing I have encountered in my professional career has been racist letters coming from supporters, most of which I have to say have come from Everton fans. After I scored that hat-trick against them over the Easter period, the letters I was getting back were disgusting. I was doing my job for QPR and I was getting racist letters for scoring a hat-trick. They got sent to the club most of the time, and while they weren't from any particular far-right political group, they would have the swastika or some sort of offensive drawing on them. That was the first time I had received that sort of thing and I knew it was because of what I had done on the pitch. It made me all the more pleased that I had scored those three goals at Goodison Park. That's no disrespect to the players or the good supporters of Everton, but that is how I felt. I never passed the letters on to the police; I don't think there was much they could have done about it.

Over the years, the supporters have got a lot better as well. I've experienced problems at Everton and at West Ham, those were probably the worst. What does anger me is when you see parents doing it in front of their kids. When Newcastle played at Goodison Park on the opening day of the 1996–97 season, I picked up an injury and needed treatment on the perimeter track. As I sat by the touchline, dads in the stand were hurling all kinds of abuse at me, much of it racist, as their sons sat beside them. Those kids will grow up thinking it's perfectly normal to carry on like that. What I can't understand is that sort of attitude coming from followers of a team which has included Daniel Amokachi and Earl Barrett. If parents are going to set that kind of example, I doubt whether we'll ever be able to stamp the problem out completely. I know it is now a criminal offence to use racist language at matches, but how do you pick out one or two voices among 30,000 people? Still, at least the game is taking the issue seriously and is trying to tackle it head on.

The abuse that you get isn't just racist. At Aston Villa last season, I was walking along the sideline going to take my seat and someone shouted out, 'Ferdinand, you fucking wanker.' He had his little kid sitting next to him. So I picked him out and said to him, 'That makes a lot of sense doesn't it? Look at your little boy sitting there, and that's what you are shouting out to people.' He actually got embarrassed about it. I know I turned down Villa to go to Newcastle a couple of seasons ago, but that doesn't warrant that sort of thing. Later on in the game, I was at the other end warming-up and one of the supporters shouted something. It wasn't abusive, so I turned round and smiled at him. Then we started having a conversation and having a laugh and joke, there was no malice intended. That's what football should be about. Some people just don't think. Once football supporters get through the gates of a stadium, they are like Worzel Gummidge, the scarecrow that could change his heads. They put on a different head and you can't believe it's the same person.

I have now become involved in football's campaign, Let's Kick Racism Out of Football, and having put my name to a lot of things and spoken out publicly, I was then asked by Nike to become involved with an advert they were putting together with Eric Cantona. It came after the incident when Eric attacked a supporter at Selhurst Park, and I felt that advert was a good thing because it highlighted racism not just towards black players but to anybody, whether they are French or whatever nationality or colour. Unfortunately, I didn't have an opportunity to talk to Cantona about what he had experienced, as we filmed the advert separately.

I think it's important for footballers to use their role in society to try and do something about racism, not just for black players but for all types of players. Why should I be judged on my colour? We should all be judged on our performances. If I was crap, then I will hold my hands up and say so. But because I score a goal against somebody, why should I be racially abused? I think the message is beginning to get through now. What the FA and the clubs have done is fantastic, but that is only inside the stadiums. Outside, it is difficult to control.

The issue was an important consideration for me when I signed for Newcastle. It was one of things I actually spoke to Kevin Keegan about. It's no secret in the game that Newcastle used to be one of those clubs which had a reputation for having a racist element among their support. When there was speculation that I might sign for them, I was sent a racist letter from the North East. I showed it to Kevin and he told me that there were people who didn't want success for Newcastle, that the rivalry between them and Sunderland was so intense that you would get a Sunderland supporter perhaps sending something like that so that I wouldn't sign for Newcastle. I looked at the situation very seriously. I knew that a few years before, this had been probably the most racist club in the country and I thought to myself, 'You don't lose that overnight.' Obviously, Andy Cole had come up to Newcastle and made great strides towards solving the problem. He made it better for the likes of me, Shaka Hislop and Tino Asprilla, but I still feel there is an element of it about. At one of our games last season, I heard a supporter shout something at a black player from the opposition. Another supporter pulled him up and said to him, 'What's your problem? We've got three black players on our side.' The guy claimed he didn't mean to say it, but if that was the case then it wouldn't have entered his thoughts in the first place. You can't accept that as an explanation. It just goes to show that the problem is still there. Newcastle is an area where you don't get too many black players or black people, so it is to be expected in today's society – but not accepted.

Before I joined, I did speak to Andy Cole about it. I asked him what it was like up in Newcastle from that point of view and he told me that I wouldn't have a problem. There had been one incident with his family – they were queuing up for some tickets and somebody had a go at them – but that situation could just as easily have occurred at QPR, Tottenham or Arsenal; it only takes one idiot. No matter what football club you go to, there are always those people. Andy found that he soon won them over, not necessarily the minute he pulled on a Newcastle shirt but because of what he achieved in that shirt. Talking to him did put my mind at rest with regard to the racist issue at Newcastle. If I had been the first black player to go and play up there, I'm not sure whether I would have joined. It wasn't a major factor in my decision, but it was important enough for me to think about it and discuss it with people.

After joining Newcastle, I got involved with a campaign up there. I was in the campaign video and I went into a few schools to talk to the kids at assembly and that sort of thing. It's important to get to the kids, because that is where it starts from. They may be taught one thing by their parents and not know any better until they speak to someone about it, or see someone they recognise – and hopefully look up to and respect – bringing it to their attention.

One thing I will say is that I don't know any black player who has said to me personally that he has experienced racist abuse from another player in professional football. The spotlight has been on that recently with the Ian Wright–Peter Schmeichel incident, but among the guys that I know, it has never been mentioned. When we get together with England, obviously you have a lot of the top black footballers in one place and the whole racist issue is one we talk about from time to time. We do talk about certain clubs and their policies. We know there is racism among supporters, but I think that at some clubs it goes a lot higher than that. I'm talking about people at boardroom level and chairmen, people like that who are actually racist themselves. What makes me think that? Because I have been told certain things by certain players about the chairmen at certain clubs, about what they want and what they would like, i.e. basically no black players. I believe there are managers who personally have racist attitudes. I couldn't go on record and say this manager is or that manager isn't, it's just a feeling I get within myself, from talking to other players and from what they tell me about what goes on at their particular club.

But it's not just an issue in football, it goes a lot deeper than that. It's a social problem to do with how people are brought up. How it can be solved is a difficult question. Obviously, you try to change people from a young age. My parents educated me so that I wasn't racist towards anyone. I had a conversation with Warren Barton recently and we were talking about this subject. He said to me that his best pal was probably Robbie Earle, who he played with at Wimbledon, and one night he went to a club with Robbie, John Fashanu and some others, where he was the only white face. What struck him was that he had never realised what it was like for someone like myself or Robbie to be in an environment where there were lots of white people. Warren said he felt very intimidated by it and did not feel comfortable at all. There was no reason for him not to be, but it was such an unusual situation that he found himself in that he could appreciate the problems for somebody else in the reverse position. I am now used to that kind of thing, so I don't give it a second thought.

I know in my heart of hearts that if I go out, I can get into certain places because I am Les Ferdinand. If I was a normal black guy trying to get into the same places, I would be looked on in a totally different light. I suppose that's what helps me keep my feet on the ground.

When you look at the Premier League, things are improving because clubs now have the finances to launch high-profile schemes and things like that. In the lower leagues, there are still problems because clubs do not have the ability to put a real effort into stamping out racism. There are new things like close-circuit television to catch people who are now committing a criminal offence, but lower down the leagues that is not always possible.

One area where I think things could definitely improve is in television coverage of matches. In years gone by, we have all sat and watched *Match of the Day* where you can clearly hear racial abuse from the terraces towards a player. Instead of condemning it out of hand, more often than not the commentator will just gloss over it, brushing it aside by calling it 'terrace banter' or something similar. That is totally wrong. I suppose they don't want to draw attention to it because it gives football a bad name. It's insulting for the black people watching the game, because it is like they are trying to make out we are idiots and don't know what is going on. I remember that myself very clearly from when I was younger.

Another part of the game I have discussed many times with coaches and other footballers is attitudes towards young players. You will often get a situation where there is a young white player at a club and a young black player, and it always seems more difficult for the coach, or whoever else it is at that particular club, to get close to the young black player or understand what is going through his mind. They'll make excuses for the white player if, in training, for example, he is having difficulty with something, but with the black player, the reason the coach can't get through to him is that he has got 'a chip on his shoulder'.

If he makes a mistake, he is disappointed with his mistake and the coach will try and explain something to him. But often the player is so disappointed, he is thinking more about what he has done than what the coach is saying to him – and because the coach can't get through to him, he'll immediately assume that the boy has got a chip on his shoulder. That happened to me as a young player many times and I've seen it with other people. It happened at QPR, and to me it is a form of racism. The coach won't take time to understand what is going on in this player's mind, they just saddle him with this label straight away. It was never said to me directly, but I heard it said about other players and a couple of times I pulled people over and said to them, 'Why do you think he has got a chip on his shoulder, is it because you can't understand him?' I would give them examples of people whose attitude was similar to this particular black player, but they made an excuse for that. Part of the Afro-Caribbean culture is to be laid-back and take things in your stride, but people who don't understand that interpret it as not caring, or having no respect for authority. That is one of the things that really annoys me. As soon as someone can't understand a black player, that is nearly always the conclusion they jump to.

The other area where I have noticed a racist element is with the national team. Obviously, here it is well-known that there is a far-right political influence among the support, and it is more evident at away games than at home. The particular incident I remember involved Paul Ince and some West Ham supporters, when we were playing in an away game. They were abusing him racially and also because he had left West Ham for Manchester United. We were warming-up at the time and so there was not a lot of atmosphere in the ground, and we could all hear what they were saying very clearly. In that situation it is possible to pick people out, but Incey didn't react. It's a terrible feeling when you hear that sort of thing. You think to yourself, 'We are all here for the same cause and then something like that happens.' It makes you feel like you are banging your head against a brick wall.

CHAPTER TWELVE

Sampdoria?

It was during the season when I broke into the England team that people first began to speculate about my future at QPR. There were rumours that I would be moving to one of the bigger clubs – or even abroad.

There have been so many different stories that I'm now not sure which was the first club I was linked with. One of the strangest examples was a story which was written by a guy called Ben Bacon, who was with *Today* newspaper. It was still quite early in my international career, but I was scoring a lot of goals for QPR so there was more and more interest in the media.

At the time, Des Walker was playing at Sampdoria and some of the press guys had obviously noticed that he was one of the players I became friendly with when I first got into the England set-up. So Ben Bacon came to the training ground at QPR and spoke to me. He said there was speculation that an Italian side was interested in me and would I go to Italy? I told him that if the opportunity came around and it was the right move, then I would consider it. I had played abroad before and had really enjoyed it. He then asked me whether I had talked about it with Des. I replied that we talked about a lot of things but yes, I had discussed with him what it was like in Italy. I had spoken to Bacon before, because he used to be around QPR quite a lot and when the press want to talk to you after a game, they wait for you in the corridor near the players' area. My dad also used to wait for me there and he got talking to Bacon because Ben had lived on St Lucia when he was younger and had family still there.

So I did this interview with him, but it ended up in the paper as me saying I wanted to leave QPR, that I wanted to move to Italy, and that I had spoken to my close friend Des Walker about it and had sounded him out about possible clubs. It was totally over the top. I never saw Ben Bacon again after that – I'd told people that I would hammer him the next time I saw him, but I never got the opportunity.

Generally, it was sort of flattering to see your name linked with some of the biggest clubs in the country but because nothing ever came of it, I just used to assume it was all newspaper speculation and that there was no substance to it. Gerry said not to let it affect me, that when someone does well at a smaller club these things always happen – as far as the papers are concerned, that person is too good for that club now and needs to move somewhere else to pursue his career. Gerry said he would tell me when someone came in for me genuinely, and if he thought I was ready for it. I had no agreement in my contract that I should be informed. The way I always see it is that if your club comes to you and says that another club have made a bid, then they must be thinking about selling you. That isn't a problem for me, but at that point in my career I didn't want to move from QPR. Gerry was quickly onto me when all the speculation first started, so it didn't unsettle me the way it has done with other players. He turned it into a positive thing by saying that if they were writing about me all the time, then I must be playing well.

The amount of times that I would go to my dad's house on a Sunday and he would get the papers out and there would be articles like 'Fergie gets his man' or 'Graham gets £4m Les', it just became laughable in the end. I think in one of the pieces where I was 'signing for Liverpool' I was actually up there, was going to have the medical the next day and all I had to do was agree personal terms! My dad said to me that had he not seen me there the same day, reading the papers with him when I was supposed to be in Liverpool, he would have believed I was signing for them. In the end, it just got to the stage where I said to him that if I was ever going to move, he would know about it before anyone else. I actually made a decision to stop buying the papers a couple of years ago because I got fed up reading things about myself that were absolute nonsense. I'll still read one if it's lying around, but I won't go out of my way to get a paper now.

The speculation just kept on coming, especially going into the following season, 1993–94, when I was becoming a more permanent fixture in the England set-up. We had some crucial World Cup games coming up, especially after the bad results we had had in Poland and Norway which were then followed by the defeat by America during the summer tour.

Our next game was against Poland at Wembley, quite early on in the new season, and there was a lot of pressure on the players to get a win this time. Anything less and we would almost certainly have been out of the World Cup. We definitely felt the pressure and the criticism. There had been a lot of things said about us and the manager and we were upset; pride was hurt and it was a very important game for us.

Things couldn't have started better for me. In the first few minutes, David Platt sent over a through ball and I raced on to it, brought it down with my left foot and side-footed in. When I scored my first goal against San Marino, some people said that the ball had already crossed the line before I knocked it in, but I was credited with it and I regarded it as my first international goal. This was my second.

After the game, the players were significantly lifted. On the night, we gave a really good performance and won the game comfortably, 3–0. It wasn't just the loss against Norway, the defeat against America had really been felt by the team as well. We knew we had let everyone down and it was important to play well.

The next game was the key one, against Holland, and here I got embroiled in controversy even though I didn't play. As it turned out, the game itself was highly controversial as well, and by the end of it we were basically relying on a miracle to get us through.

I'd hurt my back and although I joined up with the squad, the QPR people had told the England staff that I might be OK after a couple of days' treatment but it would be touch-and-go. Because of the importance of the game, Graham Taylor said that he needed all the players he was taking to be 100 per cent fit; so in that case, he said, he would leave me behind. I accepted that and understood the reasons for it. It so happened that the England game was on the Wednesday and I played for QPR on the following Saturday against Newcastle. Right up until that Saturday, I was still unsure whether I was going to make it, but Gerry came to me and said he needed me to play even if it was only to give him 45 minutes. He knew the situation, I hadn't trained all week and it was going to be touch-and-go. The thing is, you can do that for your club but you can't really at international level. A player might play for his club at 75–80 per cent, but for England it's different: you get found out at that level, you need to be 100 per cent or as close to it as possible.

But because I had such a good game for QPR that day – I scored one and set the other goal up for Bradley Allen – people questioned whether I had really been injured for the Holland game, implying that I had bottled it mentally and made out I was more injured than I was. Nothing could have been further from the truth. The decision not to travel was not mine, it was made by Taylor and his medical people. They knew I was struggling and hadn't been training properly, and that's no way to go into such a crucial match. Gerry did well for me because he came out publicly and explained the situation to nip the rumours in the bud. In fact, England had tried to send me to a hospital and have my back manipulated to try and get me fit. Gerry found out about it and said there was no way that was going to happen. It was just a stop-gap treatment to get me through the game. When I spoke about it to the guy who looks after my back, he said they could have caused a lot of damage by doing that – but when they proposed it to me, I had been willing to try it because I wanted so much to play in the game. Players nearly always think like that, especially when it comes to playing for your country in a game of such importance. So to be honest, it didn't really bother me that much when people questioned whether I was actually injured or not.

With all the lads out in Holland, I ended up watching the match at home. I really wanted to be there and felt helpless sitting at home. I am a terrible armchair-watcher at the best of times. The game became infamous for the incident when Ronald Koeman pulled down David Platt just outside the penalty area and wasn't sent-off. Up until then, England were playing well and I can remember thinking we were going to do it. Then everything seemed to go against us all at once. There was Koeman not being sent-off, and then him getting a free-kick on the edge of the box and the referee ordering it to be retaken, from which he scored a crucial goal. It just seemed like it wasn't to be.

When I first started out in football, I hadn't consciously set my heart on playing in a World Cup. It's a dream everyone has, scoring the winning goal in the final, right from when you are a little boy. But since being in professional football, I hadn't really thought about it. Now I could see the chance disappearing in front of my eyes. What made it worse in many ways was that even after losing to Holland we still had an outside chance of qualifying, but a very outside chance. Holland had to lose their last game in Poland and we had to win in San Marino by at least 7–0. It was a very unlikely scenario and all the players knew it. It was a strange atmosphere going into that last game, very similar to Newcastle in 1996 when we lost the title – on the last day, we needed to win and Man United needed to lose and you just couldn't see it happening. We knew we would beat San Marino, but Holland had to lose and that seemed unlikely. The players didn't talk about it but you could sense the tension in individuals and in the squad as a whole. It was no longer in our hands, we had no control over it. Our attitude had to be that we had a target to get and anything could happen. We won 7–1 and I scored one. We found out after the game that Holland had won as well, so there was a feeling of real dejection in the team. Ian Wright scored a hat-trick that night but he didn't even want to go and collect the ball. I think David Platt went to get it for him.

I felt empty, numb. England had not qualified for the World Cup. Obviously no team has a divine right to be in the World Cup, but thinking about it without England, that was almost impossible. The criticism inevitably followed and you have to cope with it. The fact was, we didn't qualify and we just had to get on with things. All the players really felt for Graham Taylor. He picked teams he believed were going to get us there and OK, it didn't work out, but when his private life and his family were affected – one of the tabloids had his head in a pile of horse-manure and then there was the turnip thing – I thought to myself, 'This is not on. They are not reporting about football, this is just personal and vindictive.' I think most of the players felt like that.

We saw the manager suffering from the pressure. As players, you can take that two ways. You can let it affect the way you play, or you can take the attitude that the manager is under pressure and we should help him get out of it. The players really wanted to do that for him, and of course none of us didn't want to qualify for the World Cup.

When the TV documentary came out, it gave an accurate portrayal of what was going on but I think if Graham had seen what it was going to be like at the end, he wouldn't have agreed to do it. I am sure the programme itself gave a lot of people a real insight into international management, but when it was written up in the press afterwards Graham was made out to be a laughing stock, rather than the public witnessing how much pressure the job creates and feeling sympathetic about the amount of stick the manager had to put up with. He was ridiculed as a result, and I thought that was a shame.

The players were only aware of the cameras on occasions. Most of the time they were way off in the background and he was just miked, but to be honest, when I saw the footage there were specific times when I hadn't realised he was miked up, or how often. People say the public does have a right to know what goes on and the documentary did give an insight into that. It showed the banter that goes on among players and how they are able to laugh at themselves.

There was also a lot of attention given to how Graham's backroom staff, Phil Neal and Lawrie McMenemy, came across. The players dealt most of the time with Neal, and a lot of people remember that he came over particularly badly on the pro-gramme. I must admit it did raise a few laughs when I saw certain things again. But a manager picks his backroom team because he thinks these guys are going to help him, and you have got to appreciate that.

My overall view of Taylor is that he gave me the opportunity to play for England and I will be eternally grateful for that. I think the problem he had was the press from the start. They never had any respect for him because he had never played at the highest level and they questioned how could he coach top players. I didn't find it a problem at all and I don't think most of the other players did. He had been successful at Watford and Villa and that was without having the experience of playing at that level, so why shouldn't he have done it with England? At the end, I think the players still had a lot of respect for him. I certainly did but I can't speak for everybody. It was just unfortunate that we didn't qualify. Not playing in the World Cup is like not playing in an FA Cup final, the whole experience just left me empty. I went away on holiday to St Lucia that summer and everybody I spoke to was saying the World Cup is not the same without England, how did England not qualify? I only watched bits and pieces, because I kept thinking I should be there.

That whole season, 1993–94, was a fairly unspectacular one with QPR. I scored 16 goals in the league, not as many as the year before, but then the whole team didn't play as well and we ended up ninth. At the end of the season, I won a whole load of awards at the club: Player of the Year, Supporters' Player of the Year and things like that. It was nice to get the recognition from the fans and although I had my problems early on with them, they were generally always good to me.

But there are two particular incidents that I remember from that season. The first was getting sent-off against Liverpool at Anfield on my birthday in December. I remember it vividly because the conditions that night were probably the worst I have ever played in. It was blowing a gale and hail-stoning. When we went out for the warm-up, Trevor Sinclair hit this ball in the air and it just stopped in mid-air and fell back at his feet. We all thought, 'We can't play in this!' But the game went ahead. I scored the first goal and we were playing quite well and scored again. They then got a goal back and Simon Barker got sent-off for two bookable offences, so we were down to 10 men. I had already been booked in the first half for dissent by the referee, Vic Callow. Liverpool went 3–2 up in the second half and then I was sent clear in on goal. I didn't hear the whistle for offside and I made a complete hash of the shot and was really embarrassed about it. When I turned round, everyone had stopped and the referee was walking towards me. He then pulled out the red card.

I was astonished. I asked him what the matter was, and he said I was wasting time by kicking the ball away. Now we were 3–2 down at the time, so what was the point in me wasting time? By now I was getting really angry. I went mad, I just couldn't believe he had sent me off. I had curbed my temper pretty well by this stage of my career but here I lost my head totally. It was the first time I had been sent-off in a league or cup game for QPR. I don't know what I was going to do to Callow, but Neil Ruddock, Jan Molby and Ray Wilkins had to physically restrain me from going at the referee. Gerry Francis had to come onto the pitch to calm me down and it was probably a good job they all did, because there was every chance I would have hit Callow and been banned for life from playing football as a result. The old red-mist from my younger days came down; you can never tell when it is going to happen. I don't know if it had anything to do with being stuck in a hotel on my birthday, but something just went inside my head.

There was speculation afterwards that it might affect my England career because to be honest, it didn't look very good and obviously if you are an England player, your behaviour is under scrutiny more than other people's. Gerry knew it was a one-off for me, that it took a lot for me to get angry and that I had been pretty hard done-by with that decision. He just said, 'You can't react like that,' and that was it. I got banned for three games and was called up for a disciplinary hearing at the FA. They actually said to me that they knew it was unusual for me to react like that, but they were worried about what I would have actually done had I got hold of the ref! Callow had a reputation at the time for sending-off quite high-profile players, but I don't think I ever saw him again because he retired at the end of the season.

That was just about the highlight of my season, although there was one other incident which was quite funny. When we got knocked out of the FA Cup at Stockport in the third round, the pitch was frozen and the referee had to do a check before the game which was actually shown on *Football Focus*. We were out on the pitch at the time and he was running up and down and his studs were clattering on the frozen ground. We were all looking on, thinking there was no way this game could be played, when he walked over and said the ground was fine.

We couldn't believe it. We told him it was dangerous but he said there was nothing wrong with it. In fact, the ground was so hard that in the first half Trevor Sinclair played with moulded studs and in the second he changed to trainers. I wouldn't say we were in the wrong frame of mind, but it didn't help. Gerry told us we just had to get it out of our minds, but on the day it was the same for both sides and they played better than us.

A few of the boys were talking on the coach on the way to the ground about how they had never been knocked out in the third round at a smaller club. I think Simon Barker was one of the few who had, when he was with Blackburn. It was probably a bad time to be having that conversation – we lost 2–1.

CHAPTER THIRTEEN

A Big Decision

The following season proved to be a turning point not only for me but also for QPR. The clash of personalities between the chairman Richard Thompson and Gerry Francis led to the man who was my mentor in many ways leaving the club in the middle of the season. Not long afterwards, I had made a similar decision: that it would be time to move on in the summer. But funnily enough, I went on to have my best goalscoring season for QPR that year, 1994–95.

I got on well with Richard as well as Gerry, but for some time you could see a situation developing between them. There were many stories in the press around that time, with Gerry saying how he had not been given any money to spend and was continually having to sell players to buy players, that sort of thing.

I had signed a new contract that summer. Gerry had asked me whether I would stay another year, and at that stage I felt I was still picking things up at QPR. I had improved my game every season under Gerry and thought there were still things I could improve with him. My goalscoring record showed progress every year and, as it turned out, continued to do so through this season.

This wasn't the first time there had been problems between Gerry and Richard. In the two previous seasons there had been the occasional war of words, and the fans were uneasy as well. There had been demonstrations after matches where the fans would come onto the pitch and complain about Richard and the way he was running the club. He got quite a lot of stick, so it was obvious to the players that things weren't plain sailing all round.

But when it actually came down to Gerry leaving, we were all very shocked and it came as a real surprise. The night he went, we were playing Liverpool at Loftus Road at the end of October. It was my first game back after suspension (I had been sent-off earlier that season against Tottenham) and we won the game 2–1. I scored the winning goal in the last couple of minutes.

Before the game, we were all sitting in the dressing-room and everyone was talking about what was in the press that day about QPR. There was a story everywhere that the club were going to bring in Rodney Marsh, who had been a famous player at QPR in the 1970s, as chief executive. Some people were saying it was well known that Gerry and Rodney, even though they had played together in the same QPR team, didn't get on well and that there was a real clash of personalities. This would make it impossible for them to work together.

Gerry resigned straight after the game. After he left, there was never another mention of Rodney Marsh taking over, which everyone found pretty confusing.

I had a very good relationship with Gerry, but the strange thing about this whole episode was that during it, there was no uneasiness or difference about him in the way he was day-to-day with the players, even the senior players like myself. OK, we read the stuff in the papers but there are always differences of opinion in football and there was nothing to suggest it would end with anything this drastic. Results hadn't been going so well for us – we were near the bottom of the table early on in the season so there were a few problems, but nothing that seemed too significant. Because Gerry was such a favourite with the supporters and everyone else, we just couldn't see him leaving QPR. So when it happened, it just seemed really strange.

People used to slag off Richard Thompson left, right and centre, but I used to get on with him really well for some reason. We were friendly on a superficial level, just chatting after matches, that sort of thing. He never discussed the situation with me either, nor with any of the other senior players. People were saying that a lot of the problems between Richard and Gerry had been caused by their falling out over me. There was speculation that Richard wanted to sell me but that if he did, Gerry would resign. Again, Richard never spoke to me about it at the time. The only time we really had that kind of conversation was when I was actually leaving. He said that the year before, QPR could have got £4 million for me and now they were getting £6 million, so next year it would probably be £8 million. It was like something out of a cartoon, with the pound signs in his eyes.

Personally, I felt the departure of Gerry was a big loss to QPR after what he had done for the club over the previous four seasons. It seemed very strange that it should end this way.

During the close season, I had signed an extended deal to stay at Loftus Road. There had been a lot of speculation, as usual, that I would be off in a £4–5 million move that summer. Some clubs had come in with a firm bid, like Blackburn Rovers, and I knew that others had expressed interest, but QPR told them I wouldn't be leaving. I talked the situation through with Gerry, and he felt I was still learning and that it would do me no harm to stay another year. I sat down and looked at the whole situation and felt pretty cool with it, it made sense to me. It wasn't the right time to move just yet. Everything happened to me very quickly once I had established myself at QPR. I went on to play for England pretty soon after, in what was really my first good season. I was getting a lot of publicity and I just didn't want to get carried away with it. I was happy and settled at QPR. There were phone numbers in terms of money being thrown around, which was tempting, but I'm a great believer in fate and felt that if big wages were there for me to have, then eventually I would. I didn't feel that I needed to grab the chance then because it might never come again. By that stage, I had enough confidence in my ability to believe that things would keep improving for me and the 'other things' would inevitably follow. I was on a very good wage at QPR anyway, so the money wasn't a great concern. I had negotiated a better deal for myself and I was happy with that. As you get older in football, you get a rough idea what people are earning and if you speak to experienced people like Ray Wilkins or Peter Reid – who was at QPR for a time –

you get to find out what a real deal is. As you get older, you get wiser, and I knew what I could get if I went somewhere else.

Gerry had obviously been one of my mentors at QPR but another person I was very close to was Clive Berlin, who had been managing director at the club and is now chief executive. I used to speak to him a lot. He used to invite me into his office even when I wasn't in the team. I used to have coffee with him and tell him what a good player I would be if only I was given the opportunity, and he used to say 'yeah, yeah' and joke with me about it. Whenever I see him now, he always says to me that he remembers our chats and how I used to say I was going to be the next Pele, and starts laughing. Clive encouraged me to keep going when I was struggling to get in the side in the early years, and you need someone like that to help your confidence when it is low. It was very much appreciated by me. I used to leave his office and he would say if he was the manager he would pick me, and then have a chuckle to himself.

The way I actually found out about Blackburn's bid was quite funny. I used to get on very well with the girls who worked in the offices at QPR, and when Blackburn faxed their bid of £3.5 million one of them told me, even though they weren't supposed to. I confronted Gerry with it. He had to admit that they'd had a bid, and other interest, but the club didn't want to sell me. One thing he said to me was pretty truthful: he said the reason he hadn't told me was because he didn't want to lose me. He said that if the club wanted me to go, they would have told me about the bids and accepted one. I went away to consider what he said and I thought that was true enough. I wasn't one of those people who wanted to know if this club or that club were in for me.

Gerry was different to a lot of managers in that he would always take time to come and talk things through with you. He would come in after a game and say he wasn't happy with this, that and the other. But he wouldn't have a go or pull anyone out in front of the rest of the team. He would ask us what we thought went wrong and then he would say not to worry, we'll have a look at it on the video on Monday. We knew when we got in on the Monday that we would be watching a video of the previous game. If you didn't have a particularly good game, he

My biggest regret is that my mum didn't live to see what I've achieved.

Colorsport

Popperfoto

Outjumping the Tottenham defence at White Hart Lane, March 1991. I had always supported Spurs as a boy and gave serious thought to signing for them when my transfer from QPR was being negotiated. I was delighted to join the north London club in August 1997.

In action for QPR, November 1992. It was around this time that I got called into the England squad by Graham Taylor.

On England duty, first against Holland at Wembley in April 1993 in a crucial World Cup qualifier which we drew 2–2, then in a tournament in the USA where we lost to the home side in the first match. Things were not going well for the national side.

Celebrating my second international goal, against Poland at Wembley in
September 1993. Despite winning the game 3–0 England still failed to qualify for
the 1994 World Cup finals.

Having a laugh with Paul Ince – we've become like brothers.

Empics

Shaking hands with England team mate David Seaman – I'd managed to get the ball past him in our 2–0 win against Arsenal in our first game of 1996!

Empics

When we lost 4–3 to Liverpool on 3 April 1996 I thought, 'That's it, we weren't meant to win this championship.'

In the thick of the action against Everton at the start of the 1996-97 season.

I finished the season with 21 goals, which wasn't bad considering all the injuries I'd suffered.

We beat Ferencvaros 4–0 in the UEFA Cup second round, second leg. I got the last goal in the 90th minute.

Testing the Leicester defence but goalkeeper Kasey Keller saved everything I threw at him. We ended up losing 2–0 and things got worse before they got better.

The first game of the 1997-98 season and I make my Premiership debut for Spurs at White Hart Lane, against defending champions Manchester United.

Colorsport

Colorsport

A great honour – receiving my 1996 Players' Player of the Year award from Pele.

would pull you aside in training and have a word with you about it. He would ask if everything was alright. He used to talk you through your game and ask you if there were any problems, but never having a go. He took time with you, and that is important for a lot of players.

He didn't really break the news to us about him resigning. It was in the papers already, he didn't tell the players first. I'm not sure if any of the players wanted to go and see Richard Thompson to find out the situation; I didn't. It's one of those things that happens in football and we all had to get on with it.

One of my last games for QPR was against Spurs in May 1995, and of course that meant I saw Gerry again as he had taken over at White Hart Lane. It was the penultimate game of the season and I scored both goals in our 2–1 win. I hadn't seen Gerry since he left the club, although I had spoken to him on the phone a few times. I didn't really speak to him after the game but as I left the pitch and shook his hand, he called me a little name and then we smiled at each other, because it had been my goals that had beaten them.

Ray Wilkins took over very soon after Gerry left and the view of the team was that he was the ideal choice. He had gone to Crystal Palace after a very successful time playing for QPR. Everyone looked on him as someone who had management qualities, with his experience and the way he used to talk to players. All of us had incredible respect for him and we knew it wouldn't be a difficult transition for him to make. He came back as player-manager, although he was out for quite a while at first because he had broken his foot in his first game for Palace.

Although I was very close to Gerry, his leaving didn't affect me that much because I went on to score a load of goals that season. I knew what I had set out to achieve for myself but as the season went on, although I was scoring, I felt I wasn't improving anymore as a player at QPR. That had been my reason for staying, but by the middle of the season I felt that wasn't happening. It was the first time I had felt like that and was the reason I decided to make my move the following summer. Whether it had anything to do with Gerry leaving I'm not sure – I think things were beginning to move in that direction while he was still there. It wasn't that I didn't want to play for Ray. I felt I could learn from someone like him just as I had done from Gerry, but I also felt I had reached a new stage in my career. So although during pre-season I had felt it was better for me to stay, a few months later I made the decision, in my mind, that by the following summer it would be the right decision for my career to move. I felt it was becoming too comfortable for me at QPR; I needed a fresh challenge. I spoke to my dad and my girlfriend about it, and the obvious question was where did I want to go? I just replied, 'We'll wait and see who comes in for me in the summer and take it from there.' I didn't want to rock the boat at QPR and I didn't want to think about the decision too much, because it was still a few months down the line.

There were possible complications with it. I was now living with Angelea and Aaron, he had grown from a baby into a boy and we had become very close now that we were all living together. I didn't really think about leaving London and what would happen if I did. Spurs were obviously one club to be mentioned. If you look at Gerry's record, he has a reputation for bringing players he has worked with before to his new clubs, and a lot of the guys at QPR joked that I'd be joining Spurs because Gerry was my dad, and that sort of thing. If any player does well under a particular manager, the other players always think you're his favourite and make jokes about it.

Ray's first game was against Leeds in November 1994 and there was a lot of talk that I was unhappy, that I wanted to leave and had demanded 'showdown talks' over my future. Those people that know me well, know that I don't do that sort of thing. Ray laid the speculation to rest in the press conference after the game.

I had just scored two goals in our 3–2 win. Ray and I had already talked about the situation and had decided that the time to discuss it was at the end of the season. Ray said all this in the press conference, that I had not come to see him because I was unhappy but we *had* talked about the future and had come to a decision. He also said that he had been at many clubs where players were unsettled, and it had always shown in their performances. Unhappy players didn't play like Les Ferdinand did against Leeds, he added.

However, there is a funny story to go with this whole scenario about my future, involving Ray. While he was still at Crystal Palace, he called me one night to say that he had just had Alex Ferguson on the phone. Ray said he thought the time was right for me to leave QPR and that United wanted to sign me. According to him, Ferguson had not been interested in what sort of money I was on, what my faults were as a player or anything like that. All he wanted to know was what sort of character I was, would I settle in Manchester and fit in with the rest of the team from a personality point of view? Ray had told him that there would not be any problems with me on any of those fronts.

To be fair to Ray, he was honest with me and said that he thought United would be in for me very soon. The next week, Ferguson made a bid but QPR told United there would be nothing happening until the end of the season, as I had committed myself that summer to Gerry and the club. Within a few weeks of that, there was more speculation that Stan Collymore was going to Old Trafford and then not long after that, Andy Cole actually signed for them. So who knows what might have happened if things had been different that autumn?

When Ray came in as manager, I reminded him about the conversation we had had a few weeks previously. It was funny because here he was now, saying how he wanted me to stay at QPR, when before he thought it might be better for me to leave! We had a laugh about it. He said circumstances change what you think, and I realised that now he was my manager, he was bound to take the opposite view.

None of this affected me during the season. The prospect of United making a bid was obviously exciting but if it was going to happen, it would happen; if I forced it, it might turn sour. So you just go on with how events unfold. Until the summer came along, I would be giving my best for QPR.

In many ways, the events of the season became almost a sideshow to all the speculation, but in the end I scored 24 goals in the league, my most ever. Once again, though, I suppose you could say one of the 'highlights' of the year was my sending-off at White Hart Lane against Spurs in October. The previous season

I had been sent-off at Liverpool, which had been the first time for a while that I had let my temper get the better of me.

I remember I was booked early on during the game at Tottenham, and then later I went in for a tackle and someone came in with a high boot which was very late. I grabbed hold of them and pushed them away, saying that was really out of order. Then Kevin Scott, the Spurs defender, came across and said, 'I'll have some of this.' So I said OK, and we squared-up to each other for a punch-up. It was a bit of handbags really, but the referee sent us both off (although later, for some reason, Scott got his sending-off revoked and I still had to serve my suspension). I'm not sure if I was getting more fiery as I got older. I think a lot of it was that I was getting a bigger name, more defenders were looking out for me and were dishing out more heavy treatment. I remember when I joined Newcastle, Peter Beardsley told me about the time QPR played Everton when I scored that hat-trick and he was playing against me. Because I had scored three a couple of days earlier against Forest, they had told Ian Snodin, who was a tough player, to hassle me early on and put me off my game. Peter said that was the worst thing they could have done, because I went on to totally destroy them that day.

In the summer, the team went off on an end-of-season tour to Barbados and this was where the final decision was made. I was sitting beside the swimming pool in a hotel with Ray and all the lads had gone off to do other things. He had already said in the press that during this tour, a decision would be made. So one day, while all the boys were out, he said to me, 'Come on, let's go and have our little chat.' He asked me what I felt, and I said I thought it was time to move on. He said he was sorry to hear that but understood it, and he then said, taking his manager's hat off and talking as a friend, that he agreed with my decision for my career. That was basically it. He knew my mind was made up and that I was making the right decision. He said we would do it the right way: he was going to speak to the chairman and tell him how I felt, and Ray was sure Richard would not stand in my way because I had never kicked up a fuss about anything before! We had a laugh as well, because Ray turned round and said that they would struggle with me gone.

When we got back to England, he told Richard Thompson and Richard phoned me. We agreed that, with Ray going away, a press release should be sent out straight away to say that we had come to an agreement that I was to leave and the club was open to offers. Ray would then be around if other managers wanted to contact him. I had already told some of the players like Danny Maddix and Clive Wilson but they knew the situation already and it didn't come as any surprise.

I had no firm ideas in my mind about where I wanted to go. I knew that staying in London would make life easier, as I wouldn't have to uproot my family and everything else, but that didn't mean I didn't want to go up north. As it happened, the club didn't put out the release before Ray went away and I didn't want the situation dragging out any longer. Their hand was forced by Aston Villa putting in a bid.

Within a week, £6 million had changed hands for my signature.

CHAPTER FOURTEEN

The Six-Million-Pound Man

Once I had made my decision in Barbados with Ray Wilkins, the transfer merry-go-round started straight away. As soon as I got back at the beginning of June, Richard Thompson informed me that Aston Villa had contacted him and had made a bid. But I wanted the whole thing handled properly and out in the open, so as not to give the impression that I was letting down the fans by going behind their back. I would only talk to Villa, or any other interested party for that matter, if the club put out a statement.

Ray then went away for a few days but QPR issued a statement on the Thursday, saying that Les Ferdinand had decided to leave the club and that I was for sale. As far as I was aware, there had been quite a few enquiries as to my availability and certain clubs had asked to be kept informed if circumstances changed.

So when everything was settled, Richard and my agent Phil Smith got back in contact with those clubs who had already expressed an interest. The press had written mainly about Arsenal, Tottenham and Newcastle, and I was unaware that Villa had been in for me before. I think Everton had also bid, but for obvious reasons I wasn't too keen on going there. All the papers were saying that the two big moves of the summer as far as strikers were concerned were going to be me and Stan Collymore from Nottingham Forest, and some of the figures bandied about were like telephone numbers. I had no idea what my price tag was going to be. I've never let that worry me, because in my opinion you are worth whatever someone is willing to pay for you. I thought the transfer fee might be around £5 million.

I didn't have any real preference about where I should go. I was going to take the best deal for Les Ferdinand in terms of my career, and that was the important thing. That had been my attitude when I went to Besiktas as a 21-year-old and it had worked out. That move had been a big gamble and I was now a lot older, so in my view I was prepared for any sort of upheaval which might come with a transfer.

When there was talk of Tottenham coming in for me, I must admit that with Gerry Francis now being their manager, I did think about that seriously. I had always supported Tottenham as a boy and here was a chance maybe to join them and link up with Gerry again, having been so successful with him at QPR. Although I knew they had shown interest during the season, when it came to the crunch and I was available they didn't come in until the last minute, and by then I had already made up my mind.

(In fact, Tottenham had wanted to sign me the previous year, before Gerry took over, and I actually spoke to somebody who was on the board about it. This was just before they signed Jurgen Klinsmann, but I had already committed myself to Gerry and QPR for another season so it was a non-starter.)

The negotiations for my transfer began on the Saturday, only two days after the statement went out. I travelled up to Birmingham in the morning with Phil to talk to Doug Ellis, the chairman of Aston Villa, at Villa Park. Now Doug has a certain reputation in football – his nickname is 'Deadly Doug', because of the number of managers who've come and gone since he became chairman in 1968 – and I expected him to be a real ogre of a man, but he was very nice and made me very welcome. Also at the meeting were Brian Little, the manager, and Steve Stride, the secretary. Doug Ellis's little dog was also there in his office!

I knew what I wanted in terms of money and they made me a very good offer and did their best to sell the club to me. I knew Villa were a big club with lots of support, but at the time, in my view, they weren't a much better team than QPR. We had actually finished higher than them that season. When I spoke to Brian Little, he said to me that Villa were at the rebuilding stage and what they needed was a big-name signing to attract other players there, to show everyone they were serious about making a proper challenge for honours. But at that stage of my career, I wasn't sure I wanted to take a gamble like this. The whole reason for me moving from QPR was that I wanted to be in a team good enough to challenge for all the major honours already, and Villa were not in that position yet. All the same, they had made me a very good offer and when the meeting broke up after about three or four hours, I promised them I would consider it seriously. Moving to Villa had a lot of plus points: Birmingham was only 90 minutes from London, which was good because obviously Angelea, Aaron, my family and all my friends were still in London and I wanted to see all of them as much as possible. But it had to be a football decision, first and foremost. I had told Ray Wilkins that I would only leave to try and improve myself as a player, and in that respect I saw Newcastle as a better proposition than Villa.

When we left Villa Park we headed straight back down the motorway to meet Kevin Keegan at the West Lodge Hotel, which is in Hadley Wood, north London. In the end Villa and Newcastle were the only two clubs to put in firm bids and meet QPR's asking price, which Richard Thompson had told me was £6 million. Phil and I sat down with Kevin in the evening for dinner and stayed for four or five hours. Because I wanted to improve myself as a player, I felt that with Kevin having been a striker, the best British striker around in his day, there would be no-one better for me to learn from. Funnily enough, the only other person I had in my mind who I felt had the same aura and reputation was Kenny Dalglish, and now I have ended up playing for both of them. I have spoken to Alan Shearer about the reasons he moved to Blackburn, and he always says that Kenny was a major factor in that, just as Kevin being at Newcastle was for me.

Financially, the deals offered by Newcastle and Villa were similar. I had my set of demands and they had what they were prepared to pay. We met somewhere in the middle but we weren't too far apart, although I think Villa had been pretty surprised to learn how much I was on at QPR. I was the highest earner there, and was being very well paid as far as I was concerned. It was a lot of money for anybody, especially someone who grew up where I did, but you go with market forces. Established international players at that time were earning good money, so there was no reason for me to be any different!

It was the first time I had met Kevin in person. (I had spoken to him on the telephone about a move a couple of times, like I spoke to a few people, but at that stage I was not leaving QPR.) I talked with him about what it was like up in Newcastle, how I would fit into the team from a playing point of view and whether I could settle up there personally, although I didn't see that as a particular problem after my time in Turkey. In the past it has been a real barrier to a lot of players, but I knew that part of it would be fine. What Kevin had to say about the playing side of things was very encouraging. They already had good players at Newcastle, but he said I was going to be just the first of a few major signings and that the club was really going to have a go for the title. That was the sort of thing I wanted to hear. I knew I was going to be his main striker and that the team would play to my strengths and give me lots of opportunities to score goals. They had already tried to sign Dennis Bergkamp and Roberto Baggio, so that showed the calibre of player they were after.

I had told Villa that I would not make a decision straight away and I said the same to Kevin. They both knew I had talked to the other club, but I think at the back of my mind I knew it was going to be Newcastle for me.

Despite all this going on, nothing was going to stop me from going out that night. I had promised to meet Danny Maddix and some other friends at a club, so after dinner I was quite keen to get away from the discussions. It seems funny, but there was no reason to stop partying even if I was in the middle of a decision that would change my life!

I had already talked it through with Angelea and my dad. She is not really into football and her view was that I should do whatever was best for me, even though it meant moving away for a while, away from my Aaron who was now eight or so, which is the age when things really begin to develop between a father and son because they are beginning to grow up. I thought we would discuss the issue of them joining me when I was finally up there and settled. It wasn't a decision that could be made right away.

One other person I had spoken to quite a lot about Newcastle was Andy Cole. He could not speak highly enough of his time on Tyneside. I have known him for some time and I had several chats with him about Newcastle even before the deal was actually on, because in the back of my mind they were one of the clubs that I had marked down as a possibility. Andy told me there could be no better place for a striker to play than St James' Park.

I suppose Danny Maddix was the first person to know that I had virtually made up my mind, mainly because I saw him that night as soon as I had left the meeting. He asked what I had been doing that day and I said I had been speaking to Villa and Newcastle. He then naturally asked who I was going to choose. Things were very much stacked in favour of Newcastle, but there was no reason for me to be rushed into making a decision. That isn't my way and I was just going to enjoy a night out with my friends.

We went to the Emporium nightclub and didn't get back until five or six in the morning. Although the move was obviously on my mind, it couldn't have been worrying me too much because I didn't get up until that afternoon. Phil was on the phone to me early, to see how I felt. It was an exciting time for him as well, because this was his first major transfer deal and I had put my trust in him to do the right thing for me. He was getting calls from all sorts of people asking what was happening. He had become my agent some time before, when we had worked together on some commercial stuff and endorsements while I was at QPR. We had a good chat about what I was expecting from him and we worked up a good relationship together. Although this was his first really big transfer, I had every confidence that he would do a good job for me and we didn't think it was going to be a particularly difficult deal to pull off. I knew the going rate for an established England international, and you don't buy a player for £6 million and pay him the same wages as someone who cost £500,000.

I was very relaxed about the whole thing. My attitude to life is very much, 'What will be, will be' and I wasn't going to make a rash decision and end up having to go back on my word. Things do play on your mind, though, and you have to be sure you are making the right decision when it comes to something as important as this, so I chatted it through with people close to me, like my dad. He was very excited about it and gave me some fatherly advice. He was sure I was making the right move by going to Newcastle, and told me so.

When I look back on the start of my career and the way things were going for me at QPR in the early days, I never really thought I would be in a position where I was going to be sold for £6 million. I was certainly proud that things had got to this stage, but I never let it bother me. At the time, it was one of the highest fees paid anywhere in the world and I had a little chuckle to myself when I thought about the days at Southall, Viking and the Harrow Club.

Everywhere in the papers there were all sorts of figures being bandied around about how much I was earning. Even on television, Richard Littlejohn was doing his show and he opened up a briefcase with £15,000 in cash in it and said that was how much I was going to earn in a week. He was having a go really, saying how could I earn this amount of money? I missed the programme but someone told me about it the next day and I had a little laugh about it. When I heard things like that, it made me realise the extent of the fee and everything surrounding it. It helped put it all in a bit of perspective and keep my feet on the ground. There must be a few people in the London area whose wallpaper fell off after they'd had a visit from me when I was younger. It was all a long way from the days of the wallpaper shop on the Harrow Road, the delivery van and steam-cleaning cabs. Then, I was just a teenager living on my wits in a tough neighbourhood, dreaming of making it as a professional footballer. And here I am now, moving clubs for £6 million.

By the end of the weekend I had made my decision and early the following week we phoned Kevin Keegan to tell him. But soon after, I got a call from Gerry Francis. He told me that Tottenham were interested and he wanted to speak to me. If it had been anybody else, I would have told them on the phone that my mind was already made up and there wouldn't be any point in talking. But I owed it to Gerry to tell him personally, so I went round to his house to have a chat with him. If Spurs had come in properly earlier, it might have been different; but I had made up my mind. I let Gerry have his say first. He said to me that we could work together well again and could really do things at Spurs. Then I told him I was going to Newcastle and although he was disappointed, I think he appreciated my position.

Once all the relevant people had been informed, I got myself away on holiday to St Lucia to relax and think about what was ahead. I was very excited and looking forward to it. It was going to be a new chapter in my life and there had been many of those already. It was a new challenge. Many players had been up north and failed to settle, and I was determined that wouldn't happen to me. If things didn't work out, it would be down to pure footballing reasons, nothing else.

Most of the people I knew couldn't believe how easily I had taken the whole thing in my stride. David Bardsley used to say to me that he was amazed how calm I was with all this speculation going on around me. Most footballers take the view that one tackle could end your career, so it is normally best to grab the first good opportunity that comes along to better yourself as a player (and obviously get paid better). I never took that view, as I am very much a fatalist. I am sure that has come from the background in which I grew up and the things that have happened to me along the way. My outlook on life changed when my mum died, and that had a lot to do with my way of thinking.

The whole transfer from start to finish probably took no more than a week. At the last minute, there was also interest from Paris St Germain. When David Ginola signed for Newcastle, he told me that not many people had heard of Les Ferdinand in France, but all of a sudden I was all over the papers there. I didn't really know anything about it and never spoke to PSG. But the fact that players like David were also signing for Newcastle was a positive sign. Kevin told me that I had been top of his list, that I was the man he wanted and that he had been following my situation at QPR for a long time. That is the sort of thing a player wants to hear from his manager. He said I was just the first step, and I knew I had made the right decision.

CHAPTER FIFTEEN

A Big Club

When I signed for Newcastle in June 1995, I felt like I had when I left to go to Turkey, but on a much bigger scale. I was going up north and leaving home again.

The actual signing was done very hush-hush. The day before I signed, the club put me up in a hotel close to Teeside airport rather than in Newcastle. The press had already got wind of the fact that I was coming into Newcastle airport and staying in the Gosforth Park Hotel and they had lined the airport up for my arrival. But I slipped into Teeside instead to avoid them, which was the way the club wanted to do it.

I went to the hotel, had the medical in the morning at the local hospital and then went to the ground to sign. When I saw the stadium, I thought to myself, 'I can't wait to start playing here in front of all these people.' I wanted the season to start there and then. Warren Barton had already signed, and I began thinking straight away of the players they had and who else they might sign before the new season came around.

After I put pen to paper, I went outside to meet the fans and there were loads of them out there. It was different to QPR. I just couldn't believe how many people there were outside just to see me. It brought home to me very quickly just how much football means to the people in Newcastle.

Once I had signed the contract, I went to have lunch with some of the directors. The chairman, Sir John Hall, was away but the lunch was with his son Douglas, Freddie Shepherd and Freddie Fletcher at the Gosforth Park Hotel. Afterwards, I got a flight straight back to London and then went off to St Lucia on holiday.

While I was out in St Lucia, my family were talking to me about the move. They were really pleased for me, especially my dad who thought I could really test myself. Most of my relatives had heard of Newcastle but funnily enough, my auntie, who had lived in England, and my grandad both said to me when they heard I was joining Newcastle, 'Isn't it racist up there?' There was a bit of concern about that, but I told them that was all in the past and I would be fine.

I am becoming quite well-known in St Lucia now. When England didn't qualify for the World Cup and I was over there during the tournament, I did quite a lot of TV work covering it for the local station and now it is widely known that Les Ferdinand who plays for Newcastle is of St Lucian parentage. There are even a few bars that have got posters up of me. I was surprised last year when people started walking up to me on the streets and saying hello to me because they knew I played for Newcastle. When I was in the hotel, my room was facing the beach and kids used to come up to the hotel when I was out on the patio, to try and get me to come down and play football with them. I messed about with a few of them on the beach and it is nice to be recognised, but it is still nothing like what happens over here.

I needed to get away to take stock of everything, but I realised when I got back that I only had a week or two in London before I had to organise getting all my stuff up to Newcastle, so there wasn't a lot of time to relax. It also meant there wasn't a lot of time with the family either. Here I was leaving again, like when I went to Turkey, to move somewhere else. Obviously Aaron was now a lot older and could understand what was happening. He knew I was going up to play football. I hadn't decided yet whether they were going to come up with me – I was going to get up there first and see what the lie of the land was. It was difficult for him: I was going from being there every night to being away. But we sat down and talked about things and he knew it wouldn't mean I would stop seeing him. They came up every now and again, but it was difficult while I was still in the hotel because every time they stayed I had to change rooms for a bigger one. The thinking was that it would be wrong to take Aaron away from his school and the life where he was settled. For them to have moved up north would have been a big upheaval, and it wouldn't have been fair of me to drag them up to Newcastle from London without knowing what it was like first of all. I used to go back regularly and the club were brilliant about that. Keegan was fantastic. He actually changed the training regime to accommodate me. If we didn't have a game early in the week, he would let me go back for Sunday and Monday and I would be back at training on the Tuesday. They gave me half-a-dozen free flights as well, as part of my contract, so the club did everything they could to keep me settled.

My first six weeks or so were spent in the Gosforth Park Hotel. I knew I was going to be in a hotel, but after only a week I began to get fed up with it. It's very nice getting all your meals cooked for you and being able to phone up at 2am if you're a bit hungry, but you do not get the same privacy or space as you do when you are in a flat or a house.

The club were fantastic about this as well. Kevin Keegan explained to me that Andy Cole had had some problems when he first moved here because he went and lived up in a mining village outside the city, where he was isolated and remote from everyone else. They said they didn't want to create the same problems for me with regard to settling in. Andy bought a flat in town eventually, which I later rented from him. In the end, he was only in it for a couple of weeks before he went off to Manchester United.

The club did all they could to sort out places for me, and Kevin took a great interest, saying that Andy's flat was the best place for me to be. It's close to town and handy for training. I'm quite friendly with Andy, and of course the first thing that was said to me was how did I feel about replacing him at Newcastle? He had been the number nine and scored loads of goals, and they had not really replaced him when he was sold. I didn't feel that it was a case of me stepping into Andy Cole's shoes. I felt I was going there to play for Newcastle, and although Andy had scored a lot of goals for them, I said to people, 'All I'm going to do is play how Les Ferdinand plays and hopefully that will be good enough for me to score lots of goals.' There are obviously big differences between us as players as well. It is only now that Andy's play involves other people. When he was at Newcastle, he was the mainstay of the attack and everything was designed to go to him, to create chances for him; whereas with me, I have been making goals for people, as well as scoring them, all my career. Andy was really only a goalscorer. He has brought that other aspect to his game now he is at Man United.

Pre-season was different to anything I had been used to. I turned up on the first day and there were thousands of people there to watch you run around and train. That made me realise how passionate the people were, it was something I had never experienced before. Things do go through your mind, like how are you going to settle in, are the people going to accept you, will you miss being away from your family and friends? But I think I accepted that I was in a profession which, from time to time, dictates that you have to go to different places in order to earn your living. I was already used to that with my Turkey experience, so I never really thought it would be a problem on Tyneside. Early on, however, I found out just what it was like being in a small place like Newcastle.

During pre-season, David Ginola and Warren Barton were also staying at the Gosforth Park Hotel, so we used to go out to eat a lot together and go to the pictures. One night, we went to the cinema and stopped for a bite to eat. It was summer, there were a few people out and we decided to walk through an area called the Quayside, where there are a lot of bars, pubs and restaurants. David said he had spotted a place that looked nice at the top of the hill. So we started walking through a place that I now know is called the Big Market and went to go in a pub there. But this guy came out and said to us that we shouldn't go in there because we would get harassed constantly. Just as he said that, a few people came running out of the pub because they had spotted us, and we just took off. That helped me realise quite early on that it is difficult to walk around in Newcastle and keep yourself to yourself. It's different in London, where you can lose yourself. People there are used to seeing famous people so when they see a footballer, it's not such a big deal. And as there are quite a few football clubs in London, they expect to see the odd footballer out and about. But in Newcastle it's different. You don't get harassed as much, it's just that the supporters are so fanatical. They just want you to do well, they want to come over and talk to you and wish you luck.

On the football side, there were differences that struck me straight away as well, especially between Gerry Francis and Kevin Keegan. Gerry is the best tactician I have worked with, he worries about the opposition and how to stop them. But Kevin was only worried from a tactical point of view about his own team. He felt that if we played the way he wanted us to play, then there wasn't a side in the country to touch us. He never specifically sat us down at the beginning of the season to tell us this. It was just at his team-talks and general chats that his philosophy and way of approaching things came across. The players that were there when I joined already knew what it was all about. Kevin demanded that you train how you would play in a match situation, so training was always lively. It was always game situations, playing at match tempo things like five, six, seven-a-sides. But with Gerry, you might have a fun day where you did a bit of shooting and things like that but we rarely played five-a-side. On a Tuesday we would just run, the famous 'Terror Tuesday'. Wednesday was often a day-off if there was no game, and on Thursday and Friday it was all tactical play. There wasn't really any of that at Newcastle. Some people would say that was a good thing and others would say it wasn't. I think that as a player and as a professional, no matter how good you are, sometimes you have to be told what's needed as individuals and as a team. And at times, I felt things needed to be said and people needed to be told certain things but a lot of it was left to our own devices. Kevin just felt that if we played the way we could, there would be no other side to beat us. It was very much that if we played our natural game, things would come together. He would go through the players individually and say if you give us this and that, there isn't any stopping us.

I must admit Kevin always made us feel like a million dollars every time we went out. He was just how I imagined he would be. He got me really motivated and when he spoke, you just wanted to play football. Out on the training ground he was the same, his enthusiasm just came shining through. He had Terry McDermott with him as his number two and Terry was a terrific sidekick for him. They would laugh and joke with the players and join in the training sessions, and that made it really enjoyable and created a great atmosphere. It was still done seriously, but we could have a joke with them. Kevin could still finish brilliantly and he'd like to think he could still play a bit.

I never really picked up much from playing with him, but he used to talk to me about ways that would improve my game. He would point out that, for example, when the ball came up to me I always tried to turn too quickly to try and use my pace. Instead, I should hold the ball a bit more to bring the other players into the game. That was fair enough because the way we played, with me basically as a lone striker with Peter Beardsley behind, meant that I would have to try and beat two or three men when I got the ball because I was up on my own. (I obviously began doing what he wanted, because after a while he said I didn't turn and attack people enough by running at them and using my pace!)

Most players just want to play football in training. There are other parts of the game that are important, that players will look at and say we need to do this or that, but at the end of the day players just love playing football – and if that's what you are doing most of in training, the players will be generally happy.

Now that I was training with players I had only played against before, I did begin to see some of them in a different light. It wasn't that I didn't think much of them as opponents, I knew they were good players, but when it actually came to playing with them I realised they were a lot better than I thought. Rob Lee is exceptional, and Lee Clark is another one. I thought he was alright as an opponent, but when we lined up together I saw how good he really was.

Pre-season was unusual in that we didn't go abroad, we had a series of matches organised in this country. It was a good settling-in period for us; we didn't go too far afield and it was a chance for us to gel properly as a team, considering we had a number of new players.

Certain things struck home straight away now I was at Newcastle. I was playing with better players and expectations were a lot higher, not just within the club but among the media, the supporters, everywhere you went. At QPR, people would talk about us as possibly winning a cup or something like that, but at Newcastle they were saying, 'This is a side that can win the championship.' That was something new to me. Some players thrive on that sort of pressure and it made me realise what was expected of me. The whole situation made me feel straight away that I had made the right move. It's the same sort of feeling, I suppose, as when you walk into a house; you can go in a hundred places and know they are not right for you, but then you walk into one and just know it's the right one. There was a bit of anxiety before I signed, but once I had joined and started training I never looked back.

The style of play at Newcastle was different to what I had been used to but I didn't take too long to adapt. Every time I got the ball, I had two or three options open to me all the time, and I thought this was amazing. At QPR we played with twin strikers and when I received the ball, I had to wait for people to get up and join me.

My first game for Newcastle was in a testimonial against Hartlepool at their ground. I played the first half and a little bit of the second, but the biggest surprise for me was that Kevin Keegan had arranged for my girlfriend and sister to come up and see my very first game, so my little boy was there as well. I didn't know until I actually went out onto the pitch and there they were, sitting behind the dug-out. Keegan then called over to me while I was warming-up and there was my son, sitting over on the bench. That's the sort of guy Keegan was. For that sort of thing, he was the best manager in the world. For him, football was very important, near the top of his list, but there were other things, such as family, that came above football in terms of priority. He did little things like that for players, and that is always appreciated by them.

I was talking to Des Walker recently about Kevin Keegan leaving Newcastle and he said he had a lot of respect for Keegan. When Kevin was playing he was one of the best in the world and sometimes people become aloof with that. But Des remembered an incident about Keegan that has stuck with him, and he reminded me of it again during our conversation. It was during my first season at Newcastle and I had only been there a little while when there was a story about me and a girl all over the papers. Our next game was against Des's team, Sheffield Wednesday, live on the Sunday, and my girlfriend had arrived back from holiday that day to find all this stuff going on. Keegan said to me after the game that I should go back to London and have a few days to sort things out. I was talking to Des just before I left the ground and I had my bags right next to me. Keegan came along, picked up my bags and put them in the car for me. Des said he couldn't believe that Keegan had done that. Most managers would have wanted *you* to carry *their* bags. Des said he really took to Keegan after that. And he didn't do that sort of thing for just his star players, he did it for everyone.

My first goal for Newcastle came in my second game, which was at the non-league club Rushden and Diamonds. I remember the defender was marking me really tightly, but I scored one that was a header – which the goalkeeper should have saved, so I owe him a few quid – and another when I turned the defender on the halfway line and smashed a shot into the top corner. It's very different playing against non-league rather than Premier League defenders. In non-league, with no disrespect to them, they feel that if they can do well against you, there is a chance that people will spot them because they marked Les Ferdinand out the game. They don't necessarily give you any more rough treatment than you get in the higher leagues. I've been on that side of the fence as a non-league footballer playing against a professional, and the talk in the dressing-room is, 'Don't let them come down here and take the piss, don't lie down and let them steamroller us.' So I generally know what to expect.

The next game was at Gateshead, so it was really my first game in front of the Newcastle supporters, and I scored in that one as well. The fans seemed pleased to see me score. I had scored a couple with my head during pre-season and some of the fans were coming up to me and saying that the club hadn't had a centre-forward who could head the ball like me for a long time.

Of course, I was well aware of the number-nine shirt legacy at Newcastle, everyone involved in football is. And with Andy Cole strengthening it even more and then me coming along, I knew the sort of things that were expected of me and what it meant to the Newcastle people.

Things had gone so well during pre-season, both for me personally and the team, that we just couldn't wait for the season to start. Everything just fitted into place straight away for me and the other new players, Warren Barton, David Ginola and Shaka Hislop. Sometimes it takes time with so many new players for the rest of the lads to get used to them, but we all hit it off straight away. This was different for me, because it was a new club and a new beginning. I was starting to build relationships with people I didn't know before, and of all the players I probably got to know Warren and David the best, because we were all staying in the hotel together. I think the boys who had been at the club for a long time were a bit stand-offish towards me at first. They saw me as a little bit different, because I was down in London a lot and I would get invited to different functions and places where there were loads of famous people. I noticed it really through a couple of conversations I had with them when they asked me whether I knew this person or that person, and I would say yes. It wasn't that they were starstruck, but being from London I came from a really different social environment. They weren't unfriendly, but I could see they weren't too sure about me because I keep myself to myself. I'm not a big drinker either, so when some of the players were going out to have a few beers, I would go with them but not drink nearly as much as them, and I just think they didn't know how to take me. I do think the London thing had a lot to do with it. Maybe the £6 million price-tag did as well, I don't know. The fact that I was perceived to be the new superstar coming in didn't bother me at all, so I automatically assumed it wouldn't bother or affect the other players either. There is also a process where everyone assesses the new person coming in; maybe it's natural, but I certainly noticed it.

My nickname, Sir Les, also followed me to Newcastle. It was written about in the local papers and the supporters must have picked it up from there. The one thing that struck me immediately was just how big a club Newcastle was. The local papers have to fill their pages every day with Newcastle stuff and they are desperate for success for their teams in the North East, with Newcastle being the biggest team. It was the first place I had ever been to where I had seen football on such a big scale everywhere around the town. Of course, I knew Newcastle were a big club but the scale of it surprised me. In comparison to QPR, I couldn't believe it. When I was at Loftus Road, one of the things I never used to like was when QPR were described as a 'small club'. It was a phrase managers would use to their advantage to wind up the players when we were up against one of the so-called bigger clubs. But the statement is true. When I went to Newcastle, I realised why they are called a big club: everything they do is on such a large scale.

All of us couldn't wait for the season to start, I had never known such anticipation and expectation in a group of players before. It was as though we just knew we were going to have a good season and be challenging for honours. Obviously that was expected by the fans, but it was reflected in our attitude and in the way we were playing. I knew I was going to score lots of goals. I would be getting a lot more opportunities because of the people around me. I felt fit and couldn't wait to get started.

There was an attitude building up within the team because of the way we had been playing during pre-season. We knew we were good, and we knew we could beat teams easily if we played to anywhere close to our potential. That was emphasised by the manager all the time. Once that builds up, it is very difficult for your opponents to stop you – and that is exactly what happened in the first half of the season.

CHAPTER SIXTEEN

The Dream Start

P re-season had gone well and I couldn't wait for the first game
against Coventry. From the moment I joined Newcastle,
people were saying that if I thought I'd had a good reception
when I signed, then I would be in for a shock at the first St
James' Park game. They were right.

Saturday 19 August 1995 was a day I'll never forget. It was a
full house, and I can remember coming out of the tunnel and
the noise from the stands making me feel like I was floating
onto the pitch. I had always said that the loudest crowd I had
ever heard was at Besiktas, but this was different. The stadium
in Istanbul had a running track around it, so the atmosphere
was further away. At Newcastle it was totally on top of you.

I didn't do anything differently to prepare for the game than I
normally did. I was just hoping I would have a good game and,
with a bit of luck, score. In the dressing-room, Keegan went
round to all the players, especially the new ones. He said to me
that he knew what I could do and was capable of, that I had
nothing to prove to anybody and if I played my natural game
then everyone would see how good a player I was. He said the
crowd already knew what I could do because two seasons before,
I had had a great game for QPR at Newcastle when I scored one
goal and set up another in a 2–1 win.

As it turned out, for me it was a dream start. I was really tightly
marked in the game and I hadn't played as well as I would have
liked. But when I scored, the place erupted, the players coming
over and jumping on my back. In the dressing-room after the

game, Peter Beardsley said to me that I should be a bit more casual in my finishing. For my goal, the Coventry keeper had come rushing out of his box and I had knocked it past him. I was still quite far out but I hit it first time, and Peter said most people would have run it up to the net a bit more.

The first game, and that first goal, was very important to me. When you're a striker and you have that sort of price-tag, there's bound to be a bit of pressure, which increases if you don't start off well. But everything went to plan and my confidence just soared after that. You could sense that the team knew this was potentially going to be a great season. Everything just seemed to flow through all of us almost telepathically.

For the next few games, I was unstoppable. I scored two against Bolton, Man City and Chelsea and a hat-trick against Wimbledon, with a few single-goal matches thrown in between, and I only failed to score in two league matches out of the first 10. The way the side was playing, with David Ginola on the left wing and Keith Gillespie on the right, was ideal for a striker like me. Both David and Keith were on fire at the time. They were raining balls into the penalty area from all over the place and that was giving defences nightmares. Peter Beardsley and Robert Lee were getting into the box as well – we had so many attacking options available to us that teams did not know how to cope. We all seemed to be on the same wavelength. But it wasn't due to anything that had been worked on in training, particularly. In fact, we never really worked on anything in training in terms of tactics or drills. We just used to go out there and play. It was simply a question of us all hitting it off at the same time.

I was looking forward to playing with Peter because I had seen what his partnerships were like with Gary Lineker for England and Andy Cole. It was a pleasure and an honour for me to play with him. What he gave to my game was that he works tirelessly for the team, he gets back when he loses the ball and chases people all over the pitch. That started creeping into my game, which can only be good. You learn different things from different people. At QPR I used to go back for corners but I never really concentrated on defending from the front.

You could sense that there was a great atmosphere at the club during this time. Everywhere we went in the town, the fans would be coming up to us and things like that; but also, whenever a couple of the players fancied going out for a drink on a Monday night, you could guarantee there would be 10 or 11 players at least, if not more, who would also come out. So a great camaraderie sprang up among the players very early on.

We lost for the first time that season against Southampton at The Dell, which was our fifth league game. The only thing that went wrong in that match, after four straight wins, was that we did not play to the standard we had done in the previous games. In the dressing-room after the match, Keegan came in and said what he wasn't happy about. The players were very disappointed because we had been flying until then. Ever since Newcastle came back to the Premier League they haven't been able to win at The Dell, so here was another example of our southern jinx. When we got back to training, Keegan didn't approach anything differently. There were no videos to study where it had gone wrong, like there would have been under Gerry Francis. We knew that we were a good side, but we also knew that we wouldn't go through the season without losing a game. It was disappointing when we lost, but we are not robots and in football there are upsets all the time. That was just one of them. There was no inquest; the only way to put it right was not to dwell on it and go out and win the next game, which we did against Manchester City.

In that early part of the season there were two games that stuck out for me: my return to QPR and my hat-trick against Wimbledon, my first for Newcastle. Going back to Loftus Road was obviously a very special and emotional day for me. You always see players going back to their old clubs and being given a rough time by the home supporters every time they touch the ball. While I was at QPR I saw it happen to Andy Sinton, but I think a lot depends on the manner in which you leave the club. There were lots of ins-and-outs with his transfer and the reception he got was one of the worst I've seen. It did go through my mind that mine was either going to be absolutely superb or it would be a difficult game for me personally.

When I came in through the entrance at Loftus Road, everyone was welcoming me and the strangest thing was walking into the away dressing-room. It crossed my mind that I was in the wrong place. I got changed and went out onto the pitch to have a chat with some of the QPR boys, and said hello to Ray. I got that out of the way and then it was down to business.

The reception I got coming out for the game was one that I will never forget. At the start, when the announcer read out my name, the QPR supporters gave a really big cheer, but the strangest thing happened when I scored. I was happy to score but didn't over-celebrate and as I was looking round the ground, I could see QPR supporters cheering and clapping my goal. It was weird but I really enjoyed it.

The irony of my goal was that my best friend Danny Maddix had been marking me and I had outpaced him for it. He was marking me really tightly and every time I got the ball there were two or three QPR players snapping at me to get the ball – even Daniele Dichio was tackling back. I got the impression that the players had agreed before the game that they would do anything to stop me from scoring that day. I was talking to Danny all the way through the game, trying to wind him up by telling him I was going to score, and he was just laughing and shaking his head. He wouldn't get involved in it.

QPR were playing really well and deservedly took the lead. Then Keith Gillespie equalised with a header, which was very unusual for him. They were attacking and Danny and I were on the halfway line as Warren Barton just cleared the ball down the middle. It went over us and we both spun and started running, with Danny about a yard in front of me. Now he is no slouch at all, he's very quick – but I made up the distance, nudged the ball away from him and as he tried to come across, I just smacked it with my left foot into the net. After the game, he said to me that he knew I was quick but never realised I was that quick! Those were his exact words to me and I just laughed. In training, sometimes we used to race for a ball and he would get there before me. People say to me that I don't look as quick as I actually am. But I think once someone puts a ball in front of me in a match situation and I have to chase it, then I find a little bit of extra pace from somewhere, which you probably don't see in training.

When we had won the game, the reception the supporters gave me was so wonderful I didn't know which end to go to. I went to clap the Newcastle fans because they had made a long journey down, and then I went to clap the QPR supporters. It got quite emotional for me. All the other players had gone off the pitch and just left it to me. It was a very touching moment.

I stayed down in London after the game and met up with Danny later to have a drink or two. There was one funny thing about this whole episode, though. My dad and my sisters and uncles had come to the game, and afterwards I took my dad home. He was pleased about how things had turned out that day for me, and when we were in his house he showed me a copy of that week's *Shepherd's Bush Gazette*. I looked in the paper and it had a picture of Danny in boxing gloves, saying that he was going to tame me. I thought to myself, 'Bloody hell, thank God I scored otherwise it would have looked like he'd done really well!' When I saw him that night I said to him, 'What was all that with the boxing gloves?' He just laughed and said the paper had asked him to do it. It was quite funny.

I must have been on a real high, because I scored my hat-trick in the next game, against Wimbledon. One of the strange things about my career has been that if you look at my record, I have scored two goals on loads of occasions but not many hat-tricks – I think it's only three or four. So that was a special moment for me in front of our home fans, and I remember Arthur Cox saying to me afterwards that there aren't many players who get a hat-trick in the Newcastle number-nine shirt. It was one of those days when everything went right. We got a couple of early goals, their keeper got sent-off, Vinnie Jones went in goal and I scored the third against him. As I hit it, I was laughing – not because I was taking the piss, but because I knew it was going in. I had a big smile on my face because that was the hat-trick goal.

Of all the goals I scored in the first half of that season, a couple stick out in my mind. One was a header against Manchester City. I remember it because Andy Gray was doing his bit on Sky TV where he was measuring the speed of a shot, and one in particular was going so fast that he said, 'You'll not see many balls hit harder than that.' Then the next thing he analysed was my header, and Richard Keys said he would like to see that on the speedometer. It turned out I had headed the ball as hard as the shot. It was all down to the cross by David Ginola. He whipped in this great ball and they measured it at something like 80 mph.

The other goal I remember clearly was one against Everton. I always enjoy scoring against them. Keegan had come to me before the game and said I was contributing to the side really well with my all-round play, but had lost from my game the turning and running at defenders that I used to do at QPR all the time. He wanted me to try it a few times against Everton and that's how I scored my first goal. I turned my marker, went past a couple of players and smashed it into the bottom corner. Kevin said to me after the game, 'See what I mean?' Funnily enough, as I've said, when I first arrived at Newcastle he wanted me to do less of that and hold the ball up more, to bring other people into the game, but I suppose he thought I had gone too far the other way by not doing it at all. Another reason why I remember that game is because they analysed on Sky how fast I was running. Someone had knocked the ball past Dave Watson and he and I were racing for the ball. I'd given him a few yards start but beat him to it, and they measured me at 21 mph at my fastest. It's really funny because if you watch *Fantasy Football*, at the start there is a sequence where I go round the goalkeeper and totally miss the ball. That was the same incident! I'd got ahead of Watson and nudged it round the keeper, but I was going so quickly that when I tried to stop to knock the ball in, I swung and missed it completely. I was at an angle, but it was an open goal and I felt like a right idiot. David Baddiel came to one of our games because his girlfriend is from Newcastle, and I said to him in the bar after the game that if they didn't take that sequence off, I was going to knock him or Frank Skinner out. He started laughing and said that if there was one thing he didn't want, it was to be knocked out by me . . . but of course, they didn't take it out.

Another goal that stands out in my mind is one against Stoke in the Coca-Cola Cup. That was an important goal because it was the eighth consecutive game that I had scored in and I needed one more to set a new post-war Newcastle record of nine. That surprised me because when Andy Cole was scoring all those goals, I would have thought he must have scored in so many consecutive games. Next we played Tottenham away. I hit the bar in the first half and had a shot late in the game where it hit Ian Walker, came back to me, and Colin Calderwood cleared it off the line. That was my chance of the record gone because a few minutes later, the ref blew the whistle. The record did go through my mind – I was thinking, 'I could get it today.' Up until then I hadn't thought about it, but a lot of the local media were talking about it and in my Saturday column for the *Evening Chronicle Pink* I mentioned it, which probably put the mockers on me.

Despite everything going so well, Keegan used to pull me to one side every now and again to talk about ways I could improve my game, although he never chatted things through with you as much as Gerry did. After only a few games, Keegan said to me that the team were getting more from me than he thought they would. Even in pre-season training, he had noticed that I was really applying myself. I'm not the best runner or trainer, but I wasn't close to the back in the long-distance stuff and Kevin was really pleased. One thing he noticed about my game, which I worked on with him, was keeping on my toes all the time. He used to take me to the squash court for a game and he would stand behind me and hit balls against the wall just to keep me on my toes. Sometimes, he said, I went flat-footed and took liberties with my speed, whereas if I was on my toes all the time, I would be able to get into positions quicker and make decisions a lot quicker than I was.

With things going so well, Keegan was always in a good mood. He always had a joke to tell and he used to come and play head-tennis with the players and have a real laugh. He was not the sort of manager who was aloof from the players. He was very down to earth, as the time when he took my bags for me showed. He was very different to any manager I had played under. Gerry used to think a lot more and stand a bit more to the side from things, whereas Jim Smith always used to swear his head off.

Terry McDermott was a brilliant sidekick for Keegan. He would come in and when two people work well together, they get the banter going. Terry never took any of the training sessions and he still doesn't today, but he was the crossover between the manager and the players – although I must say, because of the way Keegan was, you didn't feel he needed a man like that. A lot of managers have number-twos that really communicate with the players well, but Keegan was doing that anyway. Arthur Cox was the one person who the players would always listen to. When he spoke, we took a real interest in what he was saying. I have respect for a lot of people in football, but Arthur would be very close to the top of the list because of the way he spoke about things; he made a lot of sense. He is very black-and-white and there are no in-betweens with Arthur. He never pulled any punches, he said what he had to say to whoever and all the players respected him for that, even if he was being critical. We used to talk about the times when he was manager and some of the things he would say to players. He used to say to me that sometimes I would put all my effort into training, and other times he would say that if he was the manager, he would have told me, 'You're wasting your time, you big bastard, just get yourself home because you're no use to anyone today.' Sometimes you meet someone and you take a liking to them straight away, and Arthur was one of those people. Now that Kevin has left, he is on the outskirts of things and the lads miss him. I suppose the fact that the players always listened to him meant there were others they didn't listen to, but it's a bit difficult to say who they are.

Even if you have a squad of players who are incredibly talented and hard-working, everybody needs guidance – although some people might think they don't. Generally, players need to be told what to do from time to time, and they look to the management for that guidance. During that early part of the season it wasn't needed so much, because it all seemed to flow and the manager just left it at that. It was rare for him to have to pull anybody up about anything.

Coming up towards Christmas, the team hit a little bit of a bad spell. We drew at Wimbledon and lost at Chelsea, and although we won the next two games, the worst thing that could have happened to us was having to play Manchester United after going through a little period like that. You know that every team will go through such spells at some point in a season and on the face of it, for any other team, dropping those points wouldn't have been a disaster. But after the way we had been playing, we went into the Man United game having lost a little bit of confidence. That was the last thing we needed going to Old Trafford. To an extent, we got hit by the London hoodoo: every time we had been down there that season we had not really performed, and we started thinking there was a jinx. It would be in the back of our minds. It may not seem to be of major importance, but it doesn't take a lot for a small amount of confidence to disappear. And the wrong time to be going into a critical game against your main rivals is when the doubts have begun to seep in.

CHAPTER SEVENTEEN

The Dream is Over

When we looked at the Man United game at Old Trafford, it was not a critical match in terms of making or breaking the championship – it was too early for that and we still had a healthy 10-point lead over them. Where it was important, though, was that it was a real test in many people's eyes of what we were made of, and it was important to give a good account of ourselves from a confidence point of view.

I think the occasion got to quite a lot of us and we didn't perform at all. We lost Keith Gillespie early in the game and he was crucial to the way we had been playing. We just didn't function at all. Keegan came into the dressing-room afterwards and told us that we had had an opportunity to show not only the whole country but the world that we were the number-one team in England, and had let ourselves down badly. You could see from all the players' faces that they knew he was right. We knew it wasn't a decider or anything like that but psychologically, if we had won, it would have been a massive boost for us. We might then have approached the rest of the season in a different manner.

I don't think we were overawed. It's difficult to put your finger on why, but it just didn't happen for us as a team. We discussed it among ourselves and most of us were saying it wasn't the end, there were still a lot of games to go. Most of those sort of discussions take place before training, when players have a cup of tea or coffee before going out. We read the press reaction to see who has been slaughtered in the papers that day for their performance, and I remember people commenting, 'Don't the papers realise that there are still 15 or 18 games to go?' The most noticeable change among the players was the disappointment that we hadn't done ourselves justice.

The result gave us a bit of a kick up the backside and we went on to win the next five games. Man United lost on New Year's Day to Tottenham and we opened up another seven-point lead when we beat Arsenal 2–0 the following night at St James' Park. Just after that run, I think the team began to feel that things were not going so well. We were not playing with the same style or confidence, it seemed to have stopped flowing through us. The loss of Keith was a blow for us. When he got injured, we had to change the system to accommodate a different formation.

These things always happen during a season – there is always a lull – but unfortunately ours came in that Christmas–New Year period which is always such an important time of the season. Winning is a great habit to get into, it just snowballs and becomes easier. But once you start losing, it's very difficult to get out of that and I think that's what we found. At the start of the season I used to go out believing we were going to win, no matter what side we put out or who we were playing. The manager said at the end of the season that there were five or six of his main players who just didn't perform in the second half of the campaign, and I imagine I was included in that. You can compensate for one or two having a bad game, but when so many players are off-form for a period of time, it makes it very difficult.

When you look at the statistics, one that jumps out is that my goals dried up in comparison to earlier. I was on a real hot streak, 21 in 22 games, and then I scored just eight in the last 22. They say strikers go through periods where no matter what they do, they just can't hit the back of the net. In the previous two seasons, I had only ever gone three games without scoring and if you look back on 1995–96, the longest I went without scoring was only three games again. But because of the way I was playing in the early part of the season, it looks like a dramatic slump.

Things changed after Keith got injured and Tino Asprilla came into the side. People said the team wasn't playing the same and that I wasn't getting the chances anymore because of Asprilla, but that wasn't the case. There was a big thing in the papers the weekend we lost to Arsenal in the league. A lot of the London press who were going to be with England the following week put it to me that Asprilla was difficult to read – and I said, 'Yes, he is, but it's my job to play with him.' Keegan had said to me, 'I haven't bought Asprilla to play with you, I've bought him for you to play with him.' He said he wanted me to understand how Tino played. I thought that was a bit strange, because I was the striker who had been scoring goals all season and was on fire. Yet he was asking his main striker to learn how to play with a new signing, rather than having *him* learn how to get the best out of *me*. I just had to get on with the job and do the best I could, but unfortunately I went through a bad period. I would never blame that on Asprilla. I just think it was strange to change things like that.

I was still getting chances, though, and I never shied away from going for them because as soon as you do that, you will definitely not score. I accept that Tino is difficult to play with. He is a fantastic individual and has got some amazing skills, but sometimes reading him on the pitch is a bit difficult. I think even he doesn't know what he is going to do sometimes.

His signing wasn't a surprise to me. After the Arsenal game in the Coca-Cola Cup in January, Keegan told me he was going to get someone in to help me up front, because the team was depending on me too much to score in every game. He said I had done so well that the other players were thinking to themselves, 'Les will get us a goal.' It was not something that had crossed my mind, because I was thriving on all the chances that I was getting and at the time they were going in the back of the net. When he said it, I just thought, 'Well, you're the manager, you do what's best.'

Of course, we all knew who Asprilla was when he signed, but although I'd seen him score a few spectacular goals on TV, I had never really seen him play. When he arrived, he slotted in straight away and had an immediate impact in the match against Middlesbrough where he came on as sub and turned the game, after we had been losing 1–0, for us to win 2–1. He didn't speak any English then, and still doesn't speak very much now. David Ginola and Philippe Albert have been fantastic in learning the language, but a lot of the foreign players are a bit embarrassed to speak because they know they're going to get words wrong and footballers, being footballers, will have a laugh at that and take the piss. But Tino is a bit of a character, he's always joking about. He knows that if he gets words wrong his team mates will all get stuck into him, but he understands enough English to get by.

When we first started playing together, we didn't work on anything in training to try and make the partnership gel. We were expected to go out there and get on with it. But after a few games, I think the manager realised it wasn't going to be as easy as that, and that's when he came to me and said that I needed to adapt my game to Asprilla's. He said Tino was very talented and that he was going to play, so I had to do my best to make it work. Keegan said that with Tino, I had to expect the unexpected, which is a bit difficult in football. If you make a run to the near post for a whipped-in cross, he'll check back; and when you expect him to shoot, he'll pass to you; so in the end, you just have to gamble. Sometimes it comes off, sometimes it doesn't. Like I said, I thought it was a bit strange. If I was a manager and had a striker who had scored 21 goals in 22 games, I wouldn't be buying someone and saying to that striker, 'I want you to play to him.' I would be saying, 'I've bought someone who's going to help you get 40 goals.' But he was the boss and we had to comply with what he wanted.

As things started deteriorating, you could see that things were beginning to get to Keegan, and this was quite a long time before the famous TV interview right at the end of the season. A lot of people had commented to me before then that the manager had changed. When I think back on it, you could actually see it coming. He *had* changed. I wouldn't say the enthusiasm was gone, but he was a lot more subdued on the training ground. All the laughing and joking had cut right down and he now became very, very serious. That was the biggest difference, and I noticed that from around February onwards.

I think that began to rub off on the players as well. The atmosphere was less buoyant than it had been earlier on in the season, and I began to see that probably after the match against West Ham in late February. That was the first league game we had lost since the defeat at Old Trafford and it was a real turning-point for us and also for me: it was confirmation that things were just not going my way. I had first begun to think that against Chelsea in the FA Cup in January. I hit a shot in that game which hit the inside of the post and came back out again. I can remember thinking that on the pitch at the time. I had never seen a shot hit the inside of the post and come out like that. I had beaten Kevin Hitchcock hands down, but the ball stayed out.

At Upton Park, there was one incident which seemed to sum it all up for me. I had a shot that nine times out of ten would have gone in. It was at an angle, and I've hit hundreds like that in training into the bottom corner. This one looked like it was going to do the same, but then deviated at the last minute and went the other side of the post. The lads were already running over to me because they thought it was in. Looking back, I would say from then on I really struggled to score goals. Whereas in the early part of the season I was hitting things – or the ball was hitting me – and they were ending up in the back of the net, I was now striking them as sweetly as anything but they were going the wrong side of the post or over the bar. I basically got into the situation where the harder you try, and the more you think about it, the harder it becomes. I got too tense, instead of relaxing. When players are confident, it's like being on auto-pilot; but when things start going the other way, you start noticing little things that get inside your mind. Following the defeat at West Ham, we drew at Man City and so went into the match against Man United at home having taken only one point from two games. They had closed the gap to four points after an incredible run of victories. Clearly, while the match at Old Trafford had been important this was an absolutely crucial one for both of us. David Batty had just been signed and he played his first game for us that night. I thought it was a good signing: I knew David from England trips and he had won the league twice before with Leeds and Blackburn. I think the manager thought it would give us an extra boost at this key part of the season, and I think if you asked the supporters who their player of the year was over the second half of the season, nearly all of them would say David Batty.

In the first 45 minutes of that game, we produced some of the best football seen that season, even by our standards. We didn't approach the match any differently; for games like that, the manager doesn't need to motivate his players. If you can't motivate yourself for a game like that, you are struggling. Not too much needed to be said about it beforehand, we all knew what it meant. Our confidence was not as high as it could have been but given the way we started the game, you would never have guessed who the in-form team was. I came out and felt really good. We had chance after chance and Peter Schmeichel made two saves from me, the second of which he knew nothing about, it just hit him. I thought, here we go again – and then Philippe Albert had a shot that came off the bar and dropped in the six-yard box, Gary Neville went to whack it away but missed it, and I skied the shot over the bar. It was one of those games where you could see the ball wasn't going to go in and the other team would come away and score a goal. We've all seen it so many times and of course, that is exactly what happened. Cantona got the goal and that was it. I don't think the players thought that was the turning point, although it was a very important game. We still believed we could win the title, but what that game showed us was that it was going to be a lot more difficult than we thought. The way we were playing well into January, when we were 12 points clear, it looked like we might have the title wrapped up by April. Looking down the fixtures after Christmas, we couldn't see ourselves getting beaten many times, and maybe that attitude crept into our game a bit. We lost the rhythm of our play and once that happened, we couldn't get it back. I wouldn't say it was complacency, but when we lost three points, the attitude was, 'It's only three points, not to worry, there are still X games to go,' instead of being really downhearted. Psychologically, you keep doing that and then all of a sudden the 12 points is down to one point and then you fall behind. Once that freefall starts, it's very difficult to stop it.

There are times when the manager will come into the dressing-room after a match and have a massive go at the team because they have lost 1–0 and played absolute crap. But Keegan came in and said he couldn't fault anybody on that performance, it was just one of those nights. He didn't come in ranting and raving, he was as disappointed as anyone else. You always knew when he was going to go off at the team, because he would be as calm as anything as you walked into the dressing-room. I was always one of the last in, and he used to say, 'Come on, there's going to be some home truths now' – and as soon as he said that, I knew someone was going to get a volley. But it wasn't like that against Man United.

There was an atmosphere of dejection around the club for the following week. There were seven days until our next game at home to West Ham but we just had to get on with our preparations and try to focus on the job. We had to win our next game because if we didn't, Man United would be in front of us. So that's how we approached it. Even in the West Ham game, where Les Sealey was in goal, I had two shots that I thought were definite goals but he managed to get to them. In the end, I got my reward in our 3–0 win, but to be honest, I couldn't really have missed a volley from two yards out. I really smashed it in!

We didn't think the championship was gone yet, because we still felt it was in our hands. The win over West Ham was a major boost. People were saying that Man United would have the harder run-in as long as we could get through our next two games unscathed, which were Arsenal and Liverpool away. The Arsenal game turned out to be a disaster. We lost 2–0 and the manager went off his head in the dressing-room afterwards, particularly at one player. In the press, he said that five or six of his players didn't play (he included me in that list) and that we didn't deserve anything out of the game, which was true. Man United had gone top during the week as they had beaten Arsenal at Old Trafford, and now we were really up against it. We had been 12 points clear and now we were behind them. I don't know how the other players felt, but I never gave up hope that we could still salvage it. But that was the point: it was now a salvage operation rather than one that was fully under our control.

Then came the fateful night at Anfield, a night that for as long as I live I will never forget. It was the night the championship dream, which only weeks before had been in our grasp, was snatched away from us. This was the night the dream was over.

CHAPTER EIGHTEEN

Devastation

Going into the Liverpool game, our defenders had come in for a lot of stick. People were saying that the reason we were blowing our chances of the championship was that we couldn't defend a lead. Titles were won by winning games 1–0, not 3–2 or 4–3. We were still in a positive frame of mind, though, at Anfield, and from a personal point of view I had always enjoyed playing there and generally performed well. There is something about that stadium and the pitch.

Robbie Fowler was on fire and we were 1–0 down within two minutes. Even then, I never felt we were going to lose the game. It was a setback to go behind so early, but for some reason I had a feeling this was going to be our day. There was still a long way to go in the game. We fought back to lead 2–1 at half-time. I scored the first when Tino pulled the ball back for me and I hit a high shot into the net. Then I set up David Ginola for the second after 13 minutes and it seemed that my reaction to the early goal had been right, we were going to claw our way back. Liverpool pulled one back in the second half, then we went ahead and they equalised again.

On the face of it, a draw would have been a fair reflection of the game, but in the 92nd minute, the ball broke to Stan Collymore who blasted the winner past Pavel Srnicek for 4–3. It was a devastating blow. When that goal went in, I said to myself straight away, 'That's it, we weren't meant to win this championship.' I hadn't conceded it until that point, but when things like that go against you, it's fate.

Kevin Keegan was lost for words. What do you say after a match like that? If you are the winning manager, you say how fantastic your team was for not giving up; but when you've lost 4–3 in those circumstances, in a game of that importance, there's nothing that can sum it up. I think all Keegan said to us was, 'Get your gear and let's go.' He looked visibly drained. The pictures on the TV showed him with his head in his hands when Collymore's goal went in, and I think that picture summed it all up. It was the moment it really had all gone. No-one said anything in the dressing-room, the players were just sitting around shaking their heads, not believing that we had lost the game. There was deadly silence. It wasn't so much the defeat but the manner of it which was so devastating. The psychological damage of losing to an injury-time goal made it that much worse.

The media interest became incredible. They had been saying a lot of things about the team, but now they were saying that the defeat at Liverpool must convince Kevin Keegan that if he wants to win the title, he cannot play in such a cavalier fashion: it might be great for the neutrals to watch, but it doesn't bring titles. Kevin was his own man, though, and that wouldn't change him. For us, 99 per cent of the time, the matches were fantastic to be part of as players and fantastic for the supporters to watch but unfortunately, it didn't win us the championship. Kevin was very single-minded about how he wanted us to play, so even if some of the players had felt there was something in what our critics were saying, we would never have broached it with him or he would have turned round and said he'd find someone else to play the way he wanted to. If you look at our defenders individually, Steve Watson, Warren Barton, Darren Peacock, Philippe Albert, John Beresford and Robbie Elliott, they are all good players. But as a unit, they were not functioning. Then again, I wasn't scoring goals like I was before. I should have had another eight to ten goals and if that had happened, it probably would have all been very different.

There was no place for scapegoats, no looking for someone to blame: we were all in it together. The coach journey home that night from Liverpool was a very difficult one and the quietest I've ever been on. Everyone's head was bowed, and we had just played in one of the best games we had ever been involved in. Strangely, one thing went flashing through my mind and I have often thought of it since. It was around Christmas time and we were 12 points clear. There was a supporter at the training ground who asked me to sign the Newcastle shirt he was wearing, and when he turned round for me to sign he had 'Champions 95–96' written on it. I hate seeing little things like that, it is jumping to conclusions. I just wish I hadn't seen it, because it was a bad omen. There were also Christmas cards going around with me and David Ginola holding the Premiership trophy, saying 'The Proof is in the Pudding'. It's amazing what you think of at particular moments.

We went back after the Liverpool game to prepare ourselves for the home match against QPR. The title was in Man United's hands now, not ours. Even though we had a game in hand and were not out of it mathematically, the psychological effect of losing our lead was crucial. We could look at our games and say if we win that one and United drop points there and there, etc, but at the back of your mind you know that probably won't happen. We found it very difficult to break QPR down that day, and having got an early goal they looked like they were going to hold out for a win, but Peter Beardsley scored two late goals to scrape a victory for us. The last thing I wanted was for my former team to go down and this defeat helped contribute to that, but more than anything, I wanted Newcastle to win the championship.

The victory over QPR had kept us in touch with Man United with a game in hand. But we went to Blackburn two days later knowing we could not afford another slip-up. It was the same old story at Ewood Park. We totally dominated the match. David Batty scored his first goal for Newcastle, an unstoppable 20-yard shot, just fifteen minutes from the end, and it looked as if the type of 1–0 victory that was supposed to be so crucial in winning titles was finally coming our way. We seemed to be coping quite easily when Graham Fenton came on as a late substitute. He grabbed two late goals, the winner in the last minute, and lightning had struck twice. First Liverpool, now Blackburn. By that time, even Keegan was having difficulty finding things to say to us. He wanted the title as much as anyone, and he was struggling to communicate with the team. He was feeling the pressure as much as the players were. I felt that he and Terry McDermott had been through this situation before as players. They had won championships in tense situations with Liverpool and they knew what was needed for a side to take that one final step to win the title. They had the experience, most of us did not. Perhaps they could have given us something we needed, something that was missing, to take us that last step. Maybe it's different doing it as a manager rather than as a player, I don't know. What was needed was as much a bit of guidance as anything else, to help the less experienced ones through it, things that needed to be pointed out to the players. But there wasn't really any of that.

There was also little doubt by this stage that Keegan had visibly changed. The laughing and joking had stopped in training, he and McDermott became deadly serious. Perhaps that was the time that we needed the laughing and joking more than ever before, to ease everybody down and get rid of the tension. Certainly, I think their tenseness communicated itself to the players. The one thing I noticed about Keegan when I joined Newcastle was his fantastic ability to motivate the players, how he used to laugh with us all the time and make us feel great and completely relaxed. At the time when we needed him to do this, to break the atmosphere, it wasn't there.

The Blackburn game was a devastating defeat, but all of a sudden a glimmer of hope appeared when United lost to Southampton. It had been completely unexpected and with our victory over Aston Villa, we were now just three points behind with a game in hand. Every game was a six-pointer at this stage: one more slip and any hope would have been gone. I actually scored the only goal of the game against Villa in the second half, but I was about to be taken off at half-time. I had not been feeling very well and had vomited during the break. My head was pounding, but the manager asked me if I could get through the second half. I went back out and to be honest, it's the worst I've ever felt on the pitch. But I scored with a header just after the hour to give us a crucial victory.

The match made a lot of headlines because John Beresford was substituted after only 25 minutes. At first I thought he was injured, and it was only at half-time that I found out that John had had a bust-up with the manager during the game and had sworn at him. Keegan substituted him straight away. That has been his manner since he came into management: if someone crosses him, so be it, there will be only one winner. I think it was a spur-of-the-moment thing, and didn't have anything do with the fact that people were tense at that stage in the season.

We played Southampton in the next game and scraped a 1–0 home victory. Our next match was against Leeds on the Monday night, live on Sky. Man United had just beaten them 1–0 and then beat Forest 5–0. But the 'Leeds issue' became one that was to end in one of the most extraordinary television interviews ever seen.

Leeds could have beaten United, and the next thing we heard was Alex Ferguson saying that the Leeds players had been cheating their manager, because they had had such a poor season but had played their hearts out against United. He said he hoped they would try just as hard and not cheat against Newcastle. He also said something about Stuart Pearce's testimonial, which was coming up after the end of the season. We were due to play Forest in the league after Leeds, and Ferguson said it would be better for Newcastle to go to the testimonial as champions, to give Pearce a better crowd . . . therefore, Forest might not try so hard in the league game. It was just Ferguson's way of winding the Forest and Leeds players up; unfortunately, he also wound Kevin Keegan up as well.

I didn't give what Ferguson was saying a second thought, and I don't think the rest of the players did either. We just got on with it. The Leeds game was a hard match, which we won with a Keith Gillespie goal after 16 minutes.

It wasn't until we got home that the players saw Keegan's interview on Sky. When I saw it, I thought, 'Good on you, Kevin.' Other people interpreted it differently. When we went in the next day it was *the* topic of conversation, with people saying he went off his head and things like that. No one had seen him like that before. I saw the reports in the paper that said because

Keegan lost his cool and buckled under the pressure, so did the players, but I don't believe that's the case. We all know how passionate he was about the side and what he wanted. Unfortunately, as a manager, if you wear your heart on your sleeve, you get accused of not being strong-willed enough; but if you're a player and do that, then that's fantastic. I think if anything, he showed the players that we had a manager who was 100 per cent passionate about his team and gave the lads an incentive to do it for him. It didn't undermine my confidence in him at all.

Keegan had gone into his shell a little bit, though. It was more his physical appearance than anything he said or did that made me think he had changed. Yes, the jokes were less frequent, but it was only when someone commented to me that he looked stressed-out that I noticed it. If you see someone everyday, you don't necessarily pick these things up as you do if you go two months without seeing them. It was a gradual thing. His hair was greyer and the smile had gone away from his face. He never communicated to the players that things were getting to him, which is not surprising because no manager would do that. He was very close to Peter Beardsley, who of course was the skipper as well, but I don't know if he ever really talked to him.

Regardless of what happened, the Forest game was an absolute must-win situation. Peter Beardsley scored after half an hour and just before half-time he put over a cross for me, which I met with my head and should have scored, but didn't. While it was 1–0, Forest were always in it and with 15 minutes to go, Ian Woan hit this fantastic shot which screamed into the top corner. As soon as he hit it, I knew it was in. We had chances after that – I hit the bar with a header – but you could see the will drain out of the players after Forest equalised.

When the whistle went, I felt total dejection. Even though mathematically we could still do it, I couldn't see United getting beaten at Middlesbrough, which is what was needed. There was nothing anyone could say. I did an interview for Sky after the game and said that if you wanted to win the championship, you had to come to places like Forest and get three points. If you couldn't do that, then there wasn't much hope. It sounds harsh, but that's how I felt. I went into the dressing-room and you could feel the realisation that we had lost the title.

For me personally, it is difficult to put into words what losing the title meant. We had one hand on it for so long, and then slowly and painfully it was dragged away. Going home on the coach back to Newcastle, I started thinking about chances I had missed in games where if I had scored, we would have won the game. I went through all the games like a tape-recorder in my mind. You do that every year but this time it was different. I was trying to find an answer as to where we went wrong. How could we have played so well at the start of the season only for it all to fall away? I just couldn't put my finger on it. Keegan said that five or six of his top players didn't perform in the latter stages, and he was absolutely right.

I know I was looking towards the management to help us through the sticky period, the area where not many of us had been before. Whether the other players felt the same I don't know, because I didn't discuss it with them. When you are winning, it's easy for everyone to smile, laugh and joke, because winning creates that sort of atmosphere. When things are going against you, it's very different. That's when you need people to be bright and sharp, to help lead you through the harder times, inject a bit of fun or a change of pace.

We never analysed anything in any sort of detail when our play began to falter. We didn't really work on specifics in training, as I've said before. We didn't discuss where other teams were strong, just where we were strong. We used to play game-situations and some people would say that it worked, people loved watching Newcastle on TV because of the way we played. The manager's philosophy was that we would score more goals than the opposition. It didn't always work, but when it did, it was fantastic to watch. We went 12 points clear playing that way, and I think he felt, 'Why do I need to change it?' His attitude would have been that he just needed to get his players back to what they were and eventually the results would follow. But sometimes you get into a way of doing things and it is very difficult to get out of it, and that's what happened to us. We had got used to a certain system of playing and it was difficult for us to play any other way. Kevin started experimenting later in the

season with three at the back, but that was more because of
Tino's arrival and Peter having to play out wide to compensate
for that. At the end of it all, though, no matter what system we
played, the team didn't perform when it needed to. We had to
take the blame.

The last game of the season against Spurs was very much an
anti-climax. We knew it was unlikely that United would lose at
Middlesbrough, and in the end we drew 1–1 so the whole thing
was academic. I scored that day to take my league tally to 25,
the biggest in my career, but it didn't matter. I had been voted
supporters' player of the year, North East player of the year, PFA
player of the year, and a few others. It was nice to get individual
honours, but the only one I really wanted was the championship.
I was devastated and numb when the whistle went. I remember
walking round thanking the supporters for their backing all
season, and I was gutted for them as much as for myself because
they had been fantastic. I felt we had let them down badly. Their
support for us had been unwavering and we hadn't repaid them.
Thoughts of Man United parading the trophy around the River-
side went through my mind, and I just kept thinking, 'That should
be us now, in front of St James' Park.'

CHAPTER NINETEEN

Me and Venables

After being involved with the England team in 1993 with Graham Taylor, I was obviously hopeful that under the new manager, Terry Venables, I would be able to build on my international career. Unfortunately, that didn't really happen. Throughout the time he was in charge, I never really thought Venables fancied me as a player.

The main difference between Venables and Taylor that I noticed was that Venables had the respect of the press men straight away. This was something that Taylor had struggled to get and it had caused him no end of problems throughout his reign as England manager. It didn't matter what sort of results Venables got at first; this was the man that the press wanted, and the people wanted, as England manager.

I was in the first few squads under him and was not that concerned that I hadn't been pitched straight into the team. Then I picked up a couple of injuries and missed a few matches. I still thought I was very much in his plans, but then I was left out of the squad for the Umbro Cup tournament which took place in the summer of 1995. He never explained to me why.

In fact, I only heard about it from Brian Little, the Aston Villa manager, in Barbados when I was there on the end-of-season tour, just as I had decided to leave QPR. Villa had just arrived on the island because they were the next opponents, after us, in a game against the Barbados national team. Brian came up to me in the hotel and said he was sorry to hear about the bad news. I said I didn't know what he was talking about. He then told me that I hadn't made the squad for the Umbro Cup. I have to say I was surprised by the news. I had been in every squad up until then, and to miss out on the Umbro tournament, which was an important part of the Euro 96 preparations, and not have anything said to me was, to say the least, surprising. Even when I rejoined the squad, it was never explained to me what the reasons were for my omission. I had been playing well and scoring lots of goals for QPR, so I couldn't understand it.

In those circumstances, even though you are disappointed, players much prefer to be dealt with openly and be told the reasons behind a decision. I found, though, that Venables was inconsistent. There had been quite a few players previously that he had left out, and he had told them why or phoned them up to find out how they were. He had done that with Steve Howey so when I was left out, Steve asked me whether the boss had called and I had to say no. I thought I deserved an explanation just like anyone else and after that, I think I saw our relationship as sort of hands-off and regarded it slightly suspiciously.

When I joined Newcastle that summer, I started off the season on fire but I was still ignored for about three squads. Then I was called back in for the Portugal game in December. This was actually the first time Venables had taken any real time to speak to me. He said that I should not worry what anyone else was saying or what the press were writing, I was in the squad because he thought I was a good player and deserved my place there. Those were his words to me at the time. I didn't really react to them, I just carried on doing my own thing.

There had been a lot of speculation in the media as to why I wasn't in the squad, especially after all the goals I had been scoring. They wondered whether the two of us had had some disagreement. A lot of people thought it was a North East thing again, that Venables had a bias towards London-based players and that was why he hadn't been picking me and, before that, Andy Cole. But I played against Portugal, my first England game for almost two years, and then against Bulgaria where I scored the only goal of the game from a Teddy Sheringham pass. Every time I went into the squad, I felt I was always on the edge of things, that my place was never assured. Whether I scored or not, or played well, I always had this feeling that I would be out of the side, and as things turned out, that's more or less the way it proved to be.

When Venables first took over the job, he had made it clear that Alan Shearer was going to be his main striker and there would be one place up for grabs as his partner. Alan had missed some games through injury but he returned against Hungary in May 1996 when he came on as a substitute for me. The other strikers all knew we were fighting for one place, and it was touch-and-go whether I was going to make the final squad for Euro 96. The way I had been treated, I wasn't really fussed whether I was picked or not, to be honest. I thought I had done well when I played for England, but my opinion wasn't the one that counted. In the back of my mind, I always thought Teddy Sheringham was likely to get the other forward place in the team, and Robbie Fowler had been scoring a lot of goals for Liverpool. There was also a school of thought that Alan and I couldn't play together and in my opinion, Venables was one of the first people to start that and give it some credence.

At the age that I was, I desperately wanted to play in Euro 96 in front of our own crowds and have some kind of involvement. But the way things were looking at that stage, I could see what was going to happen even if I did make the squad. It's OK saying well, I was there on the bench – but if you don't get on the pitch, it's very different. If England had won the European Championship, I don't think I would have accepted my medal because although I was a sub and part of the banter with the lads and the build-up, I never got on the pitch and if you don't play, you can never feel you were really part of it. For footballers, it is so important to play; players are never happy when they are not out there.

The trip to Hong Kong and China was eventful, to say the least, but not from a football point of view. When we got back to England, there was a lot of fuss in the papers about the boys having a night-out, and I was at the forefront of some of the pictures that came out. Unfortunately, the press seem to do what they can to try and bring the players down and every opportunity that comes along, they do it. We are normal human beings and we make mistakes in life like everybody else, but because we are professional footballers, it seems we are not allowed to do that. OK, we are in a high-profile position, we earn good money and are looked upon as role models, but we are prone to mistakes like anyone else. We had a great team-spirit and that is why on that particular evening in the nightclub, most of the players were there. When you are away from home, you become like a family and you do things together. Unfortunately, it got a little bit out of hand, I got my shirt ripped and when I saw the pictures in the papers, I wasn't happy about it. The other thing is, I'm not a big drinker – I could have understood the reaction if I had been pissed out of my mind, but I wasn't. In my view, it wasn't front-page news.

Getting back to the football, I was not assured of my place in the squad by any means, and however well I performed out there, it might still not have been good enough. I never really knew where I stood with Venables. I scored the only goal of the game against Hong Kong, but even then, I didn't take anything for granted. Virtually every time I started a match, people were saying, 'This is Les Ferdinand's last chance to prove himself' and in the end, I became almost immune to it. Even today, I go into a game and if I'm lucky enough to be selected, the first thing the press will say is 'Is this your last chance?' I might say, 'Well, I scored in the last game . . .' but it's something I can't seem to shake off. I have had it all my England career, so even after the goal against Hong Kong, I still wasn't convinced I would be in for Euro 96.

But having made the final squad, I was obviously looking forward to it. It was the first major international tournament I had been involved in, and it was an opportunity to put the disappointments of the Premier League season behind me. I was hoping I would get my chance, play well and score, and be in a position where I could not be left out again. The only thing that spoiled it was knowing that Peter Beardsley and Robert Lee hadn't made the squad. They were delighted for me and Steve Howey (who then had to drop out through injury) but I was gutted for the two of them. They had been in so many England squads that season but then didn't make the final 22.

The problems with the press continued when we got back, over the stories of drunken parties on the Cathay Pacific flight home. It was totally blown out of all proportion. I slept for the majority of that flight and I remember waking up to find that most of the lads in the upstairs section of the plane were asleep. When I got home and saw this stuff about the party, I thought to myself that it must have been that good I'd slept right through it, and I'm a light sleeper. I didn't even know what had gone on. There was talk of television screens being smashed, but I hadn't seen anything. The press were obviously trying to find out who was responsible and the England players' pool committee of Stuart Pearce, Alan Shearer, Tony Adams, David Seaman and David Platt went away and had a chat with the rest of the squad. It was decided that we were all in it together and that was the best way to deal with it. No-one wanted to be singled out, and as a team, it was our problem.

Going into the tournament, Venables still hadn't really spoken to me about what my chances were or what he expected of me. I just got on with the training. He more or less knew his side, so it was probably going to be a case of whether I would make the subs' bench or not. It was after the Holland game, when he had put Robbie Fowler on as a late substitute, that he actually pulled me aside for the first time and had a conversation with me.

He said I had been training well but that particular morning, he thought I had been looking a bit down and despondent. He told me that the only reason he had put Fowler on was to give him a bit more experience, it wasn't that Robbie was in front of me. He said that he knew what I could do at international level and we were winning the game, so it gave him an opportunity to have another look at Robbie. By this time, I couldn't even bring myself to say anything to him, I just sort of nodded my head and walked away. He had literally not had a conversation with me until that point. In the next game against Spain he put Robbie on again, and that was when the game was finely balanced. When that happened, I sort of chuckled to myself and thought, 'From one nightmare to another.' He said nothing to me again for the rest of the tournament. In my mind, I knew I wasn't his first choice behind Teddy and Alan and I felt like I had wasted my whole summer. Players wait all their lives for opportunities like this, but I never had the chance to show what I could do. Even though I was there, involved in the euphoria of the occasion, and was ecstatic for the lads at how well they were doing – I am not a jealous person and I wouldn't begrudge anybody the success they had – from a personal point of view, I would rather have been in the Caribbean somewhere.

If I was summing up my relationship with Venables, I would say there wasn't a relationship there. He sent a letter to all the players after Euro 96, apparently thanking them for their efforts. I got this letter one day at my flat in Newcastle and I opened it, wondering who it was from. I looked at the top of the letter and it was from Terry Venables' offices in London, so then I didn't even read it. I put it straight in the bin.

Of course, there were aspects of the tournament that I enjoyed. Being away with the lads is always a good laugh, you get very close to each other. There is always great banter between us, and that did take my mind off the disappointment of the Premier League. Everyone was mixing. We had a real laugh with the Liverpool players, Robbie and Steve McManaman, and I got closer with Paul Ince. We became like brothers, really. We roomed next to each other and he was always in my room, or I was in his.

Looking at things objectively and regardless of my own disappointment, the players had this belief that grew throughout the tournament that they could win Euro 96. On the day against Germany in the semi-final, England more than matched them for everything except the penalties. You could see the confidence growing with every game. It seemed to be a time where everyone, the whole nation, put all their troubles behind them. The players noticed that. Everywhere on the news there would be bars and restaurants packed with supporters, and it got everyone excited about it.

After it was all finished, I didn't have a clue where I stood with regard to my international career. Glenn Hoddle had already been announced as the new manager, but for me, it was a case of getting away from football and having a couple of weeks' break. The first game under Hoddle was against Moldova, but he didn't really speak to the players individually. I was on the bench then, but I got my chance in his second game against Poland where I partnered Alan and he scored two goals. Hoddle just said to me then to go out there and do what I did for my club, there wasn't much more to it than that. He had obviously seen things go well for us at club level. People were now saying we could play together, and Glenn wanted to continue that.

I didn't know whether I was going to keep my place for the Georgia game, especially judging by how things had gone in the past. Alan had gone in for a hernia operation, Teddy was back after injury and people were saying that Ian Wright might play, because he was banging in goals all over the place as well. But Glenn gave me the nod and just said the same thing again, to do what I did for Newcastle. The whole team played very well that day and we won 2–0, with me getting the second goal. The Italy game was a good few months away, but I had played well in the previous two matches and was hopeful that I would get my third England match on the trot, which would have been the first time that had happened.

Before the Italy game, Glenn spoke to me and explained why he was leaving me on the bench. He said he wanted something a bit different for this game and he thought Le Tissier could give him that. I had got a call from John Gorman to say that the boss wanted to see me in his room. I knew then what it would be about and I said to John, 'Do I really need to go down to see him? Just tell him to phone me and tell me.' But John was insistent, so I went to his room and was told. I was disappointed, but not particularly surprised.

It is the sort of thing that has happened throughout my England career, so in a way I'm not really bothered anymore. What will be, will be. Of course, I want to play for England and I'm desperate to do well. If I'm doing well, I'll be in the squad and if I'm not, I won't. That's my attitude to it and I won't lose much sleep worrying about it, because of the experiences I've had.

CHAPTER TWENTY

Bust-up with Keegan

I went to St Lucia for a couple of weeks after Euro 96 for a badly needed break. Some of the lads were already back in training and Keegan was a little bit reluctant to give me an extra couple of days off, because he said I hadn't played during Euro 96. In the end, though, he gave me the time-off I wanted.

But when we started pre-season, it felt like I had never been away, I had been playing that much football without what I would consider a real break from it. Psychologically and physically, even professional footballers, who get very well paid, need to get away from everything to recharge their batteries and come back fresh, and I really felt like I hadn't had that opportunity.

We had been back training for a few days when we flew off to Thailand and the Far East for a pre-season tour. While we were at the airport getting ready to check-in, some of the lads were talking about the main football speculation at the time, that Alan Shearer would be leaving Blackburn. It had been in all the papers and lots of clubs had been linked with him, including Newcastle.

Most of the lads had checked-in and walked through when Terry McDermott came running up to me, saying the gaffer wanted a quick word. I told Terry that I had to buy a book for the trip and wanted to go and get it now, so I didn't have to rush. I would speak to Keegan later. I started to go up the escalator but Terry was strangely insistent that I must go and speak to the boss straight away. Obviously, I began to wonder what was so important. Had something happened, had they accepted a bid for me from another club, what could it be?

I found a quiet corner with Keegan and we sat down. He said straight out that it looked like we were going to sign Alan Shearer and he wanted me to know immediately that it did not mean I would be sold. He was buying him for us to play together. He was convinced that we could form a great partnership, even though Terry Venables didn't think we could. He said the transfer would probably happen that day, or the next, and he wouldn't be travelling with us because it would be going through. I said great, no problem, and got up to walk away.

But I could sense there was something else, because they said, 'Hold on a minute . . .' and wanted me to come back and sit down. Keegan was very edgy and said to me that Alan had asked for one thing if he was going to sign. At the time, it just didn't click what it could be and why it should affect me. Then the bombshell dropped. He said that Alan had asked for the number-nine shirt, my shirt, as he had had it all his career, he was superstitious about it and there was also the legacy of the Newcastle number nine, which he wanted to be part of. Keegan added that he didn't want to lose the deal over this one thing.

At first, I said no way. It's never been a superstitious thing for me, but I've always played number nine and when I came to Newcastle I didn't ask for it, Keegan gave it to me, saying, 'There aren't many people who have worn this shirt, but I think you can carry on the tradition.' So I refused.

But he was very persistent. 'But Les . . . but Les,' he was saying to me, 'when I was at Liverpool, my shirt number never mattered to me, and I know you are not very superstitious about it.' Terry Mac was chipping in with the same thing, saying it was only a number. So I sat back and looked at the two of them and had a chuckle to myself. It's amazing what goes through your mind at moments like this. I thought, 'If I don't give up my shirt and he doesn't sign, it will get out that I refused to give it up. I'll get lynched by the Geordie punters and the manager won't be happy with me.' I was really in a no-win situation.

Reluctantly, and with a sigh, I agreed. I never realistically thought that Alan wouldn't sign over it, and besides anything else, I think they had already agreed it with him and were just going through the motions with me, telling me in a nice way and trying to show me a bit of respect. The fact that the manager was coming to me to ask me this meant he wanted Alan to have it anyway. They told me I could have any number I liked. As I walked away back up the stairs, I was thinking that if this partnership didn't work on the field, it would be Les Ferdinand leaving Newcastle, because there was no way that Alan Shearer would leave. It was a strange thing to consider, but that is what went through my mind.

The next day, Alan signed for a world record £15 million and he was pictured with the shirt. People were phoning me up asking what had happened, and I had to explain it to them. They were saying I should have got Newcastle to buy it off me, but that's not my way. Keegan said they wanted to get my new number sorted out as soon as possible, but I was adamant that I wouldn't take anyone else's number away from them. I didn't like it being done to me, so why should I do it to someone else? If I am honest, I was disappointed by what had happened. I didn't tell anyone on the plane, but when the story broke about Shearer and the shirt, I was asked by the journalists on the trip how I felt. I said it hadn't been a problem with me.

The shirt saga took another twist before the first game on the tour and it led to the first and only major disagreement between me and Keegan. As a result, I felt our relationship changed and was never quite the same again.

We were in the dressing-room before the match and all the shirts, number by number, had been hung up as normal on the pegs. I went to put my gear down and coach Chris McMenemy read out the team and the numbers. 'Les, number nine,' he said. Straight away, I said, 'Is someone taking the piss out of me or something?' Everyone just stopped, there was deadly silence. Kevin Keegan was standing in the corner and he asked what the problem was. I said the club had just taken the number nine away from me and now they wanted me to play in it. 'I'm not wearing that number after what's happened. You can stick it where the sun don't shine,' I said to him. I was pretty angry, and afterwards a few of the lads said well done to me for standing up for myself. But in the dressing-room, everyone kept their heads down – it was unusual for someone to say something like that to Keegan. In the end, Peter Beardsley wore the number nine and I wore his eight for the game. He said to me later that I could have his shirt for good, it really didn't bother him – but I said no, I didn't want anyone else's shirt.

At the end of the tour, Keegan and I had a heated discussion about the incident. He said he wasn't happy with what I had done in the dressing-room, and I said I wasn't happy about losing my shirt! I think our relationship changed after that. I still have a lot of respect for him and I like to think he has got respect for me, but after that, there was a change between us. Perhaps it was because I had challenged him in the dressing-room. When we had the discussion afterwards, it was at Amsterdam airport on our way home. He said he had been disappointed with my attitude in the dressing-room. He understood that I was upset and my pride had been hurt, but I had gone about it the wrong way. Then he said, 'I don't hold grudges, so let's forget it.' I still got on well with him, we continued to have a laugh and a joke and still played squash together. But something had changed; he felt it and I felt it. There was a bit of a distance between us where there wasn't before.

They kept on at me to sort the number out. In the end, I said OK, I'd have 23. Michael Jordan is one if my heroes, that's his number, and none of the other players had it, so it seemed a sensible solution. They came back to me the next day and said the board wanted me to have a number between one and 11. I said I *had* a number between one and 11 but the board had taken it away from me! They thought I should take 10, which was Lee Clark's number – there was talk of him leaving Newcastle at the time. I said I didn't want it. What made it worse was that I had been winding Clarkie up before this, saying I wanted the 10, and I knew he would be devastated if I got his shirt. He had been playing in it ever since he joined the club as a trainee. Little did I know, they had already spoken to him about it and told him he had to give it to me. Clarkie knew me well enough to understand that I didn't want it and had just been having a laugh with him. But he was upset at losing it.

The Shearer signing was a clear signal that Keegan was going to carry on his philosophy of all-out attack, despite the criticism over what had happened to our title challenge the season before. I saw it as a positive move. He felt Alan and I could play together and if you have the chance to sign the country's best striker for the club, you have to take it. The fee was a world record, but if that is what the market dictates and the club has the money, then that's fair enough. It may have been an admission on Keegan's part that the Asprilla transfer hadn't come off as he had hoped. I don't know what was in his mind.

Things did change a bit during pre-season. We didn't play as many five-a-sides as we used to and we went on more long runs, but the atmosphere was just as buoyant and jovial. Keegan was pretty lively at the start of the season, very much how he had been when I first joined, although I think he was finding it more difficult to motivate the players.

Our first main game was the Charity Shield against Manchester United. There was obviously a lot of expectation as it was the first big game with the £21 million strike-force on show – but we got thrashed 4–0. Everyone had been looking forward to it but we got steamrollered, and I remember thinking afterwards that this was supposed to have been the start of a great season. I was gutted for the supporters. They had travelled down in their thousands, it was their first time at Wembley for a long time and we had really let them down. We hadn't played to the best of our ability; in fact, we were a shambles. Keegan was angry but he knew we had simply played badly, it wasn't a case of us playing well and still being four goals worse than Man United. It was just one of those days. At that stage, even without the benefit of hindsight, Keegan did seem a little bit uptight. The championship race had taken its toll on everybody and that included him. It was a different Kevin Keegan, that's for certain, but we put that down to the fact that he was as disappointed as us about the title and would take time to get over it.

Things actually got worse after the Charity Shield. We lost 2–0 to Everton on the first day of the season and we were all convinced afterwards that Everton would be a major force in the title race during the coming season. We had a goal disallowed that should have stood, but they were much better than us on the day. Immediately, there were people saying that the Shearer–

Ferdinand partnership wasn't going to work. But we felt it needed time and certainly shouldn't be judged after just one match. Alan scored in the next game, a 2–0 win over Wimbledon at home, and then we lost 2–1 at home to Sheffield Wednesday.

The alarm bells started ringing then. The players realised that there was obviously something wrong, because the season before, we had steamrollered everybody at the start. I think it was a case of the team having to learn to play a different way to what we were used to. When Alan wasn't there and it was just me on my own up front, with Peter Beardsley dropping off, we had the two wingers. Now we were being asked to play a different way and it took time to adapt. I didn't find it difficult playing with Alan, just different. In a lot of people's eyes, I was now the junior partner in the relationship, but I didn't see it like that. We both had our jobs to do and it was a partnership. I was used to just playing the width of the penalty box and had never had to do much work in wide positions, but now I was being asked to do that. I quite enjoyed it, because it gave me more freedom to run where I wanted and it was how I used to play at QPR.

No-one was panicking, but we weren't playing the free-flowing football that we had been. The defence was also coming in for a lot of stick, but the thing was, we never worked on anything defensively and all they were doing was carrying out the manager's orders and game-plan. He wanted them to get forward at every opportunity, and we knew that would leave us short of numbers at the back.

It took me three games to get off the mark but once I did, again I couldn't stop scoring for a couple of months. My first goal was a special one, as it came in my first North East derby against Sunderland at Roker Park and was also the winner. I like to be scoring, like all strikers, but the funny thing was, in those first three games I had actually played really well without getting a break. Most of the players had a look at themselves after those two early defeats. I think we all felt we had to work to get back to what we were capable of. Peter Beardsley hadn't played until the Sunderland game and that was a factor in our poor start.

I scored two at Tottenham in the next game and it became clear that we were all now coming to terms with playing two

When Terry Venables was England coach I was in and out of the squad. I never really thought he fancied me as a player.

Two new arrivals at St James' Park: me and Warren Barton.

Putting pressure on Sheffield Wednesday's goalkeeper Kevin Pressman in one of my first games for Newcastle.

14 October 1995: My return to Loftus Road was memorable because of the tremendous reception I received.

When I played in a friendly against Portugal in December 1995 it was my first England game for almost two years.

By the time we played Liverpool at St James' Park in November 1995 Newcastle were leading the Premiership and in the middle of an unbeaten run.

My goal against Liverpool in our 2–1 home win was my 14th of the season so far. Things were going well for me and the team was on a high.

Colorsport

Losing 2–0 at Arsenal in March 1996 was a huge blow to our chances of winning the championship.

Empics

The new £21 million strike-force.

Sharing a joke with Kevin Keegan and Terry McDermott. But the laughs got fewer and further between as the manager's strain began to show.

Our 1–1 draw at Charlton in the third round of the FA Cup turned out to be Keegan's last game as manager of Newcastle United.

Empics

On our way to the quarter-finals of the 1996-97 UEFA Cup we beat the Swedish team Halmstads 4–0 in the first round, first leg at St James' Park. I scored the opening goal in the sixth minute.

Smiles all round as I sign for Spurs in July 1997 and I am reunited with my old boss, manager Gerry Francis.

Action Images

I am still ambitious to play for England in a major tournament, hopefully the 1998 World Cup finals.

out-and-out forwards. In fact, I got six in five games, including another two in an amazing game against Aston Villa at St James' Park, which we won 4–3. They were down to ten men and we had been three goals up. This was another example of great entertainment for the neutrals, but the same things were being said again about us – that we couldn't win the championship that way.

Even so, going into the home match against Manchester United, we had won six league games on the trot and one more win would put us top of the table. The game obviously had a special significance because of the previous season and our humiliation in the Charity Shield. In the corresponding game the year before, for 45 minutes we had annihilated them but couldn't get the ball in the back of the net and ended up losing 1–0. There was a lot of fire welling up in everyone's stomachs. Nothing was actually said, but you could see the determination in the players' faces in the dressing-room before the game. All Keegan said to us was that we owed this lot one. Nothing else needed to be said. We all felt we had a huge performance in us, we just didn't expect it to come against Manchester United in such a manner. When I scored to put us 3–0 up, I realised that we were doing something special that afternoon. But when people ask me what was the best game I ever played in for Newcastle, I always say the Liverpool 4–3 defeat that ruined our title chances in 1996. During that game, I felt I was involved in one of the great matches of all time – even though we lost. Both sides performed to the highest level on the night.

Against Manchester United, we played really well but they were not the Man United people were used to seeing. Whether that was because we played so well or they were just out of sorts, or both, I don't know. In their next game, they got beaten 6–3 at Southampton, so they were obviously having a few problems. No-one expected us to win 5–0 and of course the crowd were going absolutely crazy. I think the performance brought a lot of relief to us all, including the manager, because of the recent history between the two sides. The atmosphere in the dressing-room was electric, but no-one was gloating. It was just another three points.

That win sent us top and I remember hoping we hadn't peaked too early again, like we had done the previous year. I would have much preferred to be in second place, ready to come with a spurt late on. Each year at Newcastle, you go into the season thinking this is the title year. This time, with the addition of Shearer, we felt maybe it was really going to be.

But the United game proved to be a massive turning-point in our season. It set in motion a train of events and results that was to lead to the most dramatic reaction from Keegan. It also paved the way for another football legend to re-enter the game.

CHAPTER TWENTY-ONE

Musical Chairs

We came down to earth with an almighty bump in our next league game, away at Leicester. It was the first game that Alan had missed – he needed a hernia operation – and I was amazed that people were asking me how I was going to cope without him. They had short memories, considering that the previous season I had scored 29 goals as a lone striker. Of course we were going to miss him, but the team was confident enough not to let it affect us.

However, it was very much a case of 'After the Lord Mayor's show' following the Man United game, and we got beaten 2–0. I think these games are the sort where you can judge whether you are a good side or not. If you beat Man United 5–0, then you should be going to Leicester and winning the next game, whether it be with another 5–0 drubbing or a battling 1–0 victory. If you are going to win the championship, and this is no disrespect to Leicester, you have to win at places like that. On the day, the Leicester goalkeeper Kasey Keller put in one of the best goal-keeping performances I've seen in my career. He saved everything I threw at him – even when he dived the wrong way, it hit his legs – and it was clearly not going to be our day.

It soon turned out that things were going to get worse, for me personally and for the team. Two games later against West Ham, I sustained a depressed fracture of the cheekbone that was to keep me out for a few weeks. Meanwhile, the team won only one of the next nine league games after the Man United result. The injury occurred following a corner, when I challenged the

West Ham keeper Ludek Miklosko. We both ended up on the floor, but the ball was still in play and as he tried to jump up to get back in his goal, his knee caught me on the cheek.

At first, just like when I broke my jaw when I was with QPR, I didn't think the injury was too bad. As soon as the physio came on, he signalled to the bench straight away that I had to come off, but I said I was alright. He said to get the stretcher on, but I refused because I hate going off the field on a stretcher. But they brought me off and when I looked in the mirror, I could see where the cheekbone was indented by the fracture. By the time I got to the hospital, I was in agony – again, the adrenaline of the match had worn off – but I was kept waiting for ages and people kept coming in asking me for autographs. The consultant who needed to see me was at St James' Park watching the game, and they had put an announcement out over the tannoy. But he didn't arrive until well after the game and claimed he had been stuck in traffic. He operated on it that night and they thought I might be back after four weeks; but with Alan out as well, it was a major blow for the team.

Generally, the team were struggling anyway and when we were beaten by Arsenal at home late in November, it dawned on me that things were bad. St James' Park had always been a fortress. Teams were petrified of coming there and never expected to get a result. We had only lost one match at home the previous season, but now this year we had been beaten twice, as well as drawing games there. The team wasn't functioning at all, we weren't playing the football we had before. I think other teams saw that we were not the force we had been the previous season, and they were coming to us with a lot more confidence, at a time when we ourselves were not confident or convincing. As I've said before, confidence is so important in football.

There was no one reason for the way things were going. I couldn't say, even with hindsight, that our poor form was a reflection of the way things were with the manager, in terms of his state of mind. In the end, it may have come down to the basic point that Newcastle had changed the way they played. With two strikers instead of one, we had to forfeit one of the wingers and players like Rob Lee had to play out wide. It takes

184

time to adapt to that, and maybe it was a system that didn't suit all the players.

Keegan had brought in Mark Lawrenson as defensive coach at the club after we had beaten Man United. The appointment had attracted a lot of publicity, and at the time, the players thought it was a good thing. Mark had been a great player – when he was playing, there weren't many defenders better than him – and we felt that perhaps the manager had realised that we did need to work on defensive things. I think the players always thought we needed to do this and actually wanted to do it, because they were coming in for a lot of stick. So Lawrenson's arrival was seen as a positive thing, but it didn't quite work out. In fact, in the whole time up until Keegan resigned, Lawrenson never took one defensive training-session or worked with the defence separately. It's difficult to say why, because I don't know the terms under which he was brought to the club. Everyone said he was employed as a defensive coach, but whether that was the case or not, I don't know. It did strike me as a bit strange that he never took any sessions, and I heard a few of the lads say the same thing. Training never really changed. Mark used to join in the five-a-sides, and in fact he was bloody good in them! But even after Keegan left, he still didn't really take up the role of defensive co-ordinator in training.

I had been told by the doctors that I would be off for four weeks, but after three weeks I was ready to play again and I came back for the match at Nottingham Forest, where we drew 0–0. But we were struggling, and a lot of people could see there were things going wrong when we got beaten by Coventry in the next game. There was a lot of attention on Darren Huckerby in that match. He had been sold by Keegan earlier that season and he played brilliantly for Coventry against us, scoring one of the goals. The problem at Newcastle was that the players who weren't in the team were good enough to get into virtually any other Premiership side, and anyone left out had no reserve matches to play in because Keegan had scrapped that. So they never got to play at all and got frustrated. Both Darren and Paul Kitson were sold at a time when all the forwards were fit, but soon Alan and I got injured and the manager was left with only

Tino. No-one could have predicted that, of course, although Keegan still got criticised after the event.

There were a lot of stories about Huckerby, Kitson, David Ginola and Warren Barton being unsettled, and undoubtedly there were a lot of unhappy players at Newcastle at the time. If footballers are not in the side, they are unhappy, it's as simple as that. They fall into their cliques of people in the same position and then things develop from there. It is almost like two separate camps, those who are playing and those who aren't. I'm not saying you don't speak to them and get on with them like you did, but they start getting despondent and saying things to each other. There were no showdowns or anything like that in front of the other players, but there probably were one-to-one with the manager behind closed doors – and inevitably, that gets communicated to the other players.

I had a confrontation with Keegan myself a couple of games later, at half-time during the match at Blackburn on Boxing Day. This, of course, was the match where the manager went to the board after the game to say he was resigning. But at half-time, he pulled me up in front of the rest of the lads in the dressing-room and told me that I wasn't making good enough runs, I hadn't played well in the first half, I looked like I wasn't trying and he expected more from me. In fact, he said that if he had told me before the game to do nothing, he'd have said I'd carried out his orders to the letter in the first half – which I thought was a bit unfair. But unlike over the shirt situation, I didn't react. There are times when you can, but you also have to accept criticism and keep quiet. I think that as manager, he was justified in having a bit of a go, because we hadn't played well – although I didn't think I had played any worse than anyone else.

It so happened that on the day, I wasn't feeling very well and I was going to tell the boss at half-time that I was ill. But after he'd had a go at me, I didn't want all the lads to think I was only saying it because of that, so I kept quiet. I tried to go out and put it right, but we ended up losing 1–0. It wasn't unusual for Keegan to pick out a player in this way. He used to say, 'I'm not going to mention any names . . .' and then proceed to mention someone. He did this at Blackburn that day and you could see some of the guys with their heads down having a little snigger, because you always knew, once he had said, 'I'm not going to single anyone out,' that that was exactly what he was going to do!

It was only after his resignation had been announced that we found out he had gone to the board after the Blackburn game and told them of his decision to quit. We were surprised on the one hand, because nothing official had been said to us – although it had in a way, we just hadn't read the signals – but also not surprised, because we could see something was wrong with the boss. He had been much less enthusiastic than normal in the weeks leading up to that game, and there was a different atmosphere around the place. Enthusiasm was one of his strongest points when getting the team prepared, and we always got a sense that he looked forward to games – but that had disappeared.

The team had not got anywhere near the standards we had set the previous season and I think Keegan had seen that, so when he said 'I'll know when it's time to go' in the dressing-room at half-time during the Blackburn game, that was him admitting defeat in terms of being able to motivate the players to get back to those high standards. He obviously thought the players were not responding to him, although there wasn't a specific incident where a player ignored him or anything like that. It was our performance in general, compared to the previous year, that would have made him feel that way.

After the low point of the Blackburn game, we played Spurs next and the two results could not have been more different. We won 7–1. We had a big team-talk before the Spurs match and it was here that I had my third real one-to-one with the manager. Keegan came in and told us that he had said things after the Blackburn game that maybe he should have said or maybe he shouldn't, but people would cope with them in their different ways. That was obviously directed at me and the other players he had mentioned. 'No matter what I say,' he continued, 'it's always open to debate and if there are any problems, any player can knock on my door, it's open any time.' But he also said: 'Les, I know you're not a player who'll come and knock on my door.' Then he moved on to discussing the Tottenham game.

After he had finished, as I was getting ready to go out, he came over to me and said, 'You won't knock on my door, so I'll come and knock on yours.' Obviously he wanted to speak to me, so we went into his office. He asked me what was wrong in the Blackburn game, and I explained how I'd felt ill but didn't want the other players to think I was copping out because the manager had had a go at me. He admitted I had done better in the second half, but said it was still not the type of display he expected from me. Even a couple of the Newcastle directors had said to him, 'What's wrong with Les?' I got a bit angry at that point. 'Maybe it's time for me to go if you and the directors are beginning to question whether I want the partnership to work. Maybe it's time for me to leave,' I said. 'Does this mean every time I have a bad game, they are going to question me? If that's the case, then I'm not standing for that shit.' Keegan said no, no, that wasn't what he meant. He just needed to make sure everything was OK with his players, that there were no problems or anything like that.

He knew I wasn't the type to come knocking on his door, so it wasn't unusual for him to do something like this. But the timing was strange. It was rare for him to talk to a player like that just before a game. I obviously felt a lot better, because I scored two goals in our 7–1 win. The team clicked that day and got close to the type of football we had produced the previous season. We were due to thrash someone. It just happened to be Spurs, but it could have been Blackburn or someone else.

But Keegan's actions became stranger. He went straight home after the game despite the fact that we had just won 7–1. We heard reports that his wife was poorly – Terry Mac said that to the press afterwards, as he was doing the press conference in Keegan's place. We took it at face value that his wife wasn't well, although none of us had heard she was ill and it was the sort of news you would have expected to pick up around the place. After he resigned, Keegan said his decision to quit had been triggered by the win over Tottenham – he couldn't face the pressure any longer after seeing the effect the 7–1 defeat had on Gerry Francis. Keegan came back into training before the next game, at home to Leeds, and in the past, I think he would have got over-excited about the type of performance we had turned in against Tottenham. This time he didn't. We beat Leeds 3–0 and then we had the FA Cup third round match at Charlton.

It turned out to be Keegan's last game, and it was here that he walked out of the press conference after the game when one of the journalists questioned him about a story that had appeared that morning claiming he had offered to resign after the Blackburn game. I did a column in *The Pink*, the Saturday sports paper of the Newcastle *Evening Chronicle*, so I had contact with a reporter called Alan Oliver. I spoke to him after the Charlton game and he told me that the London journalists had treated Keegan badly, because as he was walking out, they heckled him and called him a baby. That was the first time I had heard any speculation about the Blackburn game, and I started to think that something was up. Keegan had been acting strangely, and the speculation made sense.

The rest is now history.

On the following Wednesday, we were gathered at the training ground and told of his resignation. For the next couple of days, people were in shock. There was a feeling during training that it was like a dream, and any minute he would walk in – or come Saturday, he would be there. But the game at Aston Villa came, we prepared in a similar way and of course there was no Kevin Keegan at Villa Park. I missed the Villa game through injury and watched from the bench. We went 2–0 up and then it was the same old thing, we gave two goals away and it ended 2–2.

There was constant speculation about who the new manager would be. The view of the players was that it was between Bobby Robson and Kenny Dalglish, but I had it in my mind that Dalglish was not going to come back into football. I took that view from what I had heard about Blackburn, and from speaking to Alan Shearer as well – he thought the same. So I assumed it would be Robson. The players wanted things sorted out quickly, it was an unsettling time, and all credit to the board for getting it done the way they did.

CHAPTER TWENTY-TWO

Dalglish and Uncertainty

The following Tuesday, I was washing my car when I got a phone-call from Terry Mac saying I needed to be at the ground in 20 minutes. I told him I couldn't come now because I was washing my car, but he said I had to and I said OK, I'd be there in half an hour. In fact, I got there 45 minutes later.

When I arrived, we were told that they wanted to tell the players' committee before anyone else knew that Kenny Dalglish had signed as the new manager and there would be a press conference at 6pm. So I said, 'That's old news, I've just heard it on the radio coming to the ground.' We had a laugh about that and then we were introduced to Kenny. I had met him on a couple of occasions before, and of course Peter Beardsley and Alan Shearer knew him well from their respective times at Liverpool and Blackburn.

My first impression was that they couldn't have replaced Kevin Keegan with anyone better than Kenny Dalglish, because of his record with Liverpool and Blackburn. From a striker's and a selfish point of view, I had always said that I would like to play for Kenny Dalglish or Kevin Keegan, because they were two of the best strikers Britain had ever produced. It was turning out that I would play for both. The players didn't sit down and have any sort of long chat with Dalglish, it was all very brief.

Over the next few days and weeks, I noticed how different he was from Keegan. First of all, he was a lot more difficult to understand because of his accent, but generally he was a lot quieter – he would get his point across, but his personality was not as outgoing as Keegan's. Kenny would join in the five-a-sides, though, and have a laugh with the lads. You could say things to him like, 'Isn't it time you hung your boots up?' and he would come back with, 'It must be a dream come true for all you boys to play with me,' so he gave as good as he got. Towards the end of the season, he put in a couple of good performances but until then, no-one wanted him on their team.

More seriously though, he plays his cards a lot closer to his chest and you never know what he is really thinking. He seems to observe what goes on a lot more, without saying anything. He also introduced a few new things. With Keegan, we never really worked on set-pieces and on defending, but that changed under Dalglish. He talks about tactics and defence much more, on the training ground and in the dressing-room. He is a lot calmer, both before and after a game. He also began to have us in the day after a game for light training, instead of having the day off, and now we always go overnight to a hotel after a midweek game, even if we are at home. We have something to eat and a few drinks (but no alcohol) and then go straight to the training ground the next day. He said he wanted to stop us from going out after a game, like most footballers do, and drinking too much, which dehydrates you. It took a bit of getting used to at first, but the intention is to prepare and recover yourself properly, so it's not a problem.

Dalglish's first game was the FA Cup replay against Charlton at St James' Park. It was too early for the Geordie public to take to the new man like they had taken to Keegan. Although there was a great air of expectancy and he got a fantastic reception, the time when the supporters finally take to Dalglish like they did to Keegan will be when he brings back that first bit of silverware for them.

From the way we were working in training and from the team selection, it became clear that we wouldn't be playing quite the style of football we had under Keegan, although the first few results didn't show that at all. Warren Barton came back into the side and Peter Beardsley dropped out for a time. The first few games didn't go too well, though. We managed to beat Charlton in extra-time, then drew 2–2 at Southampton when

Matthew Le Tissier scored an amazing last-minute goal, after we had gone 2–0 up and it was looking like we would win at The Dell for the first time in ages. Then came the shock treatment. We were knocked out of the FA Cup at home by Nottingham Forest, 2–1, after Ian Woan scored the goal of a lifetime, late on.

From being well-placed in three competitions, we were now out of the FA Cup and struggling in the league. We put it down to the changes that had taken place and the fact that we had a few injuries as well. A lot of people were saying it was the same old Newcastle, we were still conceding goals easily, and that view was reaffirmed when we beat Leicester 4–3 at home after we had been 3–1 down. Alan got a hat-trick to pull us back in that one. The Leicester game was our second win on the trot – we had beaten Everton 4–1 a few days earlier – and we followed that with a 1–0 win at Middlesbrough, where I scored the only goal. Things seemed to be taking a turn for the better, but as was so typical of our season, we couldn't string a long series of results together. We would go three or four games with good performances and then we would go through a period of scrappy draws, get beaten and then tank someone by four or five. You would think to yourself, 'What's wrong with this side, where's the consistency?'

Where Keegan might have come in and slaughtered players for their displays, I think Dalglish was still finding his feet and he was a lot calmer about things. He didn't pick people out in the changing-room but was just as hard-hitting, only in a quiet way. He would make his point, but he didn't need to shout it. In fact, because he did it in a calmer manner, it was more effective in many ways.

The next few games were crucial. Southampton beat us 1–0 at St James' Park and then Monaco did the same in the UEFA Cup. This was a bad result, although we had a lot of players out injured that night, including me. I had pulled my hamstring against Southampton. Alan was also out and Tino was suspended, so Rob Lee played up front. But the defeat left us with a massive task in the return leg against a good side, so it looked like we would be going out of the UEFA Cup as well. I tried to come back in the next match at Liverpool and wanted to start the game.

I felt good, but the boss didn't want to risk me from the start. When we were 3–0 down early in the second half, he decided to put me on. I didn't last more than 10 minutes before the hamstring went again, as I challenged for a header. It meant I missed the Monaco return, which we lost 3–0, and a number of other games.

It was another incredible match at Anfield. Whereas in the 4–3 the year before we had really deserved to get something out of the game, if we had got a point this time we would all have to have left Anfield with our masks on, it would have been a robbery. We had been 3–0 down but clawed it back before Robbie Fowler scored in the last minute for Liverpool's 4–3 win. And to be fair, they were superior to us for most of the game.

The Dalglish revolution had not quite taken off yet. People were even talking about us not qualifying for Europe, because of the way our league form had dipped. There had been injuries, that was true, but we couldn't find any consistency. Then, towards the last three or four weeks of the season, a few results went our way. Man United struggled a bit, as did Arsenal and Liverpool. All of a sudden, we were actually in with a chance of winning the title if things continued on the same path. We had three successive 1–1 draws against Wimbledon, Sunderland and Sheffield Wednesday, and then two 3–1 wins against Chelsea and Derby. The team started thinking about winning the title as well: what an irony it would be, having been so far ahead in 1995–96 and then blown it, to now come from nowhere to win the Premiership by pipping Man United at the post . . .

We were left with four games in eight days at the end of the season, and we knew it would be a tall order to maintain our momentum and keep the pressure on Man United. Three of the games were away from home and one of those was at Old Trafford. But we got off to a great start with a 1–0 win at Highbury, where I ended up playing in central defence for most of the second half when Keith Gillespie got sent off and we were really under the cosh. That was a big game, because we were vying with Arsenal for second position and a place in the Champions League. The ironic thing about it was that we were not playing well and everyone had written us off. All of a sudden, there was this light at the end of the tunnel and the thought that we could do to Man United what they had done to us the previous year.

We had to win at West Ham in the next game to keep the pressure on. West Ham needed a point to stay up and the game ended 0–0. Liverpool lost at Wimbledon that night and so Man United were handed the title without even playing. By that time, my groin couldn't really stand up to two games in quick succession and I realised then that I would have to go in for a hernia operation at the end of the season. I'd had a problem with it for about two and a half months, and in the end, it meant me missing the crucial World Cup game against Poland at the end of May.

When we went to Old Trafford, they already had the title and it was a bit of a nothing game for them. It seemed more like a testimonial than a league game. Even though for us, second place was still up for grabs, we didn't play well and it ended 0–0. Dalglish was very disappointed with the performance because we still had something to play for, and he told us so in the changing-room after. Our destiny was now out of our hands. Even if we won our last game against Forest at home, if Liverpool won, they would get second place. As it turned out, we finished on a high. I got two goals in our 5–0 win and Liverpool drew at Sheffield Wednesday, leaving us in second place again but with a place in the Champions League, which was very important for the club in the season it had been floated on the Stock Exchange.

I ended the season with 21 goals, which wasn't a bad return considering all the injuries I'd had. I had broken my cheekbone, pulled a hamstring, had stitches in my head and other little things. It was a disappointing season as far as I was concerned, though. I set high standards for myself and I felt I had dropped below those standards. True, it was a period of upheaval for the club and overall, it had been a quite incredible two seasons.

There were also continuing question marks over my future. When I was at QPR, there was always a lot of speculation and it's funny that when I signed for Newcastle, I thought it would put an end to all of that because they are such a big club. Yet it seemed to get worse! However, I didn't let it affect me. The only time I'll worry is if the manager comes to me and says I've accepted a bid for you. Then, I'll know I am no longer part of his plans and it's time to go. I understand that Dalglish wants what is best for Newcastle United. I was disappointed that it didn't include me and that, when the time came, I was unable to persuade him otherwise.

If I look back on what I have experienced, especially over the last two seasons, I have to say I am amazed. I thought professional football had passed me by when I was in non-league, and now I'm doing and seeing things you can only dream about. This season, I was supposed to have been playing in the Champions League with Newcastle and that would have been a great thing, although I feel like the club is gate-crashing a bit because we were not there as champions. I would like to play in it as champions. I've had a great career; I have a nice house and a nice car; I've got two great kids, Aaron and Lauren, who was born in November 1996; and I've had some great football accolades.

But I would like at the end of my career to have something to show for it, an FA Cup medal or title medal to say that I was a champion, and more than one if possible.

I am still ambitious to play in some capacity in a major tournament for England, and realistically, the next World Cup is the only one I have got left. After that, I would seriously be thinking about calling it a day with England, if I do play in 1998. I have an opportunity to stake a good claim if I have a good season this year. I've had ups and downs with England, but I'm hopeful that it'll turn out fine in the end.

People ask me what I will do when I finish playing. At the moment, I feel that I have played under so many good managers, people I respected as a boy when they played, like Dalglish, Keegan, Gerry Francis, Trevor Francis, Glenn Hoddle, Ray Wilkins and Terry Venables, that I have learnt little bits from all of them and it would be a shame to turn my back on football, walk away and not give some of that back to the young players coming through. Maybe not in management, but coming back in some sort of coaching capacity might suit me. I look at my career and see that there is not that long to go. Players at the top look after themselves better than ever before, and that might prolong my football life at the top level until I'm 34 or 35. Then, if I still have the passion for football burning inside me that I have at the moment, I may drop down a standard. We'll have to wait and see.

CHAPTER TWENTY-THREE

In the Public Eye

The last two seasons at Newcastle, and my time with England, have brought it home to me how much my life has changed since the days at Southall, Hayes and even QPR. It was not that long ago that an incident at Newcastle brought back into my mind my threat to quit the professional game, which had come out in a conversation with David Kerslake. It just showed how naïve I was then and how much has changed since. David still reminds me of that conversation now.

I pulled up a young trainee at Newcastle after training when he was complaining about what he had to do and wasn't taking things seriously. He said he was thinking of packing it all in and playing football part-time while he held down a regular job. As a footballer you can get spoilt. It gives you a false sense of reality because everything is done for you, all the travel arrangements, the hotels, etc. The club wants your life to run as smoothly as possible because all they want from you is for you to produce on a Saturday, and everything is geared to that. So youngsters who come through the ranks don't see the real world. I was fortunate to work for a good few years before I made it in football, working 12 hours a day, then going off to play football in the evenings and doing that week in, week out. I told the trainee that he didn't know what he was talking about. Of course, that is exactly the same thing David Kerslake said to me all those years ago after training at Loftus Road.

Here was this kid, at one of the biggest clubs in the country, and he had a great opportunity to make a successful career for himself and never have to go out to work like most people. It was a good experience for me, but if I could have become a footballer without having to do a day-to-day job then of course I would have. I told him not to throw it away because it is not easy in the outside world. I was just trying to make him aware of what could be achieved and what he could have with a little bit of hard work.

The story was publicised in the papers at the time and I got a letter from the father of a trainee at Torquay pointing out how many hours a day he had to put in and claiming that it was much harder work at a smaller club. That is probably true, but football is still a great life wherever you are.

In the early days the pressure on you as a footballer is purely professional, to prepare yourself properly and look after your body. But certainly since I broke into the England set-up I have found it has now become a social thing as well. Your whole life comes under much greater scrutiny because more and more people know who you are. The most important side of that to me is the responsibility footballers have towards kids as role models. My friend Earl Whisky is a youth leader and when the kids see me come back to Ladbroke Grove it gives them a lift. You can see it in their faces. There are a lot of negative images around that kids see, especially in that area of London. But when I speak to them I say things can be achieved, not by going out and selling drugs and getting involved in that kind of lifestyle, but through hard work and dedication. You can also achieve things in life honestly, and with that come the fast cars and nice houses and the other trappings of success, but it is how you get there that matters. It does concern me that if I am portrayed in a certain way by the media, especially if it is wrong, then that could have an effect on a kid. It puts an added responsibility on all well-known footballers' shoulders to try and conduct themselves the best they can.

There are many positive and negative pressures that come with being a football star. And one of the negative things that I am still struggling to come to terms with is the fact that you have to choose your friends very carefully. I have a lot of female friends but there are certain places I cannot go for the simple reason that I am photographed a lot and appear in newspapers. I had one indiscretion where I had an affair with somebody not long after I joined Newcastle and she decided, not through the fault of the press, to sell her story. I was branded a 'rat' and all that sort of stuff. As a result, if I am seen out with a young lady the next thing you get is 'who is this with Les Ferdinand?' That is very difficult for me, because it means you have to analyse where you go and who you go with when most people don't have to give it a second thought. I have got some very good female friends who have boyfriends that I know and they know me very well. Now, I have to be very careful if I go out to lunch with them because I worry whether the next day there might be an article or a photo in the papers. It actually makes me quite angry that I can't just go out with friends without there being a potential problem, and I think most people, be they footballers or film stars, who are under the media spotlight feel the same way.

When you start off playing football, you try and get to the highest level your ability will permit. We all love to be recognised by people who appreciate what you do; if you are walking down the road and people come up to you then that is great. That means to me that you have achieved what you set out to achieve. Playing football as well as I can has got me attention. I don't agree with people following me around, taking pictures to try and make a story. I had an argument with a particular paper because they had printed a picture of my new house and revealed where it was in London. So I said to them that I lived in Newcastle for most of the week, everyone knew that – would they be responsible and reimburse me if my house got burgled while I wasn't there? Because until then no-one really knew I lived in that particular area.

It's those invasions of privacy I don't like. Unfortunately, Angelea and I are not together even though we have two kids. I'm not going to explain publicly why that is, but what it does mean is that I am really just a single guy, so does it really matter if I am out with someone if it is not her? Because I am in the public eye my private life becomes an issue and that is something I have real problems dealing with. I realise I have to accept it. If you go into football wanting to reach the top you will become famous, and with that comes the good and the bad, I understand that.

Not everyone wants to be famous. When I became a footballer I just wanted to play to the best of my ability. I didn't want to play for England to make me famous and recognisable. I wanted to do it for myself and my family. If anyone asked me whether I would take the success without the fame, I would say 'yes'. Unfortunately there are times when you have to take the rough with the smooth and the intrusion into your private life is the rough part of the profession.

I got involved in a relationship with the girl who ended up selling her story to one of the tabloids. All footballers are human beings, and we make the same mistakes as the next man. She saw my situation as a way of making money. If a nice girl comes up to any man and starts making advances, or you are getting on really well, naturally you feel flattered.

If it had been only me who got punished, then that would be fair enough. I did wrong and deserved the consequences. But things like that affect your family and that is my major concern. Aaron is old enough to read papers and I don't want him getting the wrong impression. I remember speaking to Ray Wilkins not long after it happened and he pointed out that the incident was a lesson in how far I had come. And, to be honest, until then I hadn't actually realised how far I had come. It wasn't a question of more people asking me for autographs all of a sudden – that exposé summed up the situation like nothing else could.

I am lucky that my family and friends keep my feet on the ground. I never get big-headed about things. The one thing I am very proud of, and pretty sure of, is that if anyone asked my friends what Les Ferdinand is like, they will all say he is just the same as when he was at school. My circumstances have changed dramatically but I am still the same guy.

I have the nice things in life now. When I was younger and saw a lot of my cousin Tony we used to stand on the balcony and watch the cars go by. I always said then that when I was older I would buy a Porsche. I didn't know how much they cost at the time, but it was my dream. Now I am in a position to buy one. That is the good side, but part of the whole package is, as I've said, accepting the rough with the smooth.

I have learned to cope with fame by trial and error as I have gone along and I have made mistakes on the way which I regret. I don't think there is any way to be really prepared for the pitfalls. For example, young professionals could be media-trained to cope with football-related stuff and be given guidance on being the model professional and on how to do this or that. But when you are presented with a particular everyday situation in a club or a bar, people don't always remember these things if they have been trained to react. There are going to be times when people do things that are wrong and make mistakes. It's a difficult thing to learn.

There are certain things I will miss and certain things I won't when I finish football. But the fame, and the attention that comes with it, is something that will probably be with me whether I stay in football or not. Nowadays if you have been successful in your footballing life there is still interest in what you do afterwards, but hopefully I can come to terms with it better.

CHAPTER TWENTY-FOUR

Home for Good

The rumours about my future continued into the summer when the season finished. I went into hospital to have my hernia operation, which forced me to miss England's match against Poland and Le Tournoi in France, with everything still very uncertain. It was during the time when England were in France that Teddy Sheringham handed in his transfer request at Tottenham, and it is really from there that the speculation became rife. There was a suggestion that there would be a swap deal involving the two of us, with me coming to Tottenham.

Normally I would ignore this sort of thing, but there was nothing to quash those rumours and they were very persistent. Nothing transpired; Teddy moved to Manchester United, but still there seemed to be doubts over me at Newcastle. Tottenham were said to be trying to sign me, then Everton and Sheffield Wednesday were also apparently after me. However, when pre-season started I was still at Newcastle and ready to go on the pre-season tour to Dublin.

It was while we were in Dublin that the Newcastle chairman Sir John Hall went on record to say that Les Ferdinand would be leaving Newcastle 'over my dead body'. I wonder if he is still alive. Funnily enough, I said to Warren Barton when I'd heard he'd said that that I would be gone by the next week because that's like a manager getting the dreaded vote of confidence from the chairman. I have to admit that by now all the speculation was getting to me, so I went to see Kenny Dalglish to get the real position from him.

Dalglish said that if I was to leave the club it would not be down to a question about footballing ability, it would be a purely financial move on behalf of the club. He said he'd told the board that he wanted to keep me, but that financially every player at the club had a price on his head and if they were to get that value then they may look to sell. I said that's fair enough as long as I know what the situation is, I know where I stand.

In the middle of July, on a Tuesday, the board met and decided that if they got a bid of £6 million they would let me go. Two days later Tottenham, because their two centre forwards, Chris Armstrong and Steffen Iversen, were both injured, agreed to meet the fee even though we now know the chairman, Alan Sugar, feels like he has paid over the odds for me.

You can understand it from Newcastle's point of view: they had two good years out of me, we players are just products, and if you can use that product for two years and then still get the same amount of money back for it, that's good business as far as they are concerned. From the Tottenham point of view, I'm hoping to justify the £6 million and then the chairman may be happier. I think his pride was hurt more than anything. He had initially said Spurs would not pay more than £4 million for me, but circumstances forced his hand.

Dalglish, true to his word, came to speak to me on the Wednesday morning to tell me of the board's decision from the previous night. He told me he didn't want me to go but if they received the right offer he couldn't stop the club from selling me. Spurs' real interest started when Sheringham handed in his transfer request. Obviously they had to replace him and they spoke to my agent Phil to see if I would be interested. I said to Phil that if Newcastle were willing to sell then I would leave, as I don't want to be anywhere I'm not wanted and I would be very interested in joining them. I don't know exactly why Newcastle didn't go for the swap deal. They had just bought Jon Dahl Tomasson, who plays in a similar position to Teddy, so maybe that was the reason.

As things progressed I obviously spoke to Gerry because of our close relationship. I told him the same: as soon as Spurs get the green light from Newcastle then I'm interested in coming. I asked Gerry if the club would be buying more players, and what his plans were. When Teddy left he made it clear he thought the club lacked ambition, so I needed to know what the situation was on that score, for I am still ambitious and want to win things in this game. But he assured me he wanted to strengthen the team; they had already signed David Ginola by the time I arrived and said they wanted to sign more players after me.

I have to say I was disappointed with the way the whole thing was handled by Newcastle. It could have been sorted out a lot sooner than it was. The rumours had started from day one when Kenny Dalglish first took over, when it was said that come the end of the season he was going to have a clearout and I was one of the names on that list. I kept cropping up almost every week as being up for sale. Little was done to quash those rumours, there was never a convincing statement from the club or the manager saying Les Ferdinand is not for sale, he is very much part of the plans for next season. As a player, that is what you want to hear. I wouldn't go in and ask Dalglish what his plans were for next season; instead I just thought that while I'm at Newcastle I'll play my heart out for them and if the time comes where they decide to sell me I'll move on and play my heart out for my new club.

It was pretty unsettling. I'd been renting Andy Cole's flat and he had decided to sell it in the summer. So I moved out and came back to Newcastle for pre-season. I didn't know whether to take out a contract on another flat for six months or a year or not because of all the rumours, as I might be out of there in two weeks. Because there hadn't been a statement, I checked into a hotel for three weeks.

There are two distinct sides to Newcastle United now, the football side and the plc side. As far as Kenny Dalglish is concerned I don't know whether I really believed he was totally open with me about it. I thought a manager of his calibre and reputation could have turned round to the board and said, if he really wanted to, 'I want to keep this player because he is an important part of the squad for the season ahead.' If he had done that I don't see the manager having much of a problem.

At the time I was led to believe that it was the plc that wanted to sell me, they needed to recoup some money and so on. Since then I have been advised by people at Newcastle that it wasn't the plc board's decision but the football club board of directors who felt it was good business to sell me and money well gained. So the transfer had nothing to do with the plc or satisfying shareholders and their demands. The reason I originally spoke about the plc was that I was led to believe at first that they were behind my being sold. As a result, because it was a football club decision, I feel that the manager could have had more influence over the decision if he had really wanted to. None of the directors ever explained to me what was going on; everything I heard was from what other people had read in the papers.

I had a great two years at Newcastle, made some very good friends, the supporters were fantastic to me, but sometimes this job dictates that you have to move on whether you want to or not. I wish Newcastle all the best: they deserve to win something, if only for their fans, because they are fantastic week in, week out. I leave a lot of good friends behind in the team so I hope they get success as well. I wish my transfer had been handled differently, less controversially, but that is how things developed.

From that Thursday onwards the transfer should have been all very straightforward. I was going to meet Spurs to discuss terms and I didn't see any real problems but events took a dramatic turn.

My agent Phil was actually away on holiday in Bali when things started moving so he flew back. Alan Sugar couldn't see us on the Saturday because he had a wedding, so we had arranged to meet on the Sunday to finalise personal terms by which time Phil would have arrived back.

At 4.30pm on Saturday afternoon, Simon Greenberg, who wrote this book with me and works for the *Mail on Sunday*, phoned me to see if there had been any last-minute hitches and I told him I couldn't see any problems.

I went to the hospital to see my dad's wife, who had to be taken in over something, so I had to turn my mobile phone off while I was in there. When I had finished I picked up a message from Simon about 6.30pm that Alan Shearer had been injured and it looked serious. Just as I was walking out, my dad was coming in and said had I heard about Alan's injury and the transfer was on hold. I didn't really believe the last bit. By the time I got home the news was on Teletext. I then got a call from Jon Smith, Phil's brother, that the injury was serious and that the Newcastle chief executive Freddie Fletcher and vice chairman Freddie Shepherd were flying down to London first thing on Sunday before my meeting with Spurs.

I told Jon that, to be brutally honest, I had nothing to say to them. I was desperately sorry for Alan but they had decided to sell me, that's it. Through pride and everything else I couldn't go back now. Jon said we had to do the courtesy of talking to them. I didn't find out until the Sunday morning that a contract had been signed between the two clubs that made me a Tottenham player subject to a medical, which I had already passed by then, and me agreeing personal terms. As I was now effectively a Spurs player I couldn't talk directly to Newcastle, it had to be done through Jon and Phil. Mr Sugar was understandably not very happy that there was going to be contact with Newcastle before our meeting and I don't blame him.

My mind was now set that I was going to Spurs and a lot of that was down to Newcastle's attitude over the previous few weeks. On the Saturday night I went out for dinner to Signor Sassi's in Knightsbridge where I got another call from Jon. They now knew the extent of Alan's injury, and that he would be out for months. I then got on the phone to my dad whose advice was not to do anything hasty, sleep on it and do whatever is best for yourself in the long run. On paper Newcastle are a bigger club than Spurs at the moment. They are in the Champions League and everything else, but I felt I was doing what was right for Les Ferdinand.

The next morning I went to Jon's about 11am and the Newcastle guys arrived about 15 minutes later. I said hello and that I was sorry to hear about Alan, I was really gutted for him. There was a bit of small talk and then I said to Jon, 'Have you still got your go-cart?' So they had to stop the talks to get the go-cart out of the garage for me and while they got down to business I was whizzing about Jon's garden on the go-cart. Newcastle were not allowed to talk to me direct, so I thought I might as well do something in the meantime. Newcastle's attempts to get me to stay were basically financial and they were hoping I would be swayed by an improved deal. Their offer was very generous, probably a bit more than I got at Tottenham, but it didn't really interest me; it had gone beyond a money issue. I would have happily stayed at Newcastle on the contract I was on. In my own mind, the decision was made. So I came off the go-cart, the Newcastle directors said that they hoped to see me soon and I jumped in my other go-cart, my Porsche, and went round to Alan Sugar's with Jon and Phil.

I was obviously in a fantastic negotiating position, no player could wish for more. Sugar was there with Gerry and the club secretary. But the first thing he said was, 'Before we start negotiating I would like to speak to Les on his own.' So I said OK. We went out and had a walk round his garden – it took us about three days it was so big! He spoke about what he wanted for Spurs and I told him what I wanted to achieve. We never discussed any finance. I thought that was good. As a player I wanted to hear that he was going to make Spurs great again. I had heard and read as a Spurs supporter about the problems and thought, just like other fans, 'Bloody hell, Alan Sugar needs to spend his money.' He said he was willing to spend it but he wanted to find the right players. I think I saw a different Alan Sugar to the one the public sees. He is in business mode then, although we were also there to thrash out business, but walking round the garden was more personal and I think I saw him in a different light to most.

When I went back in, Phil and Jon got on with the negotiating and Gerry and I went outside to talk, catch up and discuss plans for the future. I was happy with what I had heard and what I got. At this stage of my career, I knew the sort of money I was going to earn so things worked out just fine. I signed at Sugar's house after being there about three hours and I was a Spurs player. I don't hate anyone at Newcastle now. They made a decision and things moved on. If I see any of the board in the future I'll have a good chat with them; there is no animosity there.

I'm now a Tottenham player and I am looking forward to that

challenge. My 'dad' Gerry has had a lot of stick over the last couple of years; I'm just hoping that, along with the rest of the team, I can override that. They have not been that consistent and when that happens supporters get automatically upset. At the moment Spurs are not talked about as a big club, and they *are* a big club. They demand success and if you don't give that to a club like Tottenham the fans complain. If Gerry had not been at the club it would have had a big impact on my decision. You had a chairman saying he didn't want to spend that sort of money on me, and although I supported Spurs as a boy and always wanted to play for Spurs, I think Gerry was a big factor in me going there. Getting back to London was important for me, but I never had a problem living in Newcastle. I did it because I wanted success in my football career. I still haven't got that silverware, but hopefully it will come. I spoke to Gerry and I liked what he had to say. Phil spoke to a few other clubs, but nothing was really firmed up with Everton or Sheffield Wednesday.

I have heard a lot about Alan Sugar and how he does things. I don't need to get on with the chairman, I just need to do the business and then I'll get on with him as long as we have mutual respect for each other. At the meeting I had with him the only concern he had was that I wanted to play for Spurs and as soon as he realised that was the case everything went well.

I'm a lot happier now everything is settled. I'm focused on playing for Tottenham although the season didn't get off to the best of starts. I was really looking forward to it but we didn't play well against Manchester United and I didn't personally either. It will take time for me to blend with the other players, for me to learn how they play and for them to get used to me. The result in our second game against West Ham was also disappointing. I got my first goal for Spurs late in the game, which was important to me, but no points from the first two games was not the start we were looking for.

I would like to think Tottenham is the club where I will finish my career. I've signed a four-year contract and I would like to see that out. If things go according to plan, I won't need to move to a bigger club again because Tottenham will be big enough.

But, as events have proved throughout my career, who knows what happens in football? When I went to Newcastle I was the first 28-year-old to go for £6 million, now I think I'm probably the first £6 million 30-year-old. Looking at things realistically, we are looking at getting into Europe and challenging for the cups this season. If we add to the squad we can challenge for the championship in a year or two's time.

STATISTICAL RECORD

(To Start of 1997–98 Season)

1966 Born 8 December, Paddington, London
1983 Joined Southall
1986 FA Vase runners-up medal at Wembley
Joined Hayes
1987 12 March, transferred to Queens Park Rangers £30,000
20 April, league debut as substitute at Coventry
1988 13 February, first full league game at Everton
24 March, loaned to Brentford
Loaned to Besiktas (Turkey)
1989 Turkish Cup winner's medal
Recalled by Queens Park Rangers
1993 17 February, scored on England debut v San Marino
At Easter, two hat-tricks in two days
1995 9 June, transferred to Newcastle United for £6,000,000
1997 5 August, transferred to Tottenham Hotspur for £6,000,000

Domestic Career

Club Season	League Apps	Goals	FA Cup Apps	Goals	League Cup Apps	Goals	Others Apps	Goals	UEFA Cup Apps	Goals
QPR										
1986–87	2	–	–	–	–	–				
1987–88	1	–	–	–	–	–				
Brentford (loan)										
1987–88	3	–	–	–	–	–	–	–	–	–
QPR										
1988–89	–	–	–	–	–	–	–	–	–	–
Besiktas (loan)										
1988–89	24	14	8*	7*	–	–	–	–	1	–
QPR										
1989–90	9	2	–	–	–	–	–	–	–	–
1990–91	18	8	1	–	2	2	–	–	–	–
1991–92	23	10	–	–	2	–	1**	–	–	–
1992–93	37	20	2	2	3	2	–	–	–	–
1993–94	36	16	1	–	3	2	–	–	–	–
1994–95	37	24	3	1	2	1	–	–	–	–
Newcastle United										
1995–96	37	25	2	1	5	3	–	–	–	–
1996–97	31	16	3	1	1	–	1†	–	4	4

* Turkish Cup
** Zenith Data Systems Cup
† Charity Shield

England International Career
13 caps, 5 goals

1992–93 San Marino (1 goal), Holland, Norway, USA
1993–94 Poland (1), San Marino (1)
1994–95 USA (substitute)
1995–96 Portugal, Bulgaria (1), Hungary
1996–97 Poland, Georgia (1), Italy (substitute)

Index